The Rule
of Lazari

The Rule of Lazari

BEN OSBORNE

Matador
5 Weir Road
Kibworth Beauchamp
Leicester LE8 0LQ, UK
Tel: (+44) 116 279 2299
Email: books@troubador.co.uk
Web: www.troubador.co.uk/matador

ISBN : 9781848762763

A Cataloguing-in-Publication (CIP) catalogue record for this book
is available from the British Library

Typest by Troubador Publishing Ltd, Leicester
Printed in the UK by TJ International, Padstow, Cornwall

Matador is an imprint of Troubador Publishing Ltd

In memory of Alma Targett, and Margery and John Osborne.

This is also for Clive and Lilian Osborne.

To win without risk is to triumph without glory.
Pierre Corneille

CHAPTER 1

10th November. Danny Rawlings' gloved hand slid reassuringly down the sweated neck of his mount, My Noble Lord. 'Settle boy, quiet.'

The strapping eight-year-old chestnut beneath him was every inch a chaser, though he lacked the maturity of his years and had failed to shed the quirks of youth.

Danny adjusted his Perspex goggles for the umpteenth time. Ghostly swirls of steam escaped his chapped lips. He was among fourteen runners circling the collecting area inside the Old Course used for the three-day Open meeting at Cheltenham, shadowed by the grey-brown Cleeve Hill to the north and the heaving grandstand to the south, an amphitheatre befitting the home of National Hunt racing.

A stinging rush of arctic air lashed his raw face and stole his breath, though he felt nothing, mind blinkered. The lush grass swirled in patterns of green. There was a bleakness, exposed to the elements, away from the surging energy of the thirty-thousand packing the stands.

Danny glanced down, collecting thoughts. Centring his mind, like a spirit level. Given the recent deluges to hit the track, he knew his rippling pink and yellow silks would soon be a dark shade of brown.

From the blurry edge of his vision, Danny made out the tweed-clad shape of the starter mounting his rostrum; a signal for the runners to file out on to the track proper. But the line they formed was messy. 'Take a turn jockeys. No good, take a turn.'

1

Danny coaxed his charge forward, nosing ahead in the jostle behind the starting tape. *Need a good sighter of the first fence*, he thought. Every jump jockey dreamt of riding a winner round here on a card widely regarded as the curtain raiser to the winter campaign.

'Better,' came the starter, softer. 'Ready.'

Danny's alert blue eyes could see the starter's grip resting on a white lever. Pre-empting the tape rising, he rousted with fervent vigour, nicking two lengths on the field. A visceral roar from the packed crowd, starved of quality jumping action over the summer, fired him on.

Moments later, he was met with a stiff line of tightly packed birch. *Three-two-one*. The ground fell away as My Noble Lord reached for the fence and, but for his size and powerful quarters, would not have made the other side with partnership intact.

'A bold jump from the early pace-setter My Noble Lord,' the commentator relayed, above the sea of race-goers wrapped in earthy winter clothes, aside from the more hardy, beer-swilling types who braved the cold in short-sleeved shirts, warmed by the alcohol. Hardy bunch, the jumping set, Danny always reckoned, more than those Flat softies.

Confirmed frontrunner, Staying Alive, had gathered momentum in the hands of Connor O'Brien to draw alongside, though he needed to work to keep his pitch. The gelding cleared the third fence with the proficiency of a seasoned campaigner and then cornered like a hare. This was only Danny's sixth competitive ride over jumps, but as My Noble Lord settled into a good rhythm and extended the lead, he felt a growing confidence, which seemed to transmit itself to the horse.

Danny struggled to hear the chasing pack and, soon after clearing the fifth, he glanced over his right shoulder. *Where were they?*

The answer: four lengths back and closing. Had he gone off too quickly?

No point in a mid-race breather, Danny reckoned, would

only send out the wrong message to his sometimes lazy mount. Instead, he reacted by pushing the pedal and a shake of the reins helped stave off the closing pack, for now.

Looking ahead, he had little time to compose and gather his charge together, but the gelding knew his job and cleared the fence with a surgeon's precision. He then grabbed the ground on the gruelling climb for home for the first time. Striding out past the packed public enclosures and lollipop marking the finish line, Danny was urged on by a rush of adrenaline and, as if sensing the magnitude of the occasion, My Noble Lord's ears pricked. But he needed to contain this excitement; there was another lap to go.

Danny scraped paint on the rail as they climbed and branched from the stands before freewheeling away from the crowds along the back straight.

As the first fence down the back side grew larger, he could hear the thunder of hooves become louder. They were catching. *Three-two-one.* But this time, the pairing got in close, a jolting mistake shunting Danny up his mount's thick neck. He could now see the buckle end of the reins and quickly worked his way back into the riding shape of a cocktail glass; a stance drummed into him from day one, before taking out a licence. He was now back on an even keel but Rabbit In The Hat, who was a hat-trick-seeking Irish raider and punters' favourite, was now upsides, drawing a roar from the crowd. Danny sat lower in the saddle and pushed his gritty charge to regain a slight edge. He wasn't eager to get into a duel this early, though he knew only too well that My Noble Lord was a born leader and sulked once headed. His mount freewheeled over the following sequence of fences, including an open ditch, before grabbing the ground as they made the ascent to the farthest point of the track. Still hugging the rail, My Noble Lord handled the turn well and stole a length on his nearest pursuer.

Danny felt like he was wearing a lead-suit, every muscle soaked in lactic acid. This endurance test was far more taxing than anything he'd faced as a Flat jockey. If it hadn't been for weight issues, he would still be competing against the Flat boys; a cushy number where falls were rare and summer climes made it less harsh.

Having crested a high point on the track, My Noble Lord was still travelling well within himself. Danny felt a tingly sense of impending victory and a slice of the forty-grand pot attached to this Grade 3 handicap chase. It only served to fire him on as they ate up ground on the turn for home.

'Come on kid,' he growled. 'Come on!' But, having glanced at the big screen pitched in the Silver Ring, his thudding heart sank. He could see the pack closing fast and with great purpose; many were still moving comfortably.

Need a flier, Danny thought, as they closed in on the next plain fence. He could sense his mount's stride shorten on the approach, losing focus - whether through exhaustion or from being out on his own for so long – he delivered a few reminder taps down the gelding's neck with his air-cushioned whip. Even so, the horse drifted sharply left, like a punch-drunk boxer. 'Jump!'

The gelding was spring-heeled and cleared the fence like a buck, daylight to spare. But the veering gave ground to the closers who kept a truer line. Danny caught sight of a couple that had nipped through on his inner, travelling with great purpose, as the field met the dip before the gruelling run for the finish line. He knew boss Roger Crane would be casting a critical eye through binoculars from the stands.

Danny pushed his weight forward with a frantic shake of the reins and growled as his whip struck his mount's flank. The roar of the crowd escalated as the runners climbed for home, every sinew of jockey and horse stretched.

The runners' girths skimmed the birch of the final fence, sending a spray of brown leaves into the air, like a puff of glitter against the cold winter sunlight.

Danny could sense his mount had no more to give, a spent force. The front three were getting away and he wasn't going to punish his ride unduly. The eight-year-old's best days were still ahead of him and, for the owners' sake, he wasn't going to bottom the gelding out. He crossed the line in second gear, holding on for a respectable fourth. His mount needed no encouragement easing to a walk. They'd started as sixth favourite and to finish above market expectations was a step forward, in Danny's eyes at least.

They were soon met by a young groom called Kelly, who led them down a woodchip path in front of the grandstand leading to the parade ring. There wasn't the usual whooping and hollering from the other side of the plastic railing, just a smattering of polite applause from the muted crowd as the outsider of the field filled the winners' spot.

Danny dismounted before loosening the breast-girth and removing the saddle.

'And what the fuck do you call that?' a voice bellowed above the crackling crowd collecting around the winners' enclosure.

Danny turned and saw Crane loom large. No sign of the owners. His impossibly black hair was greased into a side parting and his beady eyes, resembling stitches on his fleshy face, glared like beacons upon rounded cheeks. Hidden by a green quilted Barbour jacket barely containing Crane's gut, Danny could make out the shape of a hip flask, *no doubt half-empty by this hour*. A well-worn tweed flat cap was wedged under his arm.

'Well?' Roger growled. His face was a shade pinker than usual and puffy with blood pressure, as if ready to blow a gasket. Nearby, owners of the runner-up glanced over, eyes wide, as if taken aback by his brusqueness. Having worked under him as an assistant for over a year, Danny was used to it.

'One of my best rides,' he said.

'If that's so, better give the game up.'

'Ran better than the betting suggested.'

'A 50/1 nag beat you. Fuck it, we beat that one ten lengths last time they'd met each other off the same weights.'

'It's all on the day,' Danny reasoned.

'I've heard it all now!'

Trouble with Crane, Danny thought, *anything less than a win wouldn't do*. In this game of hard knocks and setbacks, success stories were the exception to the rule, probably explained his puffy face and ruddy complexion; that and the copious whisky. Those who tended to succeed were the durable, resilient types, who treated a setback as a challenge.

'Where's the owner got to?'

'Sent off to the bar,' Crane replied. 'Didn't want him to witness this.'

'Nice of you,' Danny said under his breath.

'What?!'

'Nothing.' Danny felt his jaw tighten and his eyes sought the close-cut grass of the enclosure. He wanted to swerve an argument; dodge spoiling the best moment of his burgeoning career since switching codes and taking out a licence as a jump jockey. However, it was images of running his own racing stable that helped him drift off at night, steer his mind off debt worries. No more taking orders or abuse. For now, he needed to learn the ropes as an assistant under Crane's tyrannical regime.

Danny gathered up the saddle cloth. My Noble Lord had become restless and Kelly steadied the powerful gelding, waiting for the speakers to blast, 'Weighed in . . . weighed in . . . horses away . . . horses away.'

'I'll soon be off to the stabling area, hose him down,' she said. 'Meet at the van?'

'Yeah,' Danny said and made a beeline to be weighed. He then wasted no time getting out of his sweaty and mud-flecked silks in a jockeys' room charged by palpable electricity only found at these bigger meetings.

Cream-painted walls trimmed with maroon skirting. Plumes of steam wafted from the showers off the changing room. The other doors led to a self service buffet to stoke them up between races and the medic room to patch them up. Piles of lead weights lay on several thick pine tables arranged in the centre, alongside countless saddle clothes of differing sizes and loose tack. Stray *Racing Posts* lay strewn the other end, next to diet cola cans.

Danny weaved past several jockeys in various states of dress. Being a part-timer and a recruit from the Flat, he was very much a bit player and few would even acknowledge him let alone strike up a conversation. A heady mix of leather, sweat and deodorant hung in the air, catching the back of Danny's throat. He hooked his saddle on the eye-level peg shaped something like a lacrosse racquet and unbuttoned his silks and peeled off his blue padded body protector, stuffing them into his kit bag. He slipped off his boots, made easier by wearing Sara's tights, helping to stem the winter cold and yet adding no weight. A handy accessory, though she would often see differently searching for a pair in the mornings.

Leaving, he smiled at the jockeys' valet and glanced across at an A4 poster pinned to a cork board next to the door, normally plastered with parish notices for the jockeys, or the allotted weights for the runners, helping the valets to run a smooth ship. The poster was filled by a grainy black and white photo of a face familiar to Danny, crowned by bold red lettering: *MISSING*. Danny didn't read the smaller print below; he knew the face in the photo, ex-jockey Monty McCann. Having seen the posters up on track at Ludlow and Taunton where he'd saddled runners the previous week, it came as no surprise to discover the former jockey had vanished. Memories of duels they'd had on the Flat years back were still fresh, though he'd not seen McCann since he was forced to give the game up after losing the weight allowance afforded apprentice jockeys until they'd ridden a certain amount of winners and then, like Danny, suffering weight problems before the inevitable retirement four or five seasons ago. He was never the type to do something stupid, Danny reckoned, whatever life threw at him, though people do change.

Danny returned to the car park alongside the stabling area and weaved the rows of vans, until stopping beside Crane's blue twin-loader, dwarfed by the carriers from larger yards either side. Kelly had already boarded both runners and was listening to music on her MP3 player. She pulled her earphones out when he got comfy in the driver's seat.

'You okay?' she said. 'Crane's not getting to you?'

'Just the same old,' Danny said. Pissed off by the clash with his boss, he wasted no time setting out on the arduous drive back to the yard. He took the winding A-road, cutting through thick forests, to swerve the costly toll booths at the Severn Bridge. Money was tight for such a small yard. After costs, training fees from just seventeen horses didn't stretch very far these days and no job was out of bounds, whatever your rank in the yard. No one could take a backseat, essential to keep the boat afloat, a mantra of Crane's.

Danny often found himself mucking out when one of the stable lads or lasses failed to turn up, or schooling one of the dodgier heart-in-mouth jumpers at the yard. He preferred the finer art of the trainer's job, namely poring over the fixture and entry lists, planning future engagements to get the best from the horses. This is what Danny knew best, given his proven skills with the formbook and instinct retained from helming a betting syndicate. Like most other days, he was acting as travelling head lad, while Crane stayed on at Cheltenham to go partying, though he called it 'networking for new owners.' Danny had soon come to realise the jumping set seemed to work and socialise together.

With fuel costs on the rise, Crane mostly kept runners to tracks closer to home, with Welsh venues Chepstow and the newly opened Ffos Las regular haunts, while sometimes venturing further a field to Taunton, Ludlow, Exeter and Cheltenham in an attempt to keep winners flowing and owners happy.

The dazzling lights of oncoming traffic floated almost hypnotically as Danny allowed his thoughts to drift elsewhere. *What gives Crane the fucking right to criticize? His old-school approach to training was the problem.* The yard's results had nose-dived in recent campaigns under Crane's leadership. It was his refusal to move with the times and upgrade the facilities, like the walking machine – used to help horses recover from injury – Crane had promised last summer. He took no care over placing the horses in the appropriate races or studying the race-tactics best suited to their needs.

Flashing brake-lights up ahead whisked him from the reverie. He blinked his eyes wide open, wound the window down a fraction and turned on the radio. He knew only too well his responsibility for the cargo stood behind his headrest and he wouldn't be able to live with himself if anything happened to them on his watch. He made a mental note to get an early night sometime soon as the early mornings on the gallops were catching up on him. It had been a long day. Up at five-thirty and now, must be a good twelve hours later, he was still at it. *No paid overtime in this job*, he frowned.

The crackly voice of the newsreader delivering the six o'clock headlines came from the doors' speakers. The third story made Danny's eyes widen. He tweaked the tuner dial, like a safecracker, but it only served to make the reception worse out there in the wilderness.

'Police have confirmed a body was found in Ashdown Woodland in Berkshire early this morning,' the female newsreader stated.

'Bloody 'ell,' escaped Danny's lips.

'What is it?' Kelly asked.

'Listen.'

'The body, yet to be identified, was discovered by a member of the public walking his dog early this morning. According to early police reports, a weapon was found at the scene and is currently with forensics. The death is already being treated as murder and the man in charge of the investigation, Detective Chief Inspector Jonathon Taylor, is appealing for any witnesses or passers-by who may have any information to call the following num-'

Danny tuned to a music station. He'd heard enough. *That was Monty McCann's old stomping ground*, Danny recalled, *it had to be him*. It put his troubles into perspective.

He arrived back at the yard and went to check on Silver

Belle. The six-year-old mare was one of three inmates he was solely responsible for and he'd spent much of the last ten months carefully building up her fitness and jumping prowess, despite a number of confidence-sapping failures on track. He flicked on the nightlight and saw she was settled in one corner, her dappled grey coat shimmering like chain mail. Once satisfied the horses were settled, he made for his Golf GTI parked in the grounds of Samuel House where Crane was based and sped back over Caerphilly mountain to the apartment in Cardiff.

CHAPTER 2

Keen to swerve the lunch-hour crowds down Queen Street, Danny took the more scenic route and branched off at Park Place, past the taxi rank and New Theatre, briefly recalling some play he'd once promised to endure for Sara's sake.

He swept down Boulevard de Nantes in a black quilted jacket over navy combats. The pathway, freckled by yellow and brown leaves, shimmered in the watery sunlight.

He checked his wrist and, having recalled he'd lost his watch changing at one of the racetracks last week, glanced across at the clock tower beyond the majestic bank of civic buildings, carved from greying Portland stone. *Got ten minutes yet*, he thought.

Ahead, the old Roman part of Cardiff Castle boundary wall but Danny was heading elsewhere, branching off like a homing pigeon down Greyfriars Road.

He stopped in his tracks at the bookies, glancing at the various posters decorating the window, penned with odds of upcoming sporting events and special offers, tempting punters under the banner *Raymond Barton's Christmas Hamper*. He pushed past the tinted-glass door. The bookies' floor was quiet. A handful engrossed in a late race from a morning meeting at The Vaal, beamed live from South Africa.

By design, he was early for his meet-up with Rhys, allowing him time to check the latest racing news and fluctuations in the early bird prices. He felt his shoulders go back ever-so-slightly and muscles around his eyes softened. Everybody needs somewhere they truly belong - this was Danny's church. He scanned the single-level room, themed in red, until he saw Stony punching buttons on a fruit machine. He began to approach and then stopped. Someone had emerged from the gent's toilets and stood studying form right next to Stony. He was broad and muscular, like a man mountain against the willowy frame of Stony. His face, angular and pitted, bore a week's growth and his eyes were masked by dark shades. His gel-laden hair was black as soot and pulled back in a ponytail.

Danny felt it best to hold his distance for now and faked filling in a betting slip, primed to step in if this man was as much trouble as he looked. The man grabbed one of the many blue disposable pens lying about and wrote something on a slip and pushed it across to where the fruit machine met the sideboard. Stony looked down at the slip and his eyes returned to the mesmerising flashes of the gaming machine. The man's lips moved. Danny edged closer, pretending to be engrossed in some dog race from Crayford. But he couldn't hear above the commentator calling, 'Bunny's on the spin for the 11.57 . . . they're off to a level break.' Another step closer though all he could make out was the speakers booming, 'A late charge from the five-dog, joins three on the line. That'll go to the judge.'

He saw Stony shake his head and push the slip away. The stranger spoke again and Stony nodded this time. The man scrunched the slip into a ball and flicked it into an ashtray normally reserved for losing bets or chewing gum, since the smoking ban.

Danny then watched the man turn and leave, brushing past him on the way out. A sickly waft of aftershave pricked Danny's nostrils. He rushed forward, 'You okay, Stony?'

'Need to sit,' Stony said, dropping his weight on a steel-rimmed swivel stool nailed to the floor, presumably in case an irate punter got the wrong idea.

'Man, you look rough,' Danny said.

'Thanks,' Stony replied. 'Went for a curry after a do down the social, must've disagreed with me. Terrible stomach gripes.'

'Wouldn't be the eight pints ya sunk before it?' Danny

asked, concerned his friend had been hitting the bottle again.

'Nah,' Stony replied, 'Definitely the jalfrezi. Though we did make the young 'uns look lightweight in the drinking stakes, I tell ya. Still pissed this morning, was halfway here and needed to look down, check I'd put my trousers on.'

Danny let out a nervous laugh and said, 'Done that.' Mind still on the stranger, he said, 'What did he want?'

'Oh, nothing much,' Stony said, gaze returning to the form-sheets pinned to the wall. 'Just checking what the latest going was at Worcester, so I told him.'

Stony scribbled something on a betting slip. Danny couldn't help notice Stony's free hand shaking. Was it the hangover, or nerves?

'What d'ya reckon of this one's chances?'

'Bullet Proof?' Danny sucked in air between gritted teeth.

'No chance then.'

'Bit of a bridesmaid,' Danny said. 'She's had more seconds than Oliver Twist.'

'Don't like winning, you mean.'

'Didn't say that,' Danny said. 'Some horses prefer to chase another home rather than stick their head in front, others are born winners. I dunno, Stony, your tips should carry a wealth warning.'

'What's gonna beat her then, smart arse?' Stony asked, grinning.

'If I knew that I'd be talking to you by phone from some place hot and sunny.'

Danny glanced at the runners for the opening race at Ludlow, trying to find his mate a more likely winner.

'You still got contacts, inside info?' Stony asked.

'Lost touch with most after the syndicate broke up,' Danny replied. 'Working all hours up at Samuel House lately, fallen behind on my form study too.'

'Fat lot of good you are,' Stony said. 'And I'm down to my last fiver.'

'Just don't stick it in that,' Danny said, casting a glare at the fruit machine. 'Look, I recall Jacob Donald has a decent record at Ludlow, maybe his charge has a chance.'

'Right Side Up?'

'Yeah, better bet than most there, fair price at 6/1.'

Stony had already filled his betting slip in and made his way to the end of the counter marked 'Service'.

Danny still had a few minutes in hand, so he hung around to watch the race. Stony grinned as the favourite Bullet Proof was being furiously ridden mid-race and his pilot had lost his whip following a third-fence howler, unlike Right Side Up, who was bowling along nicely in front.

'Looking good, Danny my son, looking good.' But Stony looked aghast as, with four to jump, Bullet Proof's jockey motioned to a struggling rider for his whip. He slipped the persuader into his right hand and proceeded to give his lazy mount a few sharp reminders.

Woken up, Bullet Proof responded in kind and made up three places. Stony groaned as the favourite drew alongside his bet Right Side Up, who seemed to be put off his stride when challenged for the lead and kissed the turf after belting the final fence. This left Bullet Proof with the race on a plate. Despite idling in the lead, there was no way the favourite was going to shirk this opportunity.

'Sorry mate,' Danny said. 'I'll cover your bet.'

'Won't be any need,' Stony said, 'There's gonna be a stewards' enquiry, the winner cheated for fuck's sake. Throw him out!'

'Not so sure about that, Stony, only seen it happen once before, at a midweek meeting at Towcester,' Danny recalled.

'What happened?' Stony asked. 'What happened?'

'Not a lot. They didn't disqualify the winner, nothing in the rule book says that a jockey can't borrow a rival's whip halfway round.'

'That can't be right,' Stony fumed. 'It's cheating, tell me, it's got to be cheating.'

Danny wasn't giving him the answers he wanted to hear, so he scuttled back to the counter, this time at the 'Pay Out' end.

'There's gonna be a stewards' enquiry,' Stony muttered. 'I just know it. I just know it!'

'Good luck, mate,' Danny shouted after him. Before he left, he had to know what the heavyset stranger had left on the scrunched up slip. He quickly sifted through the discarded paper until flattening out one with no horse name, race time or betting stake, just a two word question, written in spidery blue ink. Danny slumped down on one of the foam and chrome stools and read: *Daniel Rawlings?*

He glanced across at the digital clock above the multiplex of screens and then left in a hurry. He paced the short walk to The Castle Keep, popular with office workers, tourists and students alike. He excused his way past the packed drinkers both standing and seated lining the long, narrow lounge beneath thick oak beams, and wood panelled and brick walls.

Rhys was propping up the bar, pint half-full. He was only slightly shorter than Danny at five foot seven. At twenty-two, his almond eyes and face still fresh, yet to show the withering marks left by the fasting and early mornings that go with the job, beneath a shock of brilliant blonde hair. Danny recalled the ribbing this young 'un got as a teenage apprentice rider from his elder peers. 'It was the weight of this that done ya,' they'd say ruffling his thick mane, whenever Rhys got beat in a head-bobbing finish. He just laughed it off. In any case, from what Danny had seen the odd night out on the pull in town, the women couldn't get enough of his flowing golden locks. As Rhys strengthened in mind and body with age, he was the one finishing on top and the teasing went. *The type of jockey who'd follow you into a revolving door and come out ahead.*

Down the years, Danny had known many jockeys that would follow in others' shadows, fearing to step into the limelight. Rhys wasn't one of them and, once his big break came along, Danny was sure he'd grasp it. *Surprising he hadn't been snapped up by one of the larger yards offering more equine talent*, Danny often thought, *only a matter of time.* Perhaps Rhys could join his yard once he'd attained a full training licence, Danny hoped, would be an asset.

15

'Another?' Danny asked.

'Nah,' Rhys replied. 'Booked the table for twelve-thirty.'

Danny had only just handed the barman a tenner when his mobile sounded above the din of clinking glasses and flowing conversations. He felt his jacket pocket vibrate and fished for the culprit. He assumed it was Sara, checking up on him. But the display read: No Caller ID. Danny looked up at Rhys, who gave him a look back, as if to say answer the bloody thing.

'Hello?' Silence. 'Hello?' louder this time.

Danny flicked it shut and forced a smile. 'Looks like I've got an admirer.'

Rhys smiled. 'Dark horse, you.'

Danny looked away to compose, smile gone.

'Talking of dark horses,' Rhys said. 'Got good word from one of the lads working down at Shaw's yard.'

'Go on,' Danny probed.

'Better not say, promised to keep it under wraps.'

'Why tell me then, tease.'

Rhys didn't reply, finishing off his pint. Danny took the hint and downed his.

The pair left the pub.

They pushed past a door on the high-street beside the mouth of a Victorian shopping arcade and climbed the tall echoing staircase, entering the cool snooker hall on the first floor. They were met by plush blood-red carpet and brown leather seats below beige windowless walls. The faint whirr of wall fans kept the air turning. A far cry from the dark dingy halls, with the tables often worn and ripped, stood on a dusty woodblock floor.

Danny fondly recalled the many hours hanging out there in a misspent youth, when a mix of tobacco and cannabis clouded the air and a look in the wrong direction could end in a night at A&E. Like with many of the struggling pubs and clubs in the area, a big chain took it over as a going concern, gave the decor a facelift in company colours and changed the staff, turning the place round a few years back. Danny still didn't know which he

16

preferred, hankering for the old-school charm of the original, though perhaps it was nostalgia rose-tinting those memories.

It was the quiet, midday lull for this traditionally evening game. He paid the acne-ridden lad behind the bar who flicked on their table light. Another pint of lager each and they were ready.

'Start setting 'em up,' Danny said. 'Gotta choose my weapon.' He inspected a rack of club cues on the far wall opposite the table, plumping for the straightest with a domed tip on a brass ferrule. Not a patch on the one-piece maple cue his dad bought him for his ninth birthday. He'd been a pretty useful junior, even making the odd century break in his prime, though women and betting stole his interest as a teen and snooker was pushed to the back-burner.

Rhys removed his cue case from one of the many lockers against the far wall and screwed his two-piece tight while Danny continued to set the balls up.

'Tenner a frame okay?' Danny asked, lifting the wooden triangle from the reds.

'Frittering away your prize money already,' Rhys said, smiling.

'No chance,' Danny said.

'What's this 'business' ya wanted to talk about?' Rhys asked, breaking off and splitting the reds wide open.

'You said the other day Goddard was open to offers for Silver Belle,' Danny said, potting a long red from the baulk end.

'G'shot,' Rhys said. 'Still got it, Jacko.'

Jacko was a nickname that'd stuck, at least with Rhys, ever since Danny had conjured a passable moonwalk at the last Christmas party thrown at Samuel House, made all the more memorable by having backed into the trophy cabinet. This was Rhys' version of events, at any rate, Danny was too far gone to recall.

'Never lost it,' Danny replied, tongue firmly in cheek. 'You know what they say - form temporary, class permanent.'

'But I wouldn't waste ya money. The mare needed kidding

along with a circuit to go on her last hurdle start, more knackered than me she was, and I don't reckon she'll make it as a chaser, too small. Guess we'll find out soon enough, with her lined up for Chepstow.'

Danny was less convinced. She'd continually shown him plenty in schooling sessions on the gallops and he was sure there was a good deal better to come if they could find the key to her.

'I'm serious about making an offer,' Danny said. 'Still think she has a future.'

'Where would she go?'

'Keep her in the yard, one of the empty boxes, already agreed in principle with Crane.'

'Generous of him,' Rhys said, brow raised.

'Wants a hefty dock in wages to cover costs,' Danny confirmed. 'Wouldn't expect any favours, stingy bastard.'

Rhys smiled as his chin met with cue and his fingers gripped the thick baize, forming a bridge. He feathered the cue ball and then punched a red into the middle pocket, though he'd lost position with the white ball. 'Is there no end to my talents.'

He played a safety shot into the baulk area of the table. Danny got down and, fuelled by Crane and his antics, fired a red into the corner pocket with anger, watching the cue ball fizz off the side cushion to land perfectly on the black in the corner pocket.

'Bloody hell,' Rhys said. 'What's ya secret?'

'Just pictured the red ball as Crane's face.'

Rhys laughed, 'See the likeness.'

It was Danny's turn to grin. Once the table light went off, it was a cue for the pair to call time on the game. Danny was three-one up, though he waived the £20 profit.

'Nice one,' Rhys said, seemingly buoyed by the gesture. 'Wasn't gonna say nothing, but the name of that horse laid out for Chepstow tomorrow . . .'

Danny's eyes widened. Rhys was clearly loosened up by the alcohol. 'Oh yeah.' He'd normally be sceptical of such betting plot as most go belly up; *the best laid plans and all that.*

However, coming from the mouth of his trusty colleague, who was party to all the best inside info, was a different ball game. 'I'm all ears.'

'One of the lads, Jasper, down at Shaw's yard in Somerset, says he's looking after a good thing, one that's catching pigeons in his workouts and he's no morning glory, neither. Had three quiet runs and got a featherweight for his handicap debut. Tomorrow's his day to shine, so Jasper reckons any road.'

'But can he jump?'

'Like a seasoned pro,' Rhys said. 'That's the word anyhow.'

'What's his name?' Danny said, already with pen in hand and betting slip pressed against the table.

'It's all a bit hush-hush, though, so don't let on to no one else,' Rhys said coyly, fearing he'd already said too much. 'The owner's a big player, so won't be happy me spilling the beans to any Tom, Dick or Harry.'

'Rhys, you can trust me,' Danny said. 'Don't bet no more, clean for over a year now.'

'Why so keen then?'

'Just curious that's all, going there and wanna see how good a judge this Jasper is,' Danny said sheepishly. A white lie as the demon on his shoulder was telling him, *this is your chance to get the cash to buy Silver Belle without pawning the family silver.*

Rhys' almond eyes narrowed, as if still wary.

'Look, I can easily find out myself, Shaw only runs a small outfit and won't send many runners there.'

'All right, all right, it's Jacob's Revenge,' Rhys said. 'You'll know if Jasper's true to his word as he reckons the owner's gonna get stuck into it large. But keep it zipped.' Rhys' tapped his nose.

'Mum's the word.'

Rhys settled the bar tab. 'There's something else, overheard Crane and Goddard at the bar last night discussing the sale of Silver Belle, they sounded eager.'

'Why's that?' Danny asked, eyes lit up.

'Business is on the slide, apparently, needs to cut down on his luxuries and he's getting bugger all return from his horses at Crane's, so they're the first to go.'

'Doesn't sound good for the yard,' Danny said.

'Sure Crane will find some other mugs to fill his boots,' Rhys said.

'You couldn't give him a bell, try and get a private bid in for me,' Danny said. 'Before he puts the mare on the market or through the sales ring.'

Rhys sighed, as if to say Danny was pushing his luck. He replaced his cue in its case. 'Can't make any promises. You know what he's like.'

'Not as well as you, though. But knowing his businesses are going down the pan, I could be holding a winning hand,' Danny said, 'He'll be desperate to lighten his outgoings and the first to get rid of will be an underachiever like Silver Belle. Might get her for a song.'

'Don't be so sure, he's no pushover, you know the hard-nosed type,' Rhys said. 'Doubt you'll get the price down much but I'll put your name in the hat.'

'Cheers,' Danny replied. 'I'll see you tomorrow at the track, yeah?'

'Yeah,' Rhys sighed. 'Busy day at the office, got five rides.' He began to press buttons on his mobile and handed it to Danny. There was a blurry photo of an attractive young woman, strawberry blonde with fair skin. 'Pulled her last night, not bad is she.'

'Fair play,' Danny said. 'You don't do bad for a short-arse.'

'Off to see her now,' Rhys said. 'Catch ya later.'

Rhys hollered a passing cab, off to the train station, while Danny made his way back to his apartment.

CHAPTER 3

Danny stopped off at Poundville; the only shop on the high street that'd thrived since the recession. The bitterly cold mornings had played havoc with his car and he picked up a can of anti-freeze and also topped up on toilet rolls. He was surprised when the girl at the till greeted him with what appeared a genuine smile and he made the effort to return the gesture, *makes all the difference.*

He went through the fob-activated door leading to the reception area of the apartment block and showed his palm to the concierge, whose nametag read Jim Reilly, busying himself playing solitaire on his monitor. He went into the post-room and turned the key in the box marked 127. He scooped up four letters, all a depressing shade of brown, with windows. He used to look forward to checking what had arrived. Given the debts he'd racked up, the same thrill wasn't there any more, as he cradled what looked to be two credit card envelopes and an electricity bill. *Need to shred those later*, Danny thought. Last thing he wanted was Sara to find out and fret.

He saw on the news the other day, with the economic downturn, financial woes were the number one cause of break-ups. Danny feared theirs would go the same way. *What she doesn't know can't hurt her, or us*, he thought. *Soon get back on my feet once taking out a full trainer's licence.* But he wasn't sure how he'd get hold of the funds at such short notice if Goddard accepted an offer on Silver Belle, otherwise any sale would fall through.

He left the post-room.

'Someone was looking for you,' Jim called over, his voice bouncing off the marble floor and high ceiling of the reception area. 'Refused to give a name, so I didn't let him up.'

'Ponytail, built like a Sherman tank,' Danny said.

'I'm sorry, if I'd known you knew each other I'd have told him to wait over there,' Jim replied, glancing over at the seating area.

'No, you did the right thing.'

'Mind you, he kept hanging around for a while in any case, even after I'd made it clear he ought to leave.'

Danny moved closer, thoughts drifting back to the stranger in the bookies. How did he know where he lived? He craned his neck over the seated concierge's shoulder and inspected the bank of colour CCTV monitors, occasionally flicking from one viewpoint to another in this rabbit warren of a place.

'He definitely left?' Danny asked, aware that, although this was a secure block, an intruder could well sneak in, either by the side entrance, or the larger delivery doors, or the gated carport. Easy to shadow a resident with a fob key and, once in, no one would dare question his intentions.

'Must've,' Jim said, though it failed to prevent Danny's stomach turning over and over, like a cement mixer.

Before riding the lift to his flat on the ninth floor, he flicked his mobile on and punched memory dial three. He now stood on the shadowy paved forecourt fronting the towering block, out of view from the foyer.

'All right Danny, what can I do you for?'

'All right Stony,' Danny replied. 'What did the guy at the bookies want?' Silence. 'Word for word, Stony?'

'I dunno,' Stony replied, 'I didn't say nothing, not to worry you, like. Got enough on your plate. You haven't got into trouble again Danny?'

'Dunno yet. Tell me, was he angry, happy – give me something to work with.'

'He offered me money if I led him to you,' Stony said. 'Course, I said no . . . no way.'

Danny said, 'Cheers Stony.'

'Keep in touch,' Stony said.

'Will do.' Danny closed his phone and braced himself. It was the not knowing who or what he'd find that sent a shiver down his spine and pricked the hair on the back of his neck. He fished in the carrier bag and withdrew the can of anti-freeze.

'Doors closing, going up,' came a soft woman's voice of the elevator. Danny's heart was fit to burst as he watched the digital display count, 'Four . . .five . . .six . . .'

He pressed his back hard against the wall of the lift, still not prepared for the doors parting.

A soft ping. 'Ninth floor . . . doors opening.'

His leg moved forward to shield the knee-high sensor before the door closed again. He knew there was a fire-door just yards to his right and, gripping the shaken can, he edged out with imperceptible movements. A shadow flicked across the five small squares of strengthened glass cut into the heavy door, beyond which lay the entrance to his flat.

Oh fuckin' ell, Danny thought, worst fears realised. He flicked the cap off and crabbed sideways closer to the fire-door, back skimming the magnolia wall. Muffled banging filtered past the two inches of beech. And then silence. Danny held the can behind his back. The fire-door then swung open, close to smacking Danny in the face. The man he'd seen in the bookies burst through. He stopped and looked Danny up and down.

'I'm a neighbour, heard the noise,' Danny said, forcing a smile. 'Need some help?'

The man's eyes narrowed and he tugged on the hair-tie, keeping his ponytail taught. Danny could almost hear the stranger's mind ticking over.

'Not important, I'll let you get on,' Danny said and pressed the lift button. The doors parted invitingly. Danny could sense the man's growing suspicions and could barely mask the tension building within.

There was an awkward pause as both realised Danny had over-egged his eagerness for the man to leave. Next thing he knew, he felt his skull crack the glass of one of the many prints colouring the softly-lit hallway.

A sickly groan escaped Danny's lips, now pinned to the wall. He gagged as the blurry hallway began to slowly spin and the stranger began to swell and shrink before him. He blinked, searching for some focus to clear the pulses of white light pervading his vision. Dull thudding music from the flat behind stopped, soon replaced by a thumping pain in his head.

He glanced down as the man's fleshy hand made a fist and swung like a wrecking ball, ripping into Danny's honed abdomen wall, sending him doubled in agony, gagging for air. He was then straightened, like a rag doll, jaw now pinned to the wall by a vice-like grip.

Danny heard, muffled, as if he was listening through bathwater, the man say, 'A warning, don't end up like the others.' Danny couldn't decipher the rest of the words above the ringing in his ears.

The grip loosened again. The navy blue carpet came rushing towards him. A shadow fell upon him and then the words, 'The clock is ticking.'

Danny didn't notice the lift doors hiss shut followed by another soft ping. He was already trying to drag his body to the door of his flat, arms straining to move what felt like a deadweight. He fumbled for his Yale key and, still grounded, stretched and turned the lock. He fell into the laminated hallway and flicked the lock twice, leaving red prints on chrome. He then lay there in darkness for what seemed an age, trying to fend off the nauseous urges welling within. His mind wasn't ready to even try computing what had just happened.

He struggled to his feet and limped to the door. He couldn't stop his hands shaking and he found himself shivering from a mix of shock and relief, though he guessed the intruder would return.

'Fucking 'ell,' he said, past the searing pain just below his ribcage, grimacing with every breath. He pressed his face near the fish-eye before backing all the way to the lounge. He made for the kitchen sink and washed the blood from his face and hands. He then popped a couple of aspirin.

He checked the beige carpet and was pleased to see he hadn't left a trail.

He then lowered himself gingerly onto the soft leather couch and tried to fall asleep. Perhaps he'd wake up and it was all some terrible dream. *No good.*

He stood and feelingly skirted the dining table to look out at the sprawling cityscape, hand pressed against the wall-length window, helping to steer his mind off things.

A sprawl of jutting office blocks were glowing pastel shades. He'd read somewhere Cardiff was Europe's fastest growing city and he reckoned it punched above its weight in every way. Off in the distance, towering cranes spiked the sky, industriously going about their business. He smiled past the pain. He enjoyed living in the heart of Cardiff, with its vibrant, cosmopolitan feel and the nightlife also met his approval. The capital was morphing into a real trendsetter, helped in no small part by TV shows like Doctor Who and Torchwood.

Towards the north, mainly low-level buildings, allowing Danny a view of the round-shouldered hills, beyond which nestled Crane's training establishment among the foothills in the Caerphilly valley – its slopes providing ideal lung-opening workouts for the horses in the morning.

He felt groggy and opened the window, letting in some fresh air, though he also let in the rumble of a pneumatic drill, the beeping of a van reversing, above distant grinding noises from the construction sites dotted around.

Growing pains of Europe's youngest capital, Danny thought, though it remained a compact city where he saw familiar faces and places most days. However, his thoughts soon returned to more pressing matters, *did that just happen.*

He inched his shirt up, inspecting the damage. No blood was drawn, merely red blotches and grazes. He turned and went to flick on the plasma screen. A panel of women were chatting with some reality show evictee. He thought it odd that people mostly watched reality TV to escape reality. He flicked on text headlines. Glancing down the gloom-merchant stories on the economic downturn, scandals from the celebrity and political worlds and the latest health scares, he could see why reality shows were so popular. He rarely followed them though he guessed immersing himself in the racing world, which seemed at times cut off from the rest of society, was his form of escapism. Sara was a big fan of these jungle and dancing programmes but he would assume control of the remote when *Top Gear* or a big footie match was on.

He poured and downed a large measure of single-malt Glenlivet whisky, before returning to the couch.

'Medicinal,' he murmured to himself. He emptied his lungs and surrendered to a wave of warmth, sinking deeper into the soft leather, washing away his troubles for an all-too-blissful moment.

The wall-mounted screen went black and Danny placed the remote on the coffee table, next to today's copy of *The Guardian*, presumably picked up by Sara before she'd left for work. He blinked his heavy eyes and focussed on the front page. Working in the horse-racing industry, it was easy to lose sight of what was going on in the wider world. He would normally flip it over and check out the sports pages but his attention was grabbed this time by a headline in the bottom left of the front cover. It read: Body found in Ashdown Woods. His eyes skated over the piece.

Poor Monty, he thought, heavy-hearted. He lay back and shut his eyes, running over why he was also a wanted man.

'Plates!' a muffled cry came from the hallway, followed by the front door slamming shut.

Danny shook his head and ventured into the open-plan kitchen. Sara came into view cradling a brown paper bag.

He was ashamed to admit his cooking prowess left something to be desired. He rarely strayed beyond spiking the plastic on a microwavable meal or warming plates for a takeaway. 'Even cracked one of them,' Sara would often remind him, if they had guests.

Danny kissed Sara. 'Good day?'

'Had better,' she said. She pulled off her lipstick-red bobble hat and ran her hand through light brown hair that fell to her shoulders. He unpacked the various cartons and plastic tubs before tucking into a King Prawn fried rice. He balanced the meal on his lap and pulled the ring of a lager can. He needed to numb the pain somehow. Sara had gone for her usual chicken egg fried rice. The pair settled down to watch the six o'clock news on BBC1.

'Any good news?' she asked between mouthfuls.

'Nothing much. Silver Belle's debut over fences tomorrow. Got a feeling Crane will tell Rhys to race from the front with her. She needs holding up, sitting out the back for a late charge. That's what happened when I won her only race. She deserves better than that bastard.'

'We've been through this before, Danny.' She turned, resting her fork. 'We can barely pay the rent for this place. Racehorses are fairly low on the list right now–' 'I wasn't fishing,' Danny cut in.

'Good,' Sara said. 'Because it's a no-go. God, you'll be giving me indigestion before I've even finished this. You'll just have to bite your tongue and let this Crane do his thing, whether you think it's right or wrong.'

Danny said, 'Turn it up.'

'Were you listening to me?' she snapped.

'Yeah, yeah, but I know these two,' Danny said, eyes entranced by the screen.

The news reporter said, 'A body found on the outskirts of Ashdown Woods was formally named as Monty McCann, a retired jockey from the area. The execution style of the killing with the weapon being left at the scene bears a striking similarity to the unsolved murder of another rider Simon Thorpe in 1996 and there's growing speculation that police are dealing with a serial or copycat killer. Police have revealed that early results from forensics have yielded fingerprints. At a press call this afternoon, his parents, Jean and Len, paid tribute to their son.'

As Danny feared, his old sparring partner in the saddle was now dead, murdered.

The shot cut to Jean, who began saying, 'This is all such a nightmare–' She began sobbing and Len took over, 'Monty was a special person, to us and to all who met him, this has torn our family apart. I plead with anyone, absolutely anyone with any information . . .'

He felt for the grieving couple going though hell on the screen right then. It took him back to the months after his dad was no longer there, giving him encouraging words about race tactics and how to cope with a near miss. Jean managed to add, 'Monty called us last week and said he was being harassed, threatened. A man had turned up at his house, yet he didn't call the police. If only we'd . . .'

Her face vanished behind hands, tissues sprouting between fingers.

Danny began to relive the threats that'd shaken him just hours before. He'd kept his nose clean in recent years and couldn't fathom why anyone would want to leave him for dead. Perhaps the guy was an aggrieved punter exacting revenge for a losing bet on one of Danny's rides. *Certainly enough of them,* Danny thought, reliving the jeers and protests from the betting public after he'd got beat on a favourite down to an ill-judged ride.

'They'll find the bastard,' he said. 'Leaving the gun at the scene, with today's science, they'll soon close the net.'

'Were you close?' she asked, chewing on a tough piece of chicken.

'Crossed paths daily, but didn't socialise with him, the odd beer like, at the end of the season, or for another rider's birthday.'

Something in the background then caught his eye. On the wall of Monty's family home, amidst a sea of photos of races and prize-giving ceremonies, was a black-and-white picture that lit more than a spark of recognition.

Danny stared at the TV screen and saw their mouths move

yet merely heard noises. He'd tuned out. It shot him back to his riding days on the Flat. Same way he felt when catching a waft of salt and vinegar, reliving the moment his dad would come home after a shift down the mines with sausage and chips wrapped in newspaper parcels, occasionally turning up with fish as a special treat, *seven years old again*; or hearing a few chords of Oasis' 'Cigarettes and Alcohol' rekindled memories of his time as an apprentice jockey at Lambourn when it used to blare out of his flatmate's CD player every morning.

He glanced across at the trophies, medals, photo albums and books his late father had kept as a record of Danny's achievements, sadly left incomplete. They found a temporary home beneath the computer desk until he found some space to put them.

The newsreader came back on the screen but Danny was already delving in one of the cardboard boxes. It wasn't long before he'd fumbled across the photo he was after. His fingers skated across the glass and he held the scene closer. It was an action shot focused upon a handful of runners in full flow taken along the back straight somewhere, Danny assumed, noticing the distant dark strip of a grandstand off in the distance. Hard to tell what track it was, though they were going right-handed on the round course.

'Danny, your meal's getting cold.'

'Finish it if you like,' Danny replied. 'I'm full.'

'What *are* you doing?'

'Just felt like looking back at something.'

'Thought you didn't like looking back,' she said. 'Past is the past you told me.'

'Yeah,' Danny replied distantly. He enjoyed some of his happiest days as an apprentice jockey and wanted to relive some of those memories one last time. He looked closer at the photo, a porthole to his past. He recalled sending this stuff on to his Dad who displayed it with pride, showing off to his pals down the working men's club in Rhymney. But the mementos were now with him, hidden away. He wasn't ashamed of his past; he just wasn't the type to display them in a cabinet. *You'd either look like a show-off or a bore.*

He was annoyed he couldn't recall where or when it was taken. It was bugging him. Perhaps the dark area beyond the runners in the centre of the track would hold clues. Looking closer, he noticed small dots against the shaded area. He cleared the desk of a renewal notice for the TV licence, his tax form and one of Sara's magazines called *Love Pets*. He placed the photo beneath the desk lamp. The blurry marks looked like birds. *It was a lake.* Danny knew instantly it was Kempton. It hadn't immediately rung any bells as the Middlesex venue had stopped turf racing on the flat track there, preferring to race solely on an All-Weather surface in recent years.

Intrigued, he carried out an advanced search using a form database, asking for all races run at Kempton in 1996 over a mile-plus. It threw up several results. He scoured them and the only one in which Danny had a ride against Monty was a one-mile two-furlong handicap on June 15th at Kempton, 1996. Danny came second, finishing a length off the winner, ridden by Monty McCann. *Sponsors of the race must've given a photo to those finishing on the podium,* he reckoned.

Faded memories began flooding back. It was a rough ride he'd endured that day, having been penned in from the three-furlong marker. He only managed to extricate himself from the pocket close to the finish when it was far too late to reel in the winner who'd already flown. The unlucky defeats stay with you longer than the wins.

But his joy at finding the race was cut short once he glanced further down the field. The rider of third was Simon Thorpe. Can't have lived long after this was taken, Danny reckoned. He recalled the day he'd got wind of Thorpe's untimely death. He was part of Danny's past and, once he'd gone, it felt like something of him had too. A fact about the case that'd lingered with him was the smoking gun left at the scene. Even with the killer seemingly handing the police a gilt-edged piece of evidence, no one was charged and the case, according to reports in the *Racing Post* was still open, though was now very cold. He recalled Thorpe was based in Ireland at the time, only occasionally making the trip over when good rides came up but he was a popular member of the jockeys' room, rarely seen without a smile on his thin, angular face beneath foppish Hugh Grant hair.

Danny ran over the facts - the rider of the first and third murdered in a race he'd finished sandwiched in between as runner-up. *Just a coincidence*, he thought, as he tentatively pawed at the red-raw skin peppering his lower ribcage. He recoiled in agony, sucking in air. *But perhaps that was merely a taster of things to come.* The words of the thug came flooding back, haunting him, 'Don't end up like the others.'

Perhaps Monty and Simon suffered the same bullyboy tactics before having their brains blown out. He didn't believe in coincidences but, at that moment, he desperately wanted to.

It didn't make any sense, he reasoned. Why the hell would they target us?

He needed to allay his fears before they returned, possibly armed next time. He looked further down the field in the Kempton race. Casey Jones came home in fourth. *There's a blast from the past.*

Danny only just lost out to him for the apprentice jockeys' title that year. He recalled it clear as day, the countless times they'd done battle, making him briefly wonder where all the years had gone.

He couldn't rest easy until reassured by Casey that he'd not been recently attacked or harassed as well.

Danny left for the bedroom, out of Sara's earshot, and made some calls. Via an old friend of Stony, he managed to find Casey's ex-directory number.

'Hello?'

'Casey?'

'Who's this?'

'It's Danny . . . Danny Rawlings.'

Danny was about to break the subsequent silence when

Casey asked, 'What do you want?'

'Just catch up on old times.'

'You're kidding right?' Casey asked. 'Seriously, what's this really about?'

'I am serious.'

Danny wasn't expecting Casey to say, 'It's been too long, love to catch up', but he'd hoped for something to work with, not this frosty front.

'Please, mate,' Danny added.

'No offence, but we weren't exactly familiar back in the day.'

Danny could see his hopes of meeting the ex-jockey fading and changed tack, laying it to him straight. 'I'm in danger.'

Casey replied, 'And tell me why should I give a fuck?'

'I reckon you may be next,' Danny said.

'Stop wasting both our time and don't call again d'ya hear!'

'You been attacked, threatened?' Danny asked.

There was a pause. Danny added, 'Simon Thorpe and Monty McCann are–' But he stopped when the dial tone kicked in.

'Hello?' Danny called. 'Hello?'

He returned the phone to its dock. He felt unsettled, as if there was unfinished business left to do. Working such long days, he normally drifted off within minutes of his head touching the cool pillow. But that night was different, tossing and turning and bolting upright at any noise or door slam, however distant in the apartment block, much to Sara's dismay.

CHAPTER 4

Danny parked up by Chepstow racecourse with time to kill. He offloaded the two runners from the horse box near the stabling area. Before the first race, he entered the betting ring to see if there were any early prices about Jacob's Revenge.

It was after he'd racked up debts with a now defunct credit bookie in Cardiff Bay called Target Bet that Sara dragged him along to see a counsellor. Danny told the therapist that placing a hefty bet, risking enough so it hurt if it went belly-up, felt like the most glorious, harrowing, all-consuming thrill. He truly felt alive for that moment, senses aroused. Better than any drug or drink. But it was a high that left a gaping void and pangs of guilt, coupled with an inevitable downer after the rush.

If the bet won, a brief thrill followed by a craving for more, searching desperately for the next spike of adrenaline. Playing up the winnings by raising the stakes and thereby boosting the danger and excitement, until the inevitable hard luck story robbed him of all funds and more.

If the bet lost, he would be overcome with guilt for having succumbed to his demons and, to mask this ugly feeling, he'd rush into having another bet. He knew bookies loved nothing more than enticing a punter who was against the ropes, mind foggy and judgement skewed. He knew it was punting suicide chasing your losses, betting with one eye on your previous losing bet, a fatal move. And yet he used to do it, knowing it was wrong. He was an addicted gambler.

He'd once consoled himself that, according to research he'd

33

once read in gambling magazine *Best Bet*, the chemical impulses in the brain were more powerful for a gambler needing a fix than a drug addict. It was a vicious circle with no easy escape and no winners, apart from the bookies.

Doesn't make it right, he often thought. Far from it, he knew that, and desperately wanted to be rid of these destructive urges, break the vicious circle, but he feared they were hardwired into him. No amount of treatment or going cold turkey would fully rid him of this character flaw. As his mum often used to nag at his dad after he'd spent the afternoon down the bookies, frittering away his wages, 'Once a gambler, always a gambler.'

From a long line of chancers, Danny now knew what she meant, the hard way. But he didn't care much for casinos. Perhaps he was just too tired to work the horses after a night at the tables in Sparky's on the first floor just off the high-street, returning home penniless under lightening skies and market traders setting up stalls and commuters filtering in to the city for an early start. He found the times he burnt the midnight oil in those places sucked all life and soul from him. For all its James Bond glamour with glitzy decor and pretty croupiers, Danny rarely saw a smiling face in them.

He could've watched the racing from the comfort of the owners' and trainers' bar. However, he didn't want to be even in the same room as Crane, avoiding the inevitable gloating 'I-told-you-so' if Silver Belle managed to recapture winning ways later on the card. Instead, Danny found himself mixing with the punters shopping around for the best odds along the rows of bookies' pitches manned by mostly ageing men, often helped by their sons or daughters, belting out the latest prices, some penned on whiteboards and others glowing orange on electronic screens. He felt in his element in this betting jungle at the established Welsh jumping track.

'Lay the 2/1,' shouted one.

'Money without working,' another cried. 'Here we go, win or each-way, come on down, you know you want to.'

It was like birdsong to Danny. The signing tic-tac men were a thing of the past, though there'd be bookies reps pacing between pitches relaying odds via earpieces at the bigger meetings.

Before he got sucked back into his bad old ways by those powerful urges, he withdrew from the betting ring and went to the rails, watching the runners canter to post. He guessed it was like an alcoholic, swerving routes where there were pubs and off-licences to limit exposure to their Achilles heel. The desperate need for a bet would never leave him, he'd come to terms with that, it was a case of coping with it and somehow avoiding temptation but it was a day-by-day struggle.

Even knowing this, he still felt his wallet, containing four credit cards that would each give him up to £250 instant cash. He was sorely tempted to place a grand on Jacob's Revenge, who was hovering around 8/1 on the boards. *A fair price*, Danny reckoned, and would probably shorten if Rhys' contact was telling the truth. He could hear the demon on his shoulder egg him on. *Go on, the easiest eight grand you'll ever make. Would help get you on the road to buying Silver Belle, solve your problems in less than six minutes.* He replayed Rhys saying, 'Good thing, one that's catching pigeons at home.'

But Danny desperately beat off these thoughts, flooring the demon and suppressing the urges to take the plunge.

He felt the sun gently warm the back of his neck, yet he shifted his weight like someone fighting off the cold. He felt more nervous than if he'd placed the bet. Missing out on a winner often hurt more than losing money on a bet.

The crowd was relatively sparse at this low-key midweek meeting and he got a good view of Jacob's Revenge blunder his way round to fill a distant sixth. He emptied his lungs, glad that he'd not wasted good money on whispers from a stable-hand he hadn't even met before. Stood there, he couldn't believe he'd even contemplated risking it. But then rationale went out the window where Danny and betting were concerned.

Next up was the main event, for Danny at least. He went to the paddock. Silver Belle had left the stabling area and was being led around by Kelly in the pre-parade ring.

Still no sign of Crane, knocking them back while networking in the bar no doubt; *one way to call it.*

Danny took charge as the assistant and checked Silver Belle's tack was on correctly and she was comfortable. He then met Rhys in the parade ring.

'I'd sack ya contact down in Somerset,' Danny said.

Rhys replied, 'Yeah, sorry 'bout that. Talking through his arse, hope you didn't go large on it.'

'Nah,' Danny said. He scanned the eight runners slowly circling the enclosure, sizing up the opposition.

Silver Belle was made third favourite by the bookies, based on the strength of her early hurdling form, a course win in the hands of Danny.

She'd been regarded as a very bright prospect by the press back then and, while those hacks had long since lost the faith after four below-par displays in that sphere, Danny remained a loyal fan. He was convinced she retained all of her ability and it was Crane, through stubborn bloody mindedness and failure to change her current race-tactics and racing distance, who was the architect of her downfall. It hurt him to see such a talented horse never realise her potential.

From his days as a form buff, he knew for the most part, behind every good horse there was a shrewd trainer. The best in the training establishment could comfortably maintain a one-in-four strike-rate whereas lower down the pecking order, there were small yards still desperately searching for a first winner. He could vaguely recall Crane making a name for himself with a couple of Cheltenham Festival winners in the late eighties. It had been years since the last big win, however, and it was now more a case of eking out a living at the gaff tracks. Feeling among the handful working at Samuel House was that Crane had been going through the motions for years, no aspirations to get the best from his small string and Silver Belle's career had hit the wall as a result.

Danny was convinced the mare was crying out for a shorter trip, about two-miles, four-furlongs, deeper ground and to be ridden with more patience, not the take-no-prisoners trail-blazing style Rhys had been consistently instructed to employ so far. She needed settling out the back, biding her time for a telling late surge.

She still gave Danny the feel of a decent horse on the gallops, particularly when the rain got into the ground at Caerphilly. She jumped and travelled better in her races when the ground rode soft. He was also convinced that he could get the best from the mare if given the chance in the saddle. This wasn't disrespecting Rhys, who Danny freely admitted was the better jumps rider, but having worked tirelessly with her in the mornings, he felt they'd built a rapport, an understanding. Crane, or businessman owner Don Goddard, had insisted that stable jockey Rhys kept the ride. It was hoped this switch to the larger fences today would rekindle her interest but Danny was certain she'd hate these lively ground conditions and feared for her safety.

'What's Crane told you?' he asked up to Rhys, whose feet were still out of the stirrups.

'The usual, go at it hard from the front and try burn them off, bully them.'

Danny sighed. 'Anything I say wouldn't make a difference, no?'

'Danny, who pays my wages? If I go against his orders there'd be hell to pay.'

'But if you're hassled for the lead, let them go on,' Danny said. 'She'll be legless before the home straight if you don't.'

Rhys shrugged his shoulders before being led off from the paddock to the racetrack by Kelly.

The runners were organizing themselves at the post by the time Danny had slunk off to a quiet patch, away from the other race-goers. He needed to watch it alone. He'd grown attached to her and was nervous for her well-being whenever she ran, particularly as her jumping over the less daunting practice fences at home still lacked prowess. He could make out Silver Belle's flashy grey coat mingling among her bay and chestnut rivals.

A cheer went up as they were sent on their way. His eyes flicked between the big screen in the centre of the track and the runners, still tightly packed as they went out on the second circuit. Silver Belle was towing them along, as Danny feared, she seemed there on sufferance, lacking jumping fluency and running in snatches: one minute, cruising hard-held; the next, off the bridle and needing stern assistance from the saddle. With just the four fences to jump, Rhys was niggling the mare to keep her head in front as the favourite Meadow Keep produced a menacing move on the outside. It was like witnessing a car crash unfolding in slow motion, and he was stood helpless in the stands. Having seen numerous toe-curling mistakes from the inexperienced mare, Danny wasn't surprise she surrendered the lead going over the third last fence and soon faded out of contention, coming home in her own time a tired sixth, a good twenty-five lengths off the winner.

His overriding sense of relief at her safe return and the fact she hadn't boosted her value out of Danny's price-range by winning was tempered by knowing that this was yet another bad run on a seemingly endless sequence for the Crane yard and jittery owners would soon get itchy feet. They would look elsewhere to send their cherished horses.

Owners sat on top in the stratified racing industry, then trainers, then jockeys and last the stable staff. Danny had no issue with this - they paid the bills and kept the yard afloat. But he feared a lengthy drought like this would spell bad news for him looking at the wider picture. He needed the wages to keep the roof over their heads right now, even though it worked out at pittance given the hours he put in. He wasn't afraid of hard graft but he equally didn't like being used and he suspected Crane was cashing in on the fact Danny had no place else to learn his craft and get a trainer's permit.

After seeing Silver Belle back into the paddock, he checked her over. She seemed subdued, feeling sorry for herself, but still in one piece to fight another day. *Merely pride hurt*, Danny thought.

'I'll see you back at the van in fifteen, okay, Kelly?'

'Yep, no probs,' Kelly replied. 'No more though, don't wanna get back when it's too dark.'

Danny made his way to the owners' bar in the grandstand. Crane's arm was wrapped around Goddard, who grasped a whisky tumbler in one hand and ran his other through a slick of black hair. Crane was recounting a story about the time the yard's dog had got stuck in a quagmire at the bottom of the lower fields one winter's morning. Danny picked up on this from merely the half a dozen slurry words he'd just overheard. He could retell the story verbatim and had long since given up feigning interest in the tale. Clearly trying to ease Goddard's pain at just having witnessed his runner flop badly. Crane turned and said, 'Oh, it's you.'

'We're off,' Danny said, 'I take it you're getting a lift or staying overnight.'

'More to the point, what have you been teaching that poor mare in her schooling?' he asked sternly. 'She barely lifted a leg.'

Danny felt the bile rise in his gullet like molten lava. But he wasn't going to rise to this. 'But–'

'You really must put more hours in,' Crane said.

'More hours in?' Danny gasped. 'I'm at the yard more than I'm home. Me and the wife pass like ships in the night.'

'Wish that was the case with mine,' Goddard piped up.

'Did Rhys talk to you about putting in an offer for Silver Belle?' Danny asked, meeting Goddard's gaze.

'By who?' Crane asked.

'Me.'

Crane laughed but soon stopped, seeing no one else was. 'And you're complaining about the pay, Jesus.'

Goddard said, 'He did but I guess you'd have withdrawn any bid after seeing that.'

Danny wasn't keen to reveal that his eagerness to buy the mare remained intact. Poker-faced, he said, 'Yeah, didn't cover herself in glory out there but I would be interested to take her off your hands, for the right price, mind.'

39

'I'd accept say, 18K.'

Danny hid his disappointment at Goddard setting the bar so high. He said, 'Can't do more than ten.'

Goddard finished off the spirit with one gulp and said, 'Look, seeing as she'll be staying with a good home, I'll take fourteen and that's my final word, she'll be worth at least that at the paddock sales. She's a well-made mare who's won over hurdles, would have no trouble getting interest at stud.'

Danny offered his hand and they shook on the deal.

Goddard added, 'I'll get the papers drawn up.'

'But this is on condition she's come out of this race sound, okay?' Danny asked.

'Very well.'

'I wouldn't build your hopes up with this one,' Crane said, seemingly hell-bent on picking an argument. 'Always complaining about wages, so don't reckon he's got fourteen quid let alone fourteen big ones.'

Danny smirked. 'Too right, the pittance I'm working for, but got some saved up, money left by my father.' Goddard smiled, seemingly reassured, though Danny was less so. It would be tight whether he'd be able to get together the funds needed at such short notice.

'Oh yes,' Crane said. 'Your dear father, he'd be turning in his grave if he heard what you were going to do with his hard-earned inheritance.'

'Roger?' Goddard said, hand on Crane's shoulder as if to say 'enough'.

Danny bit his lip, so close to lashing out. But he knew it would do no good flooring his drunken boss. 'First off, you never met my dad and, second, what gives you the fucking right to tell me what he did and didn't want, where the fuck do you get off?'

They had a growing audience and the barman looked primed to step in.

Goddard said, 'Leave this for another time. Roger, I reckon we've had enough for one afternoon.'

'Not getting paid enough?' Crane scoffed, mind still stuck on Danny's protestations. 'You're doing it for the experience, young man. Money will come once you've learnt the ropes and honed your craft like I had to. You don't get to helm the ship without putting the years in, sonny.'

'I got a name,' Danny said, 'Should know it by now, having been your skivvy for the past ten months.' It felt good saying these things, having let them stew for so long. Whenever he'd raised the topic in the past, he might as well have been talking to a brick wall, so he wasn't hopeful of anything coming of it, particularly given Crane's current state, lucky if he'll remember a word. Or maybe that was a good thing.

'But I never signed up to work all the hours God gives.'

Crane raised his index finger, as if to say it was still his airtime, before burping and saying, 'That's what you said when you applied, I'll work till I drop you said, that's why I took you in, no one else would.' He turned and beamed yellowing teeth at Goddard.

See how far you'd get without me, Danny thought. He then pictured what Sara had said after a previous barney he'd had with Crane: *'Don't rock the boat, we need the money and you need the experience.'*

But some things just have to be said, he reconciled himself, this had been simmering for too long and it was probably best out in the open. 'And something else, you're messing up the prospects of the yard's most promising inmates, everyone in the yard thinks so, just too afraid to speak up. Don't believe me, results over the past two seasons are proof enough.'

A vein appeared on Crane's right temple. 'Watch it, you're treading a very thin line, sonny.'

'It has to be said if we're gonna turn the tide.'

Crane gritted a smile towards Goddard. 'I do apologize about this.'

Goddard replied, 'Don't worry Roger, get enough of it at home.'

The fiery eyes returned as his gaze fell back on Danny. 'I was in this game while you were sucking on your mother's tits. Don't you dare tell me how to get the job done. Do you hear?!'

'That's the problem, you're old school, too proud or stubborn to change, move with the times.'

'Would you excuse me a moment, Don?'

'No problem,' Goddard replied, slightly awkward, as if an innocent bystander witnessing a marital between friends.

Crane's hand met with Danny's back and guided him out of the room, his jovial smile left behind. 'Don't you ever talk to me like that again!' he growled demonically. 'You fucking waste of space. I could crush any hope of you getting a licence, know people at the Jockey Club, you could kiss goodbye to your dreams.'

Danny worked hard to keep up a stony-faced mask, show no weakness. He knew Crane's rant was fuelled by a mix of drink and yet another bad result for the stable. He just had to ride the storm, take nothing personally. *No one liked being on the wrong end of a right bollocking, though.*

He couldn't resort to the words he'd told Sara the other day after she'd got some grief from her work colleagues, 'just ignore them, they're none of your business', as Crane was very much his business, and could drop him whenever he saw fit.

'You should be grateful of the work,' Crane slurred. 'Christ, yards up and down the country, even the big ones, are shedding staff. You know what you are?'

Danny remained tight lipped. He had a feeling Crane was going to tell him anyway. But when Crane opened his mouth, nothing came out. His knees jack-knifed as he collapsed.

Danny returned to the bar, shouting down the steward to call for the racecourse doctor and ambulance. Soon, a ring of concerned owners and trainers had formed where Crane and Danny had argued.

CHAPTER 5

Danny felt guilty for playing his part in tipping Crane over the edge. The trainer was discharged later that evening, doctors putting it down to drink and fatigue. Though Danny suspected it was more the former.

'No lasting damage,' they said according to Kelly, though he needed a week of rest and recuperation. That meant Danny, as assistant trainer, was placed at the helm of the sinking ship. It wasn't good timing as he'd been struggling to sleep at night since the assault outside the flat and he felt dead to the world prising himself from the sunken mattress each morning. He'd often lie there staring at the ceiling, counting down from five to try and eject himself from beneath the warm duvet, needing more than one attempt on those cold winter mornings.

The one place he thought he could feel safe was no longer. With the murders of his fellow ex-jockeys still fresh in his mind, he needed to find out why they were possibly now after his blood, before it was too late.

Casey told him not to ring again, but didn't say anything about paying a visit in person, Danny reasoned. It had to be worth a shot.

After giving three of the more experienced inmates a workout over the undulating lush-green foothills, he told Kelly he was going to meet Casey in Wiltshire, just in case something went badly wrong. He didn't know what he was getting himself into but he was sure it was worth it, to get a better night's sleep if nothing else.

He was guided by the Golf's GPS to a set of towering wrought-iron gates, guarding the gap in a tall red-brick wall. *Must be over ten feet.*

He looked down at the screen to check if he'd typed in the wrong address. It matched the one he'd got from a racing portal on the web the night before. With no place to park nearby, he found a tree-lined side street to leave the car. *Should be safe here*, he thought, admiring the large detached houses set back from either side of the road. He returned to the imposing gate and buzzed the intercom to its left, beside a black and gold nameplate marked The Mews. No reply.

He buzzed again, fearing it had been a wasted journey. Perhaps he was reading too much into the murdered jockeys happened to be riding during the same period. But that didn't explain why he was being targeted.

He stood patiently, staring in wonder and some degree of jealousy at the sweeping tree-lined driveway leading to, from what Danny could make out, an equally imposing detached mock-Tudor house, partly hidden by thick canopies.

Got to be worth best part of a million and he was no better in the saddle than me, Danny found himself thinking begrudgingly. It sent him back to his days as a housebreaker during a wayward youth, though a palatial outfit like this would've been out of his league. *Used to leave these treasure troves to the big boys.* He tried filing those memories under the 'regretful' tag, a distant past that wanted staying that way.

His reverie was broken by a man's crackly voice from the speaker, saying, 'Yes?'

'Casey Jones?'

A pause was broken by the whir of a CCTV camera, bracketed high above to one of the pillars, turning to get a good shot of Danny. 'What is it?'

'It's Danny Rawlings, thought I'd come round, we seemed to get cut off on the phone.'

Nothing came from the speaker and Danny was about to press the buzzer again when Casey said coldly, 'You shouldn't be here.'

'No way to speak to an old friend, we could talk about the old days,' Danny said. He wanted to frown, given the pair barely talked back in the day, but he knew the camera was still trained on him. He began to shift his weight and blew into a shell made by his hands, hoping Casey would take pity.

'Why are you really here?' Casey said. 'Who sent you?'

'I'm on my own,' Danny said. 'Just wanna pick your brains about something that's bugging me. I'm a wanted man and I fear you may be on borrowed time also.' He'd say anything to get Casey parting those gates, even thought about scaling them, though ten feet of railings topped with razor-sharp spearheads would be no cakewalk, even for his lean and nimble body.

He was about to buzz again when there was a click and the gates purred apart. Danny didn't hesitate and squeezed through the growing gap, keen to enter the grounds before Casey had chance to change his mind. He followed the slowly arcing driveway made from red block-paving. It widened, like the mouth of a river, into a large forecourt. A Porsche and a Range Rover were parked up.

The house was every bit as grand, with pitched roofs, high chimney stacks.

This just gets better, Danny thought sarcastically. He couldn't help being sobered by the fact he was all of Casey's age and still struggling to pay the bills and make something of his life.

He approached. Herringbone brickwork surrounded the half-timbering of its facade. Danny caught sight of a light on in one of the many mullioned windows on the first floor.

'I'm in the wrong business,' Danny muttered, as he tugged on a cord hung from the pillared porch, triggering a three-note chime somewhere distant. The scrawny head of Casey poked from behind the carved Gothic oak door and glanced over both of Danny's shoulders before letting him in.

'You being threatened?' Danny asked.

'No - why do you ask?'

'Just seem on edge, that's all.'

He was led through a large hallway, past the foot of a wide staircase, and into what looked like the dining room, complete with a long, gleaming table.

'Did you stay in touch with Monty McCann?'

'Don't remember,' Casey said. 'That seems like another life, I lead a very different one now.'

'I can see,' Danny replied, scanning the plush surroundings.

'Heard the news, though,' Casey said. 'Never know when your time's up.'

Danny turned and lost himself looking over the photos of Casey's past glories covering the wall. Above one of three shelves crammed with trophies was the same black and white photo that'd led him to Casey's door. He stared at the photo.

'What's your poison?' Casey asked.

Danny turned sharply and snapped, 'What?'

Casey was stood, decanter in hand, alongside a flashy drinks cabinet, all silver and glass. He grinned, 'Looks like you need one.'

'Nothing for me,' Danny said. Although he was gagging for a calming measure of whisky, he needed to keep a sharp and keen mind.

'Never remember you as a teetotaller,' Casey said.

'I'm not,' Danny replied. 'Driving, that's all. Got some place here, Casey. Done yourself proud since hangin' up your silks, or did you marry into money?'

Casey's look made Danny add, 'How do ya earn a crust now?'

From what little he could recall, the man before him left school before taking his GCSEs and didn't seem the type to possess any entrepreneurial spirit.

Casey drew a breath before saying, 'It was my uncle, made millions from the internet boom, flew off to Oz but never got to spend it, poor sod. Heart attack. And it came to me, quit racing and set me up for life.'

'Thought for a minute you'd got into something dodgy,' Danny said and then smiled. He wasn't convinced by Casey's reply. It felt too rehearsed, well-honed spiel that tripped off his tongue too easily. He didn't appear to think while reeling it off, as if on autopilot.

Casey slugged back a generous measure of whisky and refreshed the glass. There was an awkward silence, as if an old school friend had turned up out of the blue and neither knew what to say.

'What keeps you busy?' Danny broke the stalemate, fishing for a bigger catch. He sensed Casey was holding something back and he wanted to find out.

'After dinner speeches for corporate shindigs at the races and tipping for hospitality boxes on race days, still follow the game closely. Keeps the wolf from the door.'

'Don't reckon the wolf ever comes round these parts,' Danny remarked.

'Brown-nosing won't get you anywhere, said all I've got to say,' Casey barked, mood darkening. 'You're not wanted here.'

'You let me in!'

'You refused to leave,' Casey said. 'And this is me warning you face to face that I don't ever want to see your ugly mug again. Clear?'

'Don't go all defensive Casey,' Danny said. 'All I want is the truth, before they come back and finish me off. It's in both our interests.'

'And what do you think you're on to, Sherlock?' Casey asked. Before Danny could answer, he continued. 'Always were poking your nose where it don't belong, from what little I remember of you.'

Danny shrugged off the barb and said, 'Doesn't change the fact we're both in danger.'

'Danger? My God, this is awful, what are we going to do? Quick, call the police, this man has a hunch,' Casey said and then laughed.

'I'm serious,' Danny said.

'Your imagination's working overtime,' Casey said. 'My advice, learn to keep your mouth shut, like I have, and you'll be okay, OK?'

'What makes you so sure, unless you're behind it all.'

'I've nothing against you Danny, you're just a part of my life that I'd prefer to forget, not proud of it.'

'You did all right,' Danny said, looking up at the trophies. 'And not too ashamed to show it.'

'The wife's idea to display them, helps in those games of one-upmanship played out at the tiresome dinner parties she puts on.'

Danny turned.

'What are you doing?' Casey asked firmly.

'I came second in this race,' Danny said, unhooking the Kempton photo from the wall. 'You were fourth.'

'Come here to gloat have we, some things never change, sad bastard,' Casey said and smiled though the tone didn't smack of friendly banter.

Unfazed, Danny pressed on. 'Wanna know who filled third that day?'

'I guess you're gonna tell me,' Casey replied through gritted teeth.

'Simon Thorpe.'

'And?'

'He was murdered, we went to his funeral, must remember that, for Christ's sake. And the winner, Monty McCann, was found dead last week. Two of the jockeys riding in this photo are now dead.'

'And?' Casey asked again, venom-laced this time. 'It's tragic and all the rest, but we're all going to die at some point. One of life's certainties.'

'Not from a bullet through the head.'

'And why are you so certain I'm next on the list, unless of course you're the killer,' Casey said.

'Like I said, we rode in that very same race, look,' Danny said, holding the photo forward, finger pressed against the glass.

'But so did others. They're unrelated events, would be circumstantial in any court,' Casey said. 'You've clearly far too much time on your hands since hanging up your saddle.'

'You want evidence?' Danny asked. He lifted his shirt, revealing his torso dappled in purple, black and yellow blotches, like menacing storm-clouds. 'This enough?'

'Where did ya get those?' Casey asked with a curious more than concerned tone.

'They've tracked me down,' Danny said. 'Gave me a warning.'

'You're putting two and two together and making–'

'Five,' Danny interjected. 'Maybe I am but still don't explain who'd do this, got no enemies. For whatever fucked-up reason, there's someone hunting down jockeys riding from our era. Don't blame me if they come calling,' Danny added.

'I'll set my dogs on 'em,' Casey said and then smiled.

'I'm not joking, neither are they,' Danny fumed. Whatever he said, Casey brushed it off as some kind of joke.

'What now?' Casey asked.

'Gonna find someone who does believe me.'

'Who?'

'Police.'

'Now I know you've really lost it,' Casey said. He put his drink down, eyes narrowing. 'Tell me this.'

'Go on,' Danny said, feeling a barrier had been floored.

'Do you know of the Rule of Lazari?'

Danny paused. He had a vague recollection of the phrase from somewhere in the deep recesses of his memory bank.

'Yeah, I do,' Danny said confidently. He was a terrible liar but this wasn't technically one. He knew of it but didn't actual know it.

'Whatever you've heard, don't get involved.'

'Too late, I already am,' Danny said.

'You've definitely come here alone?' Casey asked.

'Why?'

'Leave, now,' Casey said, grabbing Danny by the forearm and pulling him from the room.

'Back off, Casey,' Danny said, shaking himself free. 'Got legs you know.'

'Go the back way, out the kitchen. Follow the path to a wall, sure you can clear it. Ensure no one sees you, clear? And if anyone asks, this never happened.'

'Only came to help,' Danny said.

'You haven't.'

'And Casey, you said I'd packed the game in – I didn't, you'd know that if you still followed the game!'

No way Casey's doing the tipping for corporate boxes, Danny thought. *None of it added up.*

He followed Casey's instructions and cleared the rear perimeter wall, landing heavily the other side. He found himself stood beside what looked like a main road with a solid stream of cars racing by. He turned to see a navy Jag pull out from a bus lay-by and roll up to where he stood. Its shimmering windows, tinted silver, made him double take. It cruised at no more than twenty mph, Danny reckoned, causing drivers behind to swerve and sound their annoyance. The Jag slowed to a crawl as it past Danny. He found himself mesmerised by his reflection in the mirrored windows, time seeming to grind to a halt, though no hope of seeing those inside. But then the Jag's three-litre engine roared into life and sped away, as if they'd seen enough.

Casey's words, 'Let no one see you,' still rang in his ears.

Not wanting to hang around a moment longer, he made a beeline for the leafy side street where he'd left his Golf. He was glad it hadn't been towed away or nicked. But the relief was wiped by what lay ahead. Not forty yards away, blocking the end of the road, was the same blue Jag sat stationary side on. Were they Casey's security? *Could certainly afford them.*

Danny sat back in the driver's seat, staring ahead, not sure whether to swerve past the road block and hope they didn't follow, or go confront them on foot. He pulled down the glove compartment and rifled through empty energy drink cans and sweet wrappers he'd downed as a quick fix before race-riding. His fingers then wrapped around the barrel of a Stanley knife he'd often used to cut bags of feed, or bedding. He clicked the blade out as far as it would go and slipped it up his sleeve.

Whatever these people were after, he was sure as hell going to find out.

A deep breath and he was ready. He pushed the driver's door open, stepped out on to the road and began to close in on the Jag. He could hear his heartbeat and felt his palm tighten around the knife. Twenty yards away and closing. He didn't know what he was going to do when there. He hoped his sharp instinct and ability to react would come to the fore. He lowered the blade ever so slightly and broadened his shoulders, walking tall, though he knew none of this would make a blind bit of difference if they rolled the window down and pulled a trigger.

He stood in front of the passenger window and stared at his creased face looking back. He lifted his free hand to bang on the window when the Jag's engine went from a gentle purr to a menacing growl, making Danny stumble back. It once again pulled away and was soon gone from view. Danny began to sprint back to his car but soon slowed to a walk. It would've been no use, they were long gone.

He sat there, arms resting on the wheel and yet to belt up, wondering what the hell was happening.

His insides tightened on his way back to Cardiff. Going to see Casey in a bid to ease his concerns had done the exact opposite. *But why would they systematically kill those riding in that particular race?* There was nothing unusual about it, with a prize fund of below £6,000 and a field of eight ordinary handicappers. There wasn't enough money or kudos at stake to spark an act of revenge, particularly all these years later.

Could be an aggrieved jockey's agent or bitter trainer that'd flipped and sought recompense by slaying those who'd let them down. He couldn't cross off anything, however unlikely it seemed.

Perhaps he was reading too much into it and the killings were separate cases of brutality. But the similarity between the murders - both executed at point blank in deserted woodlands with the weapons left to be found – suggested a watertight link. And there was his aching midriff, a constant reminder that he was possibly next up.

'Makes no sense,' he said, voice drowned by the Golf's engine and the radio spewing out travel updates, as he left the M4 at junction 29 and joined the A48 en route to Gabalfa Roundabout and then the city centre.

Danny entered the lounge. Sara was making herself comfortable, stretched out on the couch. A family-sized bag of chocolates sat invitingly on the coffee table in front of her, alongside a full glass of red wine. Danny cupped the back of her head as he passed on his way to the kitchen. He slipped off his trainers and grabbed a can of lager from the fridge. It was the last one there. *Probably a good thing*, he thought, knowing he needed a sharp mind sealing the deal to snap up Silver Belle first thing tomorrow morning. He thought it best not to mention this to Sara, for now.

'You're back late,' she said, looking up.

'Just met up with an old friend.'

'Anyone I know?'

'Nah, we're talking years back,' Danny said. 'Casey Jones. Budge up.' He slotted himself beside her.

'Did it go well?'

'Not as well as hoped.'

She was struggling to break into the bag of chocolates. 'It's like bloody Fort Knox this,' she said, struggling to find the seam, driven on by the reward inside.

'Let me have a go,' Danny said.

He was about to reach for the packet, when it burst open, the release of pressure propelling her elbow into his ribcage. Danny grimaced, biting back the pain. He couldn't let on about his injuries, questions would be asked. *No more lies.*

'Barely touched you,' she said, looking over at him like a chipmunk, a chocolate in each cheek.

She retrieved one that'd got away from the beige carpet and perched it on the coffee table. 'What you gonna do with that?'

'Throw it away.'

Danny reached over her and popped it in his mouth.

'Oh, Danny,' Sara said and grimaced.

'What?' Danny protested. 'Strengthens the defences. When was the last time I had a cold?'

Sara couldn't answer.

'Exactly,' he added.

CHAPTER 6

Danny blearily eyed the glowing digital clock. 5.24 a.m. His hand rushed to beat the alarm before harsh chimes woke Sara, cocooned in the duvet beside him. He buttoned his duck-egg blue shirt and tugged on black trousers. *Better give off a good impression to Goddard*, Danny thought, *business-types are funny like that*.

He padded into the lounge and downed a cooling glass of milk before setting out on the snaking climb over Caerphilly mountain, no strain for his 2.0 Golf GTI.

He pulled into the long sweeping shale driveway taking him to the door of Samuel House. Danny crept forward in second and drew alongside the farmhouse set against the lightening sky, a modest red-bricked abode flanked by outbuildings and lost among the sloping foothills. Beyond, lay the undulating gallops worked by the yard's current crop, seventeen jumpers of mixed ability. Danny made out the portly figures of Crane and Goddard, who'd just emerged from behind the front door, *clearly keen to strike a deal*.

Goddard offered his hand and Danny reciprocated. They'd only met a handful of times before and he'd guessed this time would be more formal than pally. Lines etched Crane's jowly face from years of pulling expressions. *Mostly frowns*, Danny guessed. Perhaps he'd cut down on the race-day entertaining and actually lend a hand at the yard from now on.

Danny asked, 'How'd she come out of the race?'

Crane and Goddard exchanged glances, both saying, 'Fine.' Crane added, 'Just fine.'

Not convinced, Danny said, 'Gonna check her out. Before I sign on the dotted line, make sure there're no battle-wounds as she'd had a hard race. That okay?'

The three made the well-trod path to the stabling area. The odd whinnying from one of the yard's younger inmates broke the morning stillness. A couple of the stable-hands were leading their charges out for an early workout. Danny unbolted the box three from the end and dropped on his haunches beside Silver Belle, who was lying peacefully on her bedding of recycled paper and hemp.

Danny ran his hand down her mottled-grey neck and her eyes opened. He'd clipped her winter coat since she'd spent the summer relaxing out in the fields alongside the paddock, helping her to refresh for the jumping campaign. She struggled to her feet. 'Easy, girl,' Danny whispered. The mare's ears pricked on hearing his voice.

Goddard rested his weight against the open stable door, saying, 'Got a way with the fairer sex I see. At least this one doesn't answer you back.'

Crane smiled. Danny didn't reply. He knew what made Silver Belle tick. He often wished he understood women as well. He began checking the mare's soundness. She stood perfectly still as his hand skated over her hock down her cannon bone to her fetlock. Feeling some heat, his hand stopped.

'Feel this,' Danny said, turning to Crane.

'You're worrying too much,' Crane replied, now mirroring Danny's action.

'Possibly a muscle strain, or just mild stiffness from the race, give her a day or two R&R and she'll be right as rain.'

'All the same, I'll need the vet give her the all-clear,' Danny said, alarm bells ringing.

'Of course,' Goddard said, forcing a smile. 'There's a seven-day cooling off period in the contract.'

'Seen enough?' Crane said, 'Not like you don't know her inside out.'

'This is gonna be a big investment for me,' Danny said, 'I'd do the same if I was shopping for a second-hand car.'

'For sure,' Goddard said, exaggeratingly looking at his watch like a poor actor, before swinging the stable-door invitingly open. 'Shall we?'

Danny hated being rushed into such an important decision and he was getting the impression it was two-against-one in this deal and he was the minority. They returned to the farmhouse. The drawing room was softly lit by wall-lights and the oak creaked under their feet. Red satin drapes and dark panelled walls. Oil paintings of distant Crane family members Danny knew about only too well, having endured insufferable tales of them at one of the odious soirées where prospective and current owners were invited to mix with his 'lordship' and celebrate the year's successes or, more like, commiserate over near misses and the 'what might have beens'.

Danny had to show his face at these events, though often made his excuses and left after downing a few glasses of Crane's best bubbly. *Worse than any office party*, Danny recalled, though he had little experience of those, having never had a proper nine-to-five.

Goddard slapped the contract on a table made of some red exotic wood and offered Danny the fountain pen. He paused for a moment as he ran over in his mind whether this was the right thing to do. He questioned why Crane was so keen for Goddard to get rid of the mare, as if he knew she was dead wood. He'd always questioned where Crane's loyalties lay. In these hard economic times, Goddard was essentially bankrolling the yard with most of the inmates running in his colours. He'd once overheard Crane blab to another trainer after a few sherries at the bar that he had to act like a 'yes' man to whatever Goddard wants.

Danny quickly leafed through the three sheets on the table, pretending to examine the legal jargon. In the end, he had to trust it was all in order and signed, witnessed by Crane. He knew it was the ideal opportunity to get on the first rung of the ownership ladder though he also knew he had to max out on several credit cards to cover the £14,000 price tag around the mare's neck. No longer swimming in debt, he was drowning. *More shredding to do.*

After finishing his duties at the yard, Danny felt like celebrating with Sara by bagging a bottle of fancy bubbly in town. He had a feeling they'd both be in need of it after he broke the news of his surprise buy.

On his way back from the off-licence, he trod carefully down what was known affectionately as Chip Alley, littered and stained by the previous night's excesses. He recalled the fuzzy memories of stumbling out of one of the many takeaways, with a polystyrene carton brimming with chips and curry sauce, passing someone who'd collapsed, while another was pissing up the side of a restaurant wall, still trying to stuff his mouth full of kebab. Hardly Utopia, he thought wryly, but he did look back on those carefree days with fondness. Friday night binges with his mates, crawling home at some ungodly hour, were a no-go now. Hangovers had become all-day affairs, not mixing well with early mornings on the gallops.

He continued along The Hayes, driven on by his grumbling stomach. He swerved the statue of former mayor John Batchelor stood in the monstrous shadow of the new St David's shopping centre. A glimpse into Cardiff's dim and distant past dwarfed by its gleaming future.

A shot of adrenaline spiked his blood when his eyes focussed upon the heavy-set Neanderthal who'd left him for dead. 'Fucking 'ell, just what I need.'

Set on a collision course, Danny knew he was short on options. A sudden about-turn would no doubt catch the man's eye, yet the alternative was carry on headlong into trouble. His furtive eyes darted awkwardly, anywhere but ahead, before settling on the iron lettering 'Cardiff Market 1891' above the mouth of the building to his left. Overall-clad traders were busying themselves unloading deliveries from the lorries and vans double-parked. Danny tried shadowing one of them but he soon veered off into the market. A comforting waft of fresh fish pricked his nostrils. He spotted several steel cages packed with crates of fruit and veg as he brushed by the thug. A cursory glance over his shoulder saw the man mirror his actions, ponytail flicking behind his trunk-like neck and thick jaw. They exchanged scornful glares. Shit!

Danny broke into full stride, grabbing a stray cage and thrusting it in the path of his pursuer though it merely dealt a glancing blow, barely halting his progress. Yet Danny, more agile than he'd ever been, was confident he could outrun his bulky assailant. He duly cleared away though he didn't dare stop, weaving the backstreets he knew like The Knowledge, until safely back in the confines of the apartment. He looked down at the bottle, fit to burst. *Won't need shaking*, he thought.

Hearing the muffled bang of a kitchen cupboard, he drew a calming breath before entering the lounge.

Sara was stood where beech laminate met with carpet, Snoopy t-shirt draped over knickers. She was flattening her bed-hair with one hand, and cradling a bowl of cornflakes with the other.

'You okay?' Danny asked.

'Bit run down,' she yawned. 'Going back to bed. Have you been for a run?'

Danny wiped the tingly beads of sweat collecting in the ridges of his brow. 'Yeah, could say that.'

'What about that thing in the corner?' Sara said, looking over at the running machine. She hated clutter and that monstrosity, as she'd often called it, had merely sat collecting dust since bought on a whim by Danny on hearing of his new job at Crane's. 'Found a cobweb on it the other day, bloody spider's worked up more of a sweat on it than you.'

'All right,' Danny huffed. He hadn't banked on being too stiff and sore come the evening and body not ready for exertions first thing in the morning. After a draining day on the gallops, on the road and at the races, a spin on the running machine felt like bringing work home.

'Needed the fresh air.'

Her face dropped as she said, 'I've got some news.'

'So have I,' Danny said.

'You first,' she said.

Danny pulled the champagne from the bag and went to the kitchen to fetch their best, albeit only, crystal glasses, a wedding present from Sara's parents.

'What's this for?' she asked.

Danny paused as his fingertips stretched for the champagne flutes at the back of the cupboard.

'Just tell me,' she said. 'God knows, I'm in need of something to cheer about.'

'Well . . .' Danny started but struggled to get the words out.

Sara could read him like an open book and said, 'Now I'm worried.'

'Drink that and I'll tell you,' he said, passing her the crystal glass filled with champagne and bubbles.

'Now I'm very worried. I'm in no mood for games Danny.'

'I've bought Silver Belle,' he said. The smile he forced was wiped when Sara gave him a look.

'Tell me this is a joke, please.'

'I know it's not the best timing for us but I'll soon have her back winning races, trust me. Could be a good little earner.'

'And you were expecting me to be pleased,' she fumed, putting the glass down, champagne sloshing over the sides. 'For crying out loud, why didn't you talk to me first?'

'Cos I knew you'd say no,' Danny said.

'For a bloody good reason,' she cried, barely containing her rage. 'We've got debts as it is, that precious mare of yours will finish us.'

'What do ya mean by that?'

'I mean . . . look, I married you knowing you were a bit of a chancer, part of what appealed to me, opposites attract. But this one takes the biscuit.'

'Love, I can turn her career around, her quality and willpower is still there, it's just a matter of nurturing it from her.'

'But even if you're right, and from what I've seen of the racing game anything can go wrong, how long will it take before money rolls in?'

'I can turn the tide before the season is out, convinced I can.'

'But we can't afford our bills, let alone the ones she'll rack up.'

'Crane said I can rent a spare box until new horses come in, won't make much of a dent in my wages. Only slight worry is if the box is needed for a new owner but the way results have been lately, that's not gonna happen anytime soon. And I can buy food and bedding at cost. Vets bills shouldn't be much, she's sound as a pound right now.'

'But when it hits the fan and she goes lame, or doesn't make the grade, what then? We'll get into more debt,' Sara said. She blew her nose hard into some kitchen roll.

'Everything will be all right, always will. What's the point of worrying, never was worthwhile,' Danny said, something he'd often heard his dad say to his fretting mum. He swore he was slowly turning into his dad. Most would find that a frightening thought, but Danny revelled in it. Since he'd passed away, his father had become someone he could look up to. As he wasn't religious, dad had become a sort of guiding light. But he knew some kind of miracle was needed to get back in Sara's good books right now. 'Prize money will cover expenses on race days. In any case, already lining her up for a novice chase in the next week or two.'

'Daniel, tell me what the hell I'm going to do with you?'

'It'll be okay,' Danny said though he couldn't be sure of this. *No certainties in racing.*

'You're not listening,' she blasted. 'There just isn't enough room in this marriage for the three of us. She takes up more of your time than me as it is.'

'You always said follow your heart,' Danny pleaded. 'What've I done wrong?'

'Let me see, what part of going behind my back to buy a bloody racehorse is right, in your eyes.'

'It's on my cards.'

'Your money is mine, we share the burden, remember what we vowed, through thick and thin.'

'I know I should've checked with you, I know it's my fault as usual, I'm sorry. I just knew this Goddard wouldn't wait, putting the mare on the open market without a buy your leave and she'd be snapped up straight away if I hadn't made an offer, cut-price mind you. 14K.'

She sighed and left the room, slamming the door shut as an exclamation mark.

Danny downed the champagne. 'That went well,' he whispered. He thought about following her but he knew it would do no good and left her to simmer down. They'd had arguments before but nothing like this and it undermined his belief he'd done the right thing signing on the dotted line that morning.

After twenty or so minutes watching the TV's blank screen, he knocked on the bedroom door. No answer. He entered anyway and sat on the bed. She was lying on her side, facing away, quiet and still. Her fast breaths suggested she was awake. 'It'll work out,' he said softly, settling by her.

'No it won't,' she croaked.

'I got her for a knockdown price and they're not like buying a new car, losing value as soon as you drive off the garage forecourt. I can sell her at any point, get the money back.'

She didn't respond. He reached forward and gently rested his hand above her waist. She shook it off.

'I've never been a Steady Eddy, Sara, life is about risks and taking them. Won't get anywhere if ya don't.'

But it seemed she was still giving him the silent treatment. 'I'm sorry for not telling you my plans and for the way I told you. It was wrong for me to assume you'd be pleased about it, should've known after the times you'd warned me against it. But I'm not sorry for buying the mare and neither will you be, she's a little dynamo.'

Danny didn't mention the seven-day cooling off clause in the contract as he knew she would soon be marching him back up Caerphilly to tear up the contract. Instead, he asked, 'What about yours?'

'What?' she croaked.

'You had some news.'

'I lost my job.'

'What?' Danny asked though he'd heard perfectly.

'Got fired, laid off, us in admin were first to downsize, I was one of four from twenty to go, work those odds out Danny.'

Danny's hand reached forward again.

'When are we going to get a change of luck. Was working my fingers to the bone, for what? Didn't expect a bonus or anything, but this?!'

'Silver Belle will be our golden ticket, trust me.'

'Come back to the real world, Danny,' she said and turned to face him. 'And don't bring trust into this. That went out the window when you forked out fourteen grand on her behind my back.'

Danny returned to the lounge and poured a whisky. He logged on to the Weatherby's website and sifted through the entry stages for the Graded races in the coming months, mapping out a campaign plan for the mare, take his mind off Sara's erratic mood-swings, though it didn't work. He needed to give the mare a much-needed confidence restoring run and to do that, he looked to lower the sights and aim her for a minor novice chase where she could find a better rhythm.

He'd singled out a Class 4 event at Newbury on Saturday week. He checked the weather forecast for the coming days and, with steady rain predicted for the area, he reckoned the going might turn suitably soft by then. It was well worth entering at the five-day stage and see from there.

He then went to the section on the website for ordering owners' colours. Having virtually wiped all available funds with the purchase of the horse, he had little left in the coffers to reserve his colours. He knew the top owners snapped up the fashionable one-colour silks, like plain blue or plain pink.

It was like personalised number plates, often the simpler the more popular and prestigious. Danny looked at the bottom end of the range and resorted to a brown and green striped body, with brown sleeves and cap. Far from his first choice, with his favourite colour being blue, but he knew beggars can't be choosers. *Green and brown it is.* He clicked the button and went about ordering silks to his measurements from an independent website called *yoursilks.* His mood was lifted by doing this, feeling he was moving in the right direction for once.

Sara appeared from behind the lounge door and sat on the couch.

'You okay?'

'Given a fortnight's notice, so have to face everyone knowing they'd singled me out as a disposable asset,' she said and blew her nose again. 'And cheek of it all, seeing I was upset, Margaret, you met her once, said cheer up, might never happen. I was left standing there speechless with rage, whole room looking at me, as she walked away. Moments later, I'd come up with a killer reply that would've wiped the smile off her fat face but by then it was too late, the moment had passed.'

'Forget it,' Danny said. 'What are they to you?'

Her sobbing had subsided to a mere sniffle. She shrugged.

Danny continued, 'They're none of your business, just tell yourself that. I know it's hard but they're just trying to drag you down to join their miserable existence. Don't let 'em. Any case, you don't have to see 'em after the fortnight's up.'

'It's not as easy as that,' she said.

Danny sucked in air as if he was about to leap from his comfort zone, 'At school, this kid, Jack his name was, twice my size, pinned me down on the school field. Whole of the lunch break I was there, playground attendant didn't see, or didn't wanna see. Even spat phlegm in my face when I dared to question his sexuality, straddled over me with a grin spread over his face.'

Danny ran his hand over his closely cropped brown hair and swallowed back the threatening tears. He was caught off-guard by his own response to regurgitating those unsavoury memories after all these years.

'You never told me this,' Sara said, straightening up. 'God, that's awful Danny.'

'That was the least of it,' Danny said, 'was once forced against the wall by a pair of 'em in one of the labs, while another heated an iron rod over a Bunsen burner and scarred my lower back.'

'Why on earth would they do that?'

'For a laugh, I guess. They seemed tickled by it. Price for being the smallest in the year, pick on the weakest first.'

'Did you go to a teacher?'

'You kidding? Would've been dead meat then. Nah, took a leaf out Darwin's book and got myself fit, strengthened up. By the end, I could outrun 'em no probs and put up a fight if they'd got me cornered.'

'Why wait 'til now to tell me this?'

'Some things you don't wanna relive,' Danny said. 'Best left as a distant memory, faded. And I wanted you to know however bad things got, there's always a way out.'

'But you always said your school days were happy,' she said.

'I was outta there by fifteen,' Danny said, 'not cos I was thick.'

'But you told me you were spotted by one of the Lambourn talent scouts.'

'Begged my dad to leave, find me a placement at one of the yards and, being obsessed with racing, he was all for it. Used to lay awake, trying to shut out my parents arguing over plans 'til mum rushed off to bed in tears. Broke my heart but there was no way I was gonna stay at that dump of a school. Get away from it all, best thing I ever did.' There was a pause. 'You'll be okay' Danny said. He moved forward and rested his lips on the crown of her head, an excuse to take in the scent of her hair.

She forced a smile, though it failed to tell in her pink eyes. She then nodded.

Danny let himself fall back on the couch, arm draped over her stomach. But he soon became restless with the blackened skin of his stomach still sensitive to the touch, like a bad case of the flu.

'Gonna see Rick tomorrow, after the morning gallops. Are my jeans there?'

'Should be,' she said and followed him to the bedroom, as if not wanting to be left alone. Within the walk-in wardrobe, he fished for the jeans he always wore when visiting his brother Rick; the pair with scuffed knees soiled green. 'They've been washed,' she added, 'couldn't get those stains out.'

'Why don't you use the others?'

'Don't want to dirty them,' Danny said. 'These will do fine, Rick was never big on fashion.'

He looked around at the stuff Sara had hoarded over the years: dresses, blouses, mostly in slimming black, hats and shoes. *It was like a department store all by itself*, Danny thought, *could sell half of these and we'd clear a lot of the debts*, though he wouldn't dare broach the subject in the current air. He'd done so last year and couldn't argue back once she said, 'They're my hobby, like you've got your horses.'

CHAPTER 7

After the debacle that was Silver Belle's introduction to fences the other week, Danny felt a mix of eagerness and anxiety about renewing their partnership, like going on a first date. There was no way of telling how much confidence had drained from her. He knew racehorses weren't always able to shrug off early bad experiences when trying new disciplines. Like children, they needed handling with great care. That's why debutants are rarely unduly punished from the saddle, providing a positive memory and a solid platform for them to build a career upon. No point in thrashing the living daylights out of an impressionable horse during the initial stages of their career, they'd most probably burn out before the end of the first campaign, like some city whizz-kids.

Danny spun Silver Belle round, now facing the line of three baby brush fences. He'd schooled plenty of inexperienced or problem jumpers over these confidence-building obstacles before graduating to the more daunting regulation ones. His soft hands and good timing could get the most erratic of jumpers into a rhythm. But he could relax with those, less at stake. He couldn't ignore the fact Silver Belle was no longer just his pride and joy, but also his last shot at moving up in the racing world. She could make or break him.

Kelly had ventured over from the stabling area and was stood by the wings of the final fence. Danny could just make out, stood alongside her, the yard's dog Racket, a lively Jack Russell. He was named, according to Rhys, after he wouldn't stop yapping when first setting eyes on Crane. Danny always thought the little scamp was a good judge of character.

He felt a cramping in his stomach, not because he'd skipped breakfast. *First schooling session on Silver Belle since taking the plunge*, Danny thought, *something to put in the diary.*

Being her proud new owner, he felt as if sat on precious cargo. Like the first time he'd driven his gleaming Golf GTI back from the showroom, fearful that one wrong move could prove costly. But he couldn't do a worse job than Crane, who'd washed his hands of the mare after a string of lacklustre displays. He knew he was taking on damaged goods, mentally scarred from several bad experiences at the track, and it was now left to him to get her career back on track where it belonged and repair her once lofty reputation as a bright jumping prospect.

Stood here now, she felt like a shadow of the exuberant and precocious talent he'd sat on soon after she first arrived at the yard a year ago.

He drew in a lungful of crisp morning air. It felt cool and invigorating, like pure oxygen, compared to the city stuff he'd become accustomed to. He was prepared to set aside time every morning to send her over them for the next fortnight, or until she was clearing them fluently once more, whichever came soonest. It was like breaking her in again, building her up from scratch.

He urged her forward and was soon upon the first brush of birch. She got in close and stuttered her way over. He quickly got her organised as the second fence neared. She again mistimed her run up and brushed through the top of it. The mistake seemed to unsettle her. He swiftly ran a calming hand down her plaited mane. But she jumped far too big at the third and final fence; ballooning it with daylight to spare. He could hear Kelly clapping behind as he pulled her up sharply and began trotting back.

'Thought you'd have better things to do,' Danny said, perplexed why she would want to come and watch a routine session on the practice ground.

'Finished mucking out,' she replied. 'Thought I'd take five, see how our fallen star was.'

'You talking about me or the mare?'

She beamed a smile. 'Seemed to jump okay.'

'Bit awkward, but understandable I guess,' Danny said.

'Must be pleased with that, she made a good shape over the last fence,' she said.

'Perhaps, but she gave it too much respect, seems afraid of them after clouting so many in her last race,' Danny replied. 'Can't afford to spend that long in the air on race days.'

'Guess so,' she said.

'Gonna give her another spin over 'em, try and hone her technique so it becomes second nature. Keep everything crossed she'll translate that fluency to the track where it matters, different story in the heat of battle.'

The sun poked from behind scudding clouds, stroking her heart-shaped face, as she tucked lose strands of her raven-black hair behind her ears. 'Do you fancy a cooked breakfast back at the house?'

'You've twisted my arm,' Danny said. 'Can't leave on an empty stomach.'

'I'll see you back there in ten,' she said. Danny turned the mare and cantered back the way.

Pleased by an error-free round of jumps the second time, he trotted her back to the yard and pulled off waterproof bottoms and changed into his scuffed jeans. He met Kelly in the staff kitchen. The sweet smell of frying bacon met him as he struggled to pull on his trainers in the cloakroom.

Kelly was filling a tall glass of orange juice full of bits, as Danny liked. He sat down at the pine kitchen table. 'You shouldn't have gone to the trouble.'

'Nonsense,' Kelly said, still facing the window overlooking the gallops. 'I've trimmed the rinds off.'

'The rate we're working, ya could serve me a slab of lard and it wouldn't matter.'

She turned and prodded the bacon and tomato in the pan. It sizzled and crackled.

'Where's Crane?'

'In bed with exhaustion,' she replied. 'Doctor said it'll take weeks before he's back to his usual self.'

'Shame,' Danny said. 'Kind of like the new quiet version.'

'Danny!'

She served up the grub and Danny tucked in. 'This is great,' he said between mouthfuls. 'But you really shouldn't bother.'

'Stop saying that,' she said. 'I want to.'

Their eyes met briefly before she turned and began washing up. She said, 'Leave it there I'll finish cleaning up later.'

'Barely needs it,' Danny said, wiping the plate spotless with the last piece of thick white bread, 'Gorgeous it was.'

She smiled. 'Tea, coffee?'

'Better not,' he said chewing. 'I'm paying Rick a visit this afternoon but cheers for this, top nosh.'

He sat back, relishing the full and satisfied feeling. It wasn't often he allowed himself such a hearty meal for brunch, as he knew the pounds wound soon pile on and there was no way he was going to let anyone else on Silver Belle, not even Rhys.

He looked up at her stood against the bright orange light streaming through the large kitchen window. He couldn't deny Kelly was attractive. It was a natural beauty, the kind that could look good first thing in the morning with barely any make-up.

Danny's eyes returned to the empty plate and banished those thoughts immediately. He didn't feel guilty for momentarily fancying his colleague, any red-blooded male would've done the same, he reckoned, it was impossible not to. Her dark hair shimmering in the light, her full lips, her youthful soft face and flawless skin. Not to mention her infectious giggle at his jokes. But he was equally secure in his feelings for Sara and that would never waver. In any case, being a good decade older than Kelly, she probably wouldn't think of him in the same light.

CHAPTER 8

Danny stopped off at the flower shop in Canton and picked up his weekly order of lilies. He then drove to Llandaff – a leafy suburb full of large detached houses and flash cars. It was like the Knightsbridge of Cardiff. The parking was always a nightmare in the narrow, busy streets and he resorted to buying a ticket at the Pay and Display around the corner. He pushed past an iron gate and dropped his weight on the damp grass in front of a marble headstone marked with *In memory of Richard Rawlings Died aged 33*, shadowed by the spire of St. Teilo's church.

He'd never get over witnessing Rick's untimely death. Sara had begged him to go seek help, get his anger out in the open, as he took after his father in that he bottled everything up, too proud. *Don't need none of that psychobabble or mumbo-jumbo, pull y'self together*, his dad used to say, *worse things happen in war*.

Danny shifted his weight and said, 'Hello again, fancy seeing you here.' He began picking away at the wilting, discoloured flowers and replacing them with fresh ones. 'Mum's well, making the best of it like, keeping herself busy, you know how it is. Fretting about some speech she's got to do for her Christian group, only six others will be there apparently, but you know what she's like, worry for Britain she could. Got her a ticket for the Burt Bacharach concert at the CIA, take her mind off it. Would've jetted her out to the Costas for a week or two, but things gone a bit tight.' He paused. 'I know, I know,

70

same old story . . . some things never change, aye. I reckon my ship's just turning, not long before it comes in.' He leant forward and, with a tissue from his jeans, wiped clean a white-grey streak from the gleaming marble. 'Birds just won't leave you alone bruv, even now.' Another pause. 'Sara's well, bit tired and moody but at least she's stopped bangin' on about getting a dog, anyway-'

His train of thought was suddenly derailed. Dead ahead, beyond the headstone and railings, was a man staring directly at him. Danny looked over one shoulder, but there was no one behind. He cut a ghostly figure, as if floating, lifeless. Danny blinked. His initial feelings of embarrassment and self-consciousness turned to annoyance and anger. *Why shouldn't he catch up with his only brother without being rudely distracted by some stranger?* His gaze returned to the grave. 'Where was I? I dunno Rick, cheek of some bloody folk.'

It was less intimate now, though, fully aware of his surroundings. He didn't feel comfortable carrying on. He looked back up but the spectral shape had gone. Bunching clouds, turning battleship grey, began shedding their load.

Danny pushed off the grass and gathered together the dead flowers and his thoughts. About to leave, he noticed a shadow flick into the church. Was it the stranger? Eager to tell the man the error of his ways, Danny changed course.

Wanna set him straight about manners. On his way in, out of respect, he tossed a two-pound coin in a yellow box marked: 'Church Roof Restoration Appeal Fund.'

He entered the dark nave and was conscious of his boots slapping the polished flagstone floor. He softened each footfall and dropped his weight on the pew beside the stranger, three rows from the altar. They were alone, both looking ahead.

'What's your game' Danny hissed, 'staring me down out there?'

The man turned, his waxy skin gave off a translucent quality against the spectrum of light streaming through the towering stained glass windows either side.

'No game,' the man rasped. 'Life is too short for games, Daniel.'

Danny now eyed the stranger with suspicion. 'But I don't know you.'

'Don't be alarmed,' the man replied. 'I'm a regular here, I merely saw you a few times and asked the vicar who you were, out of mild curiosity. I too have a relative buried here, you see, it's easy to see a connection with your fellow man if you look hard enough.'

Danny said nothing for a moment. He thought about leaving. But the distant rumble beyond the thick stone walls, like tyre-tread on cobbles, swayed him otherwise.

He hated small-talk, recalling those turgid wine and cheese evenings he was dragged along to by Sara for her firm. Stuck for something to say, he blurted out, 'You religious?'

It was a subject he'd always swerved until now, seeing where he was.

The man smiled, 'No. Not in the slightest.'

The answer took Danny by surprise. He'd assumed a man of his advancing years would've turned to religion as a means of solace and comfort, believing there was a point to all of this and a place to go after it. He was wrong and made a mental note not to be so quick to judge. His mum had recently turned born-again Christian and had increasingly become involved in the weekly meetings. Although Danny was a firm atheist, anything to help her deal with Rick's death was fine by him. He hoped there wasn't a Judgement Day. If there was a hell, he was sure his place was already booked.

The man continued, 'But I get some source of serenity, peacefulness from coming here, get away from this mad world of ours.' He turned and his pale lips stretched into a faint smile again, though it failed to tell in his sunken eyes. Danny could sense the man was suffering and couldn't help feel pity towards him.

'Danny,' he said, extending his hand as an olive branch.

'James,' the man replied. 'Nice to meet you.'

'Likewise.'

The pair sat facing ahead. Two rows of heavy oak pews, leading to a pulpit and a majestic brass sculpture of Christ on the cross.

James turned to face ahead, still as a mannequin. Was he praying? 'Impressive,' Danny said, looking up at the work of art. 'Can't say I've been in here since I laid my brother to rest.'

James said, 'Not the only treasure within these walls. You're from around here?'

'Sort of,' Danny replied, always wary of revealing anything to complete strangers. 'And you?'

James shifted his weight to face Danny again. 'Born and raised in Cardiff, second generation immigrant.' He paused. 'What's your line of work?'

'Horses . . . racehorses, I'm a trainer,' Danny said, before questioning why he felt the need to give himself a promotion to impress a complete stranger. 'Well, I'm assistant, for now.'

'You want more?'

'Who doesn't?'

James arched his grey eyebrows. 'Go on.'

'Wanna run my own yard one day soon, be my own boss. Reckon I got what it takes, gonna take time, though.'

'And money I presume.'

'That as well, makes the world go round apparently.'

'Indeed.'

'And have you always been in the racing game?'

'Yep, well since I've kept the right side of the law.'

James's brow creased, perhaps surprised by Danny's honesty. 'We all have regrets. Mistakes we shouldn't have made. It's what makes us human.'

'Yeah, I guess so,' Danny said, the burden of shame easing from his shoulders.

'May I ask what happened?' James asked. 'I know it's none of my business and you can tell me to be quiet.'

Danny said, 'Course not, never made no secret of it. Got in with the wrong crowd you see, did some time for B&E.

73

Nothing big like, never armed. Not quite so nimble nowadays. Anyway, that's all behind me. Listen to me, feel like I'm in confessional or something.'

'I guess that fleet of foot helped as a jockey.'

'On a job, they used to call me 'The Rat'. Give me a drainpipe and I was up it in a flash, least I think that's why the name stuck.'

James smiled.

'Was also called on to clear walls, squeeze through gaps. While doing a stretch, I had a teacher, an old-time pro who taught me the finer things, like picking locks. Never had the need for those skills, mind you, gone clean since getting out. Hang on, never said I was a jockey.'

'Just assumed, from what little I know of the sport, most jockeys stay in the game.'

'True.'

'What really brings you here Daniel? Are you in some kind of trouble?'

'Far from it, think I'm on to something big,' Danny said, thoughts returned to Silver Belle's improved display in her homework.

James's eyes narrowed as if intrigued. He said, 'Care to reveal more.'

'Nah, keeping this one to myself, don't want to put the mockers on it, you understand.'

James sighed. 'I like you Daniel.'

'Hardly know me,' Danny replied. He was never very good at taking a compliment, always brushing them off. Yet he'd tend to scrutinize every word of criticism, or below the belt jibe.

He knew it wasn't a good attitude to adopt if you wanted to succeed in the cut-throat world of racing, where it was survival of the fittest mind and body. Nevertheless, he would be lying if he said he wasn't buoyed by the remark just now.

'I feel I know you enough to see a younger version of myself. I had dreams once. You must take every opportunity.'

Danny didn't pry whether James had fulfilled his dreams, just in case it dampened his mood. 'What did you do?' he asked, keeping it as vague as possible.

'I used to do a lot of things, can't even fish now, my knees give me terrible jip.'

'My father used to fish.'

'Really, which rivers?' James asked.

'Not sure,' Danny replied, 'just recall packing my junior rod and luncheon meat at first light. Can remember the thrill of catching my first, though, a right tiddler it was. Even then, guess I wanted to make my dad proud, prove myself. Reckon it's a man thing, hunter and gatherer.' Danny stopped and smiled, flicking over the faded snapshots of his childhood.

'Tell me,' James said, 'what's your father's name?'

'Peter.'

'Peter Rawlings,' James said, eyes lit, as if he'd just completed a crossword. 'I recall him, how the devil is he now, used to share the same banks upstream on the River Taff way back when.'

'He died,' Danny said, figuring a long time ago it was easier just to come out with it straight, not skirting round the issue, making it more awkward than it already was.

'I'm so sorry, Daniel,' James said. 'He was a fit young man when I knew him. When?'

'Years ago,' Danny said. He swallowed hard, squirming at the mere threat of showing any emotion in front of strangers. 'But it seems like yesterday when I heard the news. He supported Liverpool and I was an Arsenal fan. When I left to learn my trade in Lambourn, we used to phone each other every Saturday after the matches and poke fun if the other's side lost. First sign I knew something was wrong when the call never came that Saturday. Head-on crash, died at the scene. He was on his way to meet me.'

'Such an awful thing for you to go through, I'm sorry, I liked Peter. He was salt of the earth, genuine. So tragic.'

'Yeah, I know,' Danny said. Feeling his eyes dampen, he continued, 'Anyway, best be going, sorry I was a bit off with ya at first.'

'No, glad we sorted out our differences,' James said. 'Daniel, would it be amiss of me to offer you something, a gift?' James displayed a watch over the back of his gnarled hand, peppered with liver spots. Its silver face shimmered in the dusty light and its strap was cut from rich brown leather.

Danny didn't know how to react, conditioned from childhood not to accept anything from strangers. But he could handle himself now and he didn't want to offend the elderly man. Danny sensed he was lonely, probably got no relatives and wanted to give it to a good home. 'I'll pay you for it.'

'Nonsense,' James croaked. 'Then I would gain no pleasure from the gesture. Please, take it, a gift.'

'What's the catch?' Danny asked. Working in the racing world, Danny had built up a healthy level of scepticism, *no such thing as a free lunch*.

'No catch,' James said, offering it to Danny. 'I'm not getting any younger you see. And I want to know it will be looked after. Please, at least try it on.'

Danny examined it. On the back, there was a number engraved. 'What's this?'

'My phone number,' James replied. 'In case it was misplaced.'

Danny wished he'd done the same for his watch. He worked the strap to a tight fit, and met James' gaze. 'I'm touched, really I am. You're a dying breed.'

He needed a watch to replace the one he lost and, with finances on the brink, he was sorely tempted to accept it. 'But I just couldn't take it off you, be like daylight robbery and those days are behind me.'

'Nonsense, I will derive more pleasure knowing someone is making use of it, rather than at the bottom of a drawer somewhere.'

'Cheers,' Danny said and left before the man had a change of heart.

Back at the apartment block, he checked his post and signed for a parcel, *must be the silks*. He was right, sent by express delivery, much to his relief as they were cutting it fine. He'd have to pass them on to the jockeys' valet as soon as he got on track at Newbury tomorrow.

He took care in unfolding the pristine top and cap, laying them on the dining table. He glanced at a 'to do' list left by Sara. It read: Shop – bread, milk. Doctors. Job Centre – enrol. He pushed the list to one side and stood proud as he stared down, *my very own colours*. He smiled.

Hearing the clap of the front door told him Sara was back. 'All right love?'

'Bugger all work about.'

'Something will come along,' Danny said. 'They'll always need admin.'

She dropped on to the couch and flicked on the TV.

Danny pressed the silk against his body. 'What do ya reckon?'

'Very fetching,' she said. 'Where's the party?'

'Very funny,' Danny said. 'They came through today, have to try them on later, for size.'

'I like a man in silks,' Sara said.

'It's your lucky day,' Danny said. His hand brushed her shoulder as he passed the couch and booted up the laptop. He felt things were finally getting somewhere and it pleased him to see Sara in a better mood. Perhaps she'd forgiven him for his surprise purchase, seeing he was serious about getting her on the track in search of a return on his investment, though he didn't ask her, afraid it was too soon to test the water.

He logged on to the Weatherby's website using Crane's details. Buoyed by the solid workout from Silver Belle and James's gift, he ran over the final declarations for the chase he'd entered the mare at Newbury tomorrow. Just the seven runners and the going had eased to soft, heavy in places. *Just perfect*, Danny thought. *Must be in with a shout with the help of her seven pound sex allowance for being a mare against colts and geldings.* He could get used to this life as a trainer.

CHAPTER 9

A thick white quilt of cloud covered the closed Berkshire sky. Smudges of brightness to the north, where fingers of lemon-gold sunlight broke through.

Danny looked down at the starter, who was checking Silver Belle's girth strap was a comfortable fit. But he found himself distracted by a red dot on the green and brown body of his rippling silks. He immediately pressed his gloved hand against his nostrils. He was prone to severe nose bleeds as a kid but they hadn't resurfaced for years. He feared the pressure of sitting on the reason for his mounting debts may have brought one on. But his leather-clad fingers were stainless. He lowered his goggles and his gaze. The dot had moved from his abdomen to his chest and was shaking ever-so-slightly, dancing.

Fearing the worst, Danny placed his hand in front of the dot. It disappeared. It was his hand that was now shaking. His furtive eyes skated across the panorama, lingering on the imposing reddish grandstand at Newbury with its many turrets and lookouts, across to the dense wooded outcrop lining the back straight and then the huge storage barn to his right.

This can't be happening, Danny thought, hoping it was one of the fellow jockeys playing a prank. The seven riders seemed preoccupied with their own thoughts and concerns, focussed to do battle. *Where the fuck was it coming from?*

He tugged gently on the reins, holding the mare firm, now rooted to the spot. The other runners continued to circle patiently around him down at the start as the clock ticked towards 3.30 p.m. Danny was transfixed by the dot. It kept disappearing when a rival passed him at about the two o'clock position from where he'd stopped. Taking a straight line beyond this was the woodland. *That's where the bastard was hiding.* It was alongside the third fence they'd have to jump, leaving him a sitting duck, dead meat. He turned to shout to the starter or the racecourse vet, warn them. Perhaps say Silver Belle had gone lame, anything to stop the race. But the vet had returned to his Range Rover already primed to follow the runners on their two-mile five-furlong journey, while the starter had now mounted his rostrum and was checking his wrist. *Shit!*

His furtive eyes flitted between the wooden area and the starter. He had no option but to walk forward and join the other runners forming an orderly line. Danny knew that purposefully not starting the race would risk his jockey's licence and make headline news in the trade press. Being labelled as a non-trier was a big deal, undermining any future pretensions of taking out a trainer's licence. *Kiss goodbye to attracting new owners.* Who'd want to send their prized thoroughbreds to a trainer with a tarnished past; *bad news sticks.*

'Lead in jockeys,' ordered the starter. Danny kidded Silver Belle forward and she responded, passing a few more recalcitrant types less keen to set off. 'Come on, walk in.'

Danny couldn't stop the reins from shaking and wanted to shout, 'No!', and start sprinting in the opposite direction, away from where he believed the sniper's hideout to be. He felt sick as butterflies flapped wildly in his cramping stomach.

The orange tape disappeared and, before Danny had chance to run through any other options, he found himself galloping strongly mid-pack, first fence closing fast. With just three furlongs to where the trees became dense enough to conceal a hit-man, he had to make the impossible decision whether to jump ship, effectively leaving his mount rudderless. The mere thought of parting company with the mare hurt him but she was sensible and would most likely pop a few fences for fun before spotting the offshoot to the stabling area. He knew this was a vital prep race to boost her confidence and fitness levels but what good would that be if he was lying in a morgue somewhere, he reasoned.

Being a moving target, what if the sniper's bullet missed and hit his mount; she was after all bigger. *Couldn't live with that.*

He'd made his mind up. After skimming the first fence neatly, he began to pull on the reins. If he hit the deck, he didn't want to be trampled on by the backmarkers. She resisted at first, head carriage up, but he was in command and the pair soon found themselves trailing the field. The second fence came upon the runners quickly.

He slipped both riding boots from their stirrups and began to shift his weight off kilter. He soon felt the full force of gravity and saw the rain-saturated ground rush towards him, connecting with shoulder first and then back, aquaplaning on the wet turf to stop in the shelter of the second fence. To his relief, during the tumble he'd caught glimpse of the only grey in the field clear the fence cleanly as they streamed over, no casualties. He lay still for a moment as he gathered his bearing, still slightly dazed from the spill.

Although he'd plied much of his trade as a Flat jockey, where tumbles were rare, he was well-versed in the art of landing safely after leaping from many a first-floor window during his days as a housebreaker. It didn't faze him. He glanced around the fence, still grounded. Through plastic grilles forming the wing of the fence, he could see the runners were already passing the grandstand off in the distance, a flash of white among a field of chestnuts and bays told him Silver Belle was still on her hooves and seemingly enjoying herself. Closer, an ambulance had turned and was negotiating a rutted and puddle-ridden path on the inside of the course; his ticket to a safe journey back to the shelter of the jockeys' changing room. He felt and moved each limb, and flexed his neck, just to make sure, *no damage.*

He was then checked over in the back of the ambulance and, once given some pure oxygen and the green light, they ferried him back to face the wrath of the stewards.

Head bowed, he took the punishment dished out by the three officials, one professional stipendiary and two volunteers. A two-week ban for dangerous riding was the punishment. Danny's excuse that he'd 'lost his balance' clearly didn't wash with them. He was also given a final warning for potentially bringing the game into disrepute, with 'further action pending if subsequent audit trails from the major betting exchanges revealed to the security department of the British Horseracing Authority suspicious activity relating to the race.' Danny knew they wouldn't.

He rushed to the stabling area, make sure Silver Belle had returned safe and well. Her nose was deep in a food bag hung from the stable-box wall.

Kelly was leading the yard's other runner to the twin-loader, her face blanched. 'You okay?' she said. 'Crane phoned, turned the air blue he did. What the hell happened?'

'Why should he care? Not like it's his mare anymore,' Danny reasoned, though he knew it was still R. Crane next to her name on the racecard and it didn't look pretty out there. He didn't want to cast any further dark clouds over the yard, struggling as it was.

Danny repeated, voice still shaken, what he'd just told the stewards. 'Got short of room and lost my balance.'

'Gonna say,' she sighed, 'Worried to death that I'd not tightened the tack enough. If anything had happened to you . . . well, doesn't bear thinking about.'

There was an awkward pause. Danny gritted a smile, *nice to know there was someone batting for my side among the Samuel House team.* 'Nah, all my fault. Got the bruises to prove it.'

He lifted his shirt, revealing a honed stomach. Her eyes widened, colour returning to her face. 'We'll get you patched up when you get back.'

'No need,' Danny said. 'Looks worse than it feels.'

'You're a lot braver than me,' she said. Their eyes locked again, before Danny broke the link.

'Nonsense,' he said, before switching focus back on the mare beside him, 'More importantly, how's this one. When did she call it a day?'

'She did a circuit and a bit,' she said, frowning. 'Jumped super she did, then trotted back in her own time. Good as gold.' She ran her hand down Silver Belle, who was still snaffling and snorting at her feed.

'Eating up well,' he said. 'So can't feel too bad, aye girl.' He pinched the mare's grey ear and she flashed her tail. 'May as well make a move, hate driving in the dark. Will you load 'em, while I get changed out of these.'

'Will do,' she replied, already unbolting the stable door.

A large field of runners going to post for the next race had left the changing room eerily quiet, just the valet entranced by a small monitor in the corner.

He peeled off his soiled silks and body protector. He still felt on edge, fearing the gunman would come after him and complete any unfinished business. Rooting in his kitbag for an antiperspirant spray, he came upon a small sheet of paper, folded in two. Danny always left notes in his wallet or jacket pocket. He scanned the room again before flipping the paper open, half expecting a childish prank by one of the pros.

Being a part-timer, Danny was low in the jockey room hierarchy and was occasionally the brunt of some friendly banter, though he recalled they once went too far when throwing his kitbag containing his clothes and towel on the roof of the changing room back in his days on the Flat. He only discovered this after leaving the showers. Had to shimmy up a drain-pipe in his silks, soaked through as the culprits looked on and laughed, *like being back at school it was.* He tried brushing the incident off, though he'd be lying if he said it hadn't left its mark at the time.

Now the wrong side of thirty, Danny could look back and smile, *boys will be boys.* Though he wasn't smiling once he read the note typed in black ink: *Be wise, walk away from this or you will die.*

Danny stopped tightening his belt and dropped onto the wooden slatted bench framing the room, reading the words again, walk away from this or you will die.

Holding the slightly quivering piece of paper in his hand, he now had hard evidence to prove the recent troubles weren't just paranoia on his part.

After a distant roar sounded, the valet's interest in the TV had waned. Danny looked across at the screen. It showed the winner of the fifth race on the card being led back.

'Dear John letter is it?' the valet said, picking up some stray saddle cloths.

'Something like that,' Danny said, in no mood to joke around. He finished changing and swung his kitbag over his aching shoulder.

He carved a path through the racegoers mingling between the many bars, the betting ring and the row of tented shops selling everything from jewellery to books. He was keen to board the horse-box parked in the owners' and trainers' car park and get away, for all he knew the gunman was among those punters. A casual glance across at the paddock enclosure and he was distracted by a striking individual, wearing a grey knee-length coat and a peaked cap. The plastic railing bore the brunt of his bulky frame. He was staring right at him, unblinking, even with racegoers cutting across their path. He kept looking. Was this the gunman? Danny asked himself, though he certainly didn't look like one and why would he lurk around such a public area, *too risky.*

The onlooker remained fixed between the stepped viewing areas around the parade ring. Despite the darkening sky, Danny could see the man clearly, even the entry badge hung by string from a buttonhole on his mac. Not keen to hang about, Danny quickened his stride but was held back by the crowds spilling into the paddock area, slowing his progress. And then, a kid tugged on his jacket and squeaked, 'Can you sign this for me?'

He'd clearly seen Roger Crane Training Yard writ in bold

white on his navy kitbag. 'Sure, kiddo. Who's it to?' His eyes flitting between the child's chubby face and the figure still watching his every move from afar.

'Ryan, I want to be a jockey,' the child said.

Danny smiled and signed his name. 'Work hard and you'll do just fine.' He handed the kid back his pen. When he looked up, the man had gone. *Now it's definitely time to go*, Danny thought, unnerved.

He paced back to the van. Kelly had loaded both inmates and he could see her shadowy outline sitting patiently in the passenger seat.

Calling from behind, a voice wheezed, 'Mr. Rawlings.'

Danny sighed and turned, prepared to sign another autograph. Last thing he wanted before the three-hour drive back to the yard. But what confronted him was the man who'd just eyeballed him. He'd removed his cap. A runway of gleaming scalp topped his head and what was left of his hair was flecked grey. He was now sweating and had unbuttoned his mac to reveal a checked shirt overhanging bleached jeans, or possibly just old and faded.

'Glad I caught you,' the man said. 'It's Mike.'

He extended his callused hand and, out of politeness, Danny reciprocated, before glancing at his new watch as a not-so-subtle hint to the guy.

'I won't take a minute of your time,' Mike said, 'but I need to talk to you.'

'Go on,' Danny said past gritted teeth.

'Tell me, what just happened out there?'

'Thought that was obvious, I slipped and fell,' Danny said. 'Got the bruises and a fortnight's holiday for my troubles.'

'Did you jump?'

Who was this guy? He needed to find out before revealing anything else. Probably some hack looking for an exclusive, or was he even the psycho who'd left the note, playing some sick mind games. Getting kicks by following it up to see if Danny would rise to the threats.

'Who are you?'

'I'm sorry, I should've said.' He delved in his jeans pocket and handed him a card. 'I'm a private detective.'

But Danny refused it. 'You don't look like one.'

'I guess I'm doing my job then.'

'What were you?' Danny asked, fearing he was an army veteran capable of firing a rifle with any accuracy, or ex-police following up a cold case. Either way, he didn't want to know. 'No one ever starts out as a private detective.'

'Formerly worked for Customs and Excise.'

'You don't look like a tax man, neither.'

'Thanks,' Mike replied, smiling. 'I'll take that as a compliment.'

'Like I said, I fell off, jockey error, covers a multitude of sins.'

'Does the name Dante mean anything to you?'

'Nah,' Danny said, hand resting on the handle of the driver's door, a portent to his intentions.

'And Lazari?'

Danny's mind shot back to his visit to Casey, who'd asked him about the Rule of Lazari. 'What about it?'

'What does it mean to you?' Mike asked, seemingly bemused at Danny's apparent ignorance.

'No comment,' Danny said, squeezing the handle on the driver's door of the horsebox. He was shook up physically by the fall and mentally from the note left in his kitbag. Still mindful of its typed lettering: Be wise, walk away from this or you will die.

'Answer me,' Mike said sternly.

'Don't have to answer any of your questions. Who sent you?'

'I'm working on my own case. Have you been threatened in any way?'

Aside from running the guy down with the van, Danny knew he wouldn't be rid of him until he'd got an answer.

Mike persisted, 'Have you?'

'Yeah, found this,' Danny said, unfolding the sheet he'd discovered just minutes earlier. 'Familiar to you?' Danny asked in an accusatory manner.

Once Mike's eyes had devoured it, his free hand pinched the other corner of the note, as if to act as a steadier. He handed it back, clearly having seen enough.

'What?' Danny asked, concern growing. 'What is it?'

'This isn't easy for me to say.' Mike paused.

'I'm sure you'll manage.' Danny replied.

'The same printed words were found on Monty McCann and Simon. This isn't a joke, these people mean business.'

Danny's brow tingled with sweat yet his skin felt cold. 'Wait a minute, on the news they never revealed this detail. How the hell would you know? Unless you'd planted them.'

Mike shrugged off the accusation with a hollow laugh. 'I can assure you, I want this killer found as much as you. My contacts unearthed the details from a classified police report, waiting to go public unless the investigation fails to make any significant progress apparently.'

'So what you're saying,' Danny said, 'I'm next.'

Mike's eyes sought the tarmac.

Danny felt like the moment he'd first heard his father was dead. He noticed his jaw tremble, as if his body was slipping into shock mode. He couldn't cope with this and wanted desperately to flee, put his head in the sand, but he knew he'd only fret until the killer would be caught. 'Can't your *contacts* find out who planted this?' he asked. He tried wetting his lips but the spit wasn't there.

'I have no more details I'm afraid. Still working on it.'

'They're gonna catch the killer,' Danny said, more to convince himself. 'Fingerprints were left at the scene on the weapon for Christ's sake. They'd have to fuck up big time not to close the net with forensics on the case.'

'What have you discovered about the Rule of Lazari?'

'Speak English or I'm outta here,' Danny said. But the man stared, seemingly steadfast until getting an answer. 'No, I don't know the Rule Of . . . whatever. Casey Jones asked me the same.'

'When did you meet him?' Mike asked.

'Just the other day.'

Mike's free hand skated over his bald strip. 'Did anyone see you leave?'

'Don't think so,' Danny said, not wanting to face up to the truth.

'That's something,' Mike muttered. 'Please take this.' He forced the card in Danny's palm. 'Speak soon, we'll need each other.'

'Think what you like mate,' Danny said, slamming the door in Mike's face and then making out his muffled voice through the driver's door, 'Don't run from this, Daniel. You'll be caught.'

The man started banging on the side door. Danny felt movement behind, horses unsettled. 'That's all we need.'

'What's he want? Kelly asked.

'Nothin', just some nutter,' Danny said. 'Seem to attract them. Let's get outta here.'

Danny pulled away, joining the stream of traffic leaving the trainers' car park. 'Excuse the French, Kelly, but what a fucking day,' he fumed. 'Two hundred miles round trip for two unplaced runners and grief from some nutcase.' Danny took his frustration out on the steering wheel.

He dropped off the horses back at the yard and ensured they were settled, looking over Silver Belle with a fine-tooth comb to make certain she was still in A1 condition after her exploits following his early unseating. She didn't have a mark on her. Her legs and feet were fine and she seemed to be happy enough within herself, no sulking.

Remarkably settled, he thought, *given the day's events*. Perhaps she was maturing with age.

'Sorry about leaving you today,' he whispered, her head lolling over the stable door. 'Still, we're both fit to fight another day, just about.'

By the time he'd dropped Kelly off at her parents' house in Caerphilly and returned to the flat it was dusk. Sara had yet to come home. He read a note on the table. *Gone to dad's, back late.*

She often sought solace from her dad when times were difficult. He didn't feel any resentment that she would do this. He only wished he could do the same with his own dad when stuck in one of life's troughs.

He switched on the computer. The only link he could glean from talking with both Casey and Mike was this Rule of Lazari. He typed in a relevant search that flashed up over a thousand results. He scrolled down the screen. Most of the websites were gambling forums or horseracing portals, many to do with betting systems and strategies. He clicked on one that appeared most relevant.

It was a site dedicated to punting for profit and there was a small section about famous systems of the past. He read:

The legendary betting system known as the Rule of Lazari made headlines in the mid-nineties. There are few details of its workings but it was famed for building upon the already substantial riches of its founder Jeremiah Lazari, who cleaned up with some hefty recorded bets on-track alone. This was, according to reports, merely the tip of the iceberg in relation to his betting profits off-track.

One of the world's foremost mathematicians, Miles Crabtree, was the mastermind behind this foolproof system. The Oxford don was sponsored by Lazari to produce the ultimate racing system based on data covering the previous ten years' results and statistics. Little else is known about the factors used in the system, with Lazari and Crabtree remaining tight-lipped on the subject.

No shock there, Danny thought. If a successful betting system became common knowledge, the odds of each runner it picked would collapse and, as a result, long-term profits would be wiped out. *The fewer who knew its workings, the more its worth.*

The final line of the piece read: *The initial media coverage whipped up soon ebbed away and no further details were ever revealed.*

That one passed me by, Danny thought, though he wasn't betting at the time as jockeys weren't allowed to. As a punter, he rarely dipped his toe in the world of betting systems though he knew they were merely a structured approach to gambling using stats with a view to swinging the percentages into the punters' favour away from the bookies'. Much like in life, some betters preferred to live by a more regimented approach, following set rules and sticking to them, while others were more at home relying on instinct, more of a feel. Systems predicated on punting with the mind rather than the heart.

Having researched a few as a last resort during lean spells when advising a betting syndicate, Danny recalled they could be as simple as loyally following a certain trainer that did well at a certain track, or a particular jockey that did well, according to past records, in a particular month. Or they could be a complex multi-layered formulae, involving numerous variables. He knew it was rare for systems to work in the long run as there were so many out there putting the hours in trying to find an edge and it was never long before they'd cottoned on to the gap in the market and then force the price down. He was therefore left more than a little intrigued at how they achieved it. He carried out another search, typing in Miles Crabtree – the brains behind it all.

According to reports, since being thrust into the limelight with his name associated with the 'system to end all systems', he'd hung up his college robes and slipped into the shadows as a recluse. Nothing more heard of him since. Danny's first thought was that he'd passed away, another dead end. But after delving deeper, he came across a small feature for a local paper in Cheltenham that'd been uploaded to their website. It was a retrospective piece that suggested Crabtree, who had apparently been flagged up in the local and trade press for his association with the Rule of Lazari, was still in the area and was working on other research work, despite being well into retirement age. There was also a grainy black and white image of Crabtree.

After finishing up at the yard, he was tempted to visit Crabtree, catch him off-guard. The phone rang, making him flinch.

'Daniel Rawlings,' a voice said with a cold efficiency, as if pre-recorded. 'This is Draper. Help me find the Rule of Lazari. Meet outside St. Teilo's church grounds 2 a.m. Wednesday.'

Before Danny had chance to answer back or question who the voice belonged to, the line went dead. He felt his heart double in pace.

CHAPTER 10

Tuesday, 1.36 p.m. Danny wasn't hopeful as his knuckles struck glossy black paint on an imposing front door. It was one of several making a crescent of impressive regency houses in the historic spa town of Cheltenham.

A slim woman, early forties, answered Danny's call. Her tight curls were ruddy brown, matching her tired eyes. A black cat stealthily slipped through a slender gap and made its escape, brushing his leg en route.

'Arkle! Come back here,' she shouted but it was already gone. 'That bloody cat. Yes?'

'Is Miles Crabtree in? I've been told he lives here.'

'Who shall I say it is?'

'An old student, Danny Rawlings.' He didn't feel it was worth inventing a pseudonym. She disappeared behind the door with a 'wait here one moment.'

Several moments later, she reappeared, opening the door invitingly. 'Up the stairs, would you wait in the room second on your left, he won't be long.'

Very trusting, Danny thought, for someone who was unlikely to have heard of him. It raised his suspicions. *Was Crabtree expecting him?*

He felt a nervous tingle as he was led into the hallway. He guessed it was the building's age, with a tall ceiling and creaking floorboards. *These places give me the creeps.*

He was taken to what looked like a drawing room. 'Please, wait here,' she said.

A brass chandelier hung proudly from an ornate ceiling rose and he stood on a large Indian rug matted with animal hair and blanched by rich, fruity pink sunlight streaming through a tall sash window to his right. Wilting potted plants lined the windowsill, crying out for a watering. A musty smell of cigars and cats tainted the air.

The place was a mess, every available surface taken. Reminded Danny of a bedsit he'd shared as an apprentice jockey in Lambourn. He guessed there was a desk somewhere under the mass of files, books and folders piled high, teetering over the edges, like those coin-drop machines in the arcade halls he used to hang around during double maths years back. Two finely polished duelling pistols hung from the wall, though there were three hooks. Lost in a gallery of framed photos was a signed picture of the legendary punter Phil Bull – founder of the hugely influential *Timeform* organisation. Beneath was a quote saying something about securing the 'best possible odds for your stake as, like it or not, after that everything else was in the lap of the gods.' Another was a certificate of Crabtree's embossed in gold italics, with more letters after his name than in it.

He glanced up at a bank of six flat screens, a mix of live satellite feeds, including one showing them go down to the post for the opener at Uttoxeter. Others were displaying movements in odds for upcoming races, all muted. Below, a laptop was perched on a small desk, screensaver on.

'Yes?' a weak gravelly voice came from behind. Blocking the doorway was a frail man, draped in a mauve quilted smoking jacket. To look at him, Danny wouldn't have guessed he was arguably the greatest mind to set about solving one of the most rewarding puzzles to elude mankind - a betting system that yielded guaranteed long term profits. *More like someone you'd avoid eye-contact on a night bus cruising one of the estates skirting Cardiff*, Danny thought. His sunken eyes pierced past tortoise-shell glasses and coils of white hair framed his bristly face, thinning on top.

'Tell me, what brings you here?'

'Miles . . . Miles Crabtree?' Danny asked, though it was merely rhetorical. He matched the photo on the web.

Crabtree nodded before saying, 'Now answer my question.'

'The Rule of Lazari,' Danny said.

Crabtree emptied his lungs, as if that was the wrong answer. 'Why come to me?'

'You created it,' Danny said, 'so say old newspaper reports from the *Racing Post* and *Sporting Life*, even made a few business sections of the broadsheets.'

Crabtree paused, as if considering his choice of words, and then said, 'I was the face and name behind it. But why should it concern you, after all these years?'

'I'm an ex-jockey and two of my biggest rivals at the time have since been murdered, executed,' Danny said.

'I'm guessing you're alluding to Monty McCann and Simon Thorpe.'

'Yeah,' Danny enthused, feeling he was getting somewhere. 'But don't you think it's odd?'

'Not particularly,' Crabtree said. He skirted the brimming desk and sat in a scroll armchair of burgundy leather, fingertips making a steeple.

'I reckon I'm next on the list,' Danny said. 'Or one of the other jockeys.'

Crabtree laughed and then said, 'Now you're being ridiculous.'

'I'm deadly serious. If I wasn't, wouldn't be 'ere, would I.'

'Ask yourself why someone would systematically kill jockeys riding over a decade ago,' Crabtree rasped. 'You won't find many answers.'

'But I already have evidence they're after me,' Danny said. 'Left me in a right state he did.'

'Who?' Crabtree asked, brow lowered.

'Some thug, tracked me down,' Danny said. 'Miles, they know where I live, and, if that weren't enough, at the races the other day, I was about to line up and some infra-red beam was tracking my every move, like those ya see on guns the SAS guys use.'

'That explains your somewhat ungainly departure,' Crabtree said.

Danny asked, 'How come you know about that?'

'Daniel, I make it my business to watch every race in Britain and Ireland, yours was just one of them; my desire for the game remains undiminished. I have to keep up to minute with all the news and results.' He glanced up at the screens, still a hive of activity. 'I have a reputation to maintain you see.'

'Tell me what you know about the Rule?' Danny asked, determined not to leave without something to work with.

'Why should I?'

'I've made a cast-iron link between the Rule and the murders and I'm sure as hell gonna find out what's behind it all before they finish me off too.'

'The system put bookies out of business,' Crabtree revealed. 'Others became wary of accepting Jeremiah's bets and the founder turned to a team of associate bettors and contacts he could trust to get bets on at short notice.'

'But why don't you use it?'

'I have an analytical mind, not a punting mind,' Crabtree said. 'My interest was in the achievement of discovering a flawless system.'

'Don't give me that,' Danny said. 'Everyone's after a quick buck.'

'Don't get me wrong,' Crabtree said, leaning forward. His glasses slid down his aquiline nose, revealing dark burrowing eyes. 'I was rewarded handsomely for my role.'

'I know you were funded. But it still don't ring true,' Danny said. 'No offence, but if money was no object I'd be off sunning myself somewhere exotic, not cooped up here.'

'But I'm not interested in the trappings of wealth. For me, it was more about achieving something thousands had failed to do before me.'

'Just can't believe you managed to create a foolproof

system,' Danny said. 'I mean, with all the imponderables that go to making up racing results: suffering interference, changes in going, slip ups, slow starts and the like.'

'Jealousy will get you nowhere.'

'Why are you talking to me, a complete stranger?' Danny asked. Crabtree got to his feet. 'I'm flattered 'n all but I'm nothing to you and it looks like I'm wasting your time, with the afternoon racing on. Why give me the time of day?'

'I'm beginning to wonder myself,' Crabtree said, head tilting slightly. He glanced up at the array of wall-mounted screens to his left.

It's as if he was trying to put a stop to Danny's meddling by allaying his fears. But why?

'Now I want some answers,' Crabtree said. 'Tell me why you went to Casey Jones?'

'Who the hell did you hear that from?' Danny asked, on the back foot.

'From the horse's mouth,' Crabtree said.

'Casey?'

Crabtree nodded.

'He came to mind after I saw a photo of a Kempton race we all had a ride in,' Danny said distantly, mind recalling the Jag lurking that day. Was it Miles Crabtree inside? Danny added, 'He was an old friend.'

'No, Daniel,' Crabtree said. 'He was merely an acquaintance. You were at each other's throats in the press, I recall, in your battle royal for the apprentice title.'

'Just friendly rivalry,' Danny protested. 'How do you know all this?'

'I make it my business to know,' Crabtree rasped. 'The jockey is a vital element in the form selection process and I studied jockey form and stats during that period.'

'And that's part of the formula making up the Rule?' Danny asked.

'The top jockeys can make up the mind of the, shall we say, less willing racehorses and their superior race-tactics, being in the right place at the right time, can make the difference between winning and losing. But you would know this.'

'Still, all this was over a decade ago.'

'I'm blessed with a brain that can absorb information like a sponge and retain it, even after all these years. And I'm still left wondering why you should visit Casey.'

Why was he so concerned by this? What had Casey to hide?

'Other riders are dropping like flies and then I'm left for dead outside my flat. Can you blame me?'

Crabtree pursed his thin lips, as if less convinced.

'Just can't get my head around it that a system could be so successful,' Danny said. 'We're dealing with unpredictable animals, for crying out loud.'

'I can understand your intrigue, as a failed punter.'

'I can pick winners,' Danny snapped defensively. 'Just have trouble keeping a lid on my betting habit.'

'You're not alone, the selection process is only half the story, a staking plan is equally vital, knowing the time to place a large bet when the odds are stacked in your favour and the moment to ease off when suffering a barren patch. Perhaps the Martingale system would have helped you,' Crabtree said. 'Where you double your stake with every loser until you back a winner, hence ensuring your stake on the winning bet is always more than the previous accumulated losses.'

'That's a dangerous game if you have a losing run,' Danny said.

'But you pick winners, Danny.'

Danny paused. No way was he going to rise to this smart-arse.

Crabtree filled the silence with, 'Look, what I can reveal is that it incorporates the main pillars of form analysis: the going, distance, track, race-fitness and so on but there's a secret variable.'

'Well?'

'You know I cannot reveal that. A system can only work if the creator keeps the formula or rules to themselves.'

'And you're staying loyal to this Lazari because he paid you for the system.'

'Hardly, he sadly died years ago. Drowned in bad seas, washed from the keel of his yacht with business friend Roland Meyers in the Solent.'

'So you won't give me anything to go on.'

'All I can say, it's more complex than say betting purely on five-year-old geldings trained by Roger Crane in March and April.'

'Why choose Crane?' Danny asked, suspicions heightened.

'No reason.'

'Of all the hundreds of yards, you pick out a minor outfit I work for.'

'Daniel, relax.' Crabtree smiled. 'I'm fully aware you're assistant trainer there, like I said, I make it my business to know. If you're immersed in the game day in, day out, it would be foolish not to cover all bases.'

'What's stopping you using the system now he's gone?'

'I'm a loyal man,' Crabtree said. 'Jeremiah Lazari's son now owns the intellectual rights. It would be like walking over his father's grave. I wouldn't dream of it.'

His free hand combed through his wild locks. 'Let me teach you something, Daniel. People possess herd tendencies; they'll follow the pack rather than go it alone. They are also creatures of habit, not always learning from their mistakes. However free spirited we may like to think ourselves, ordering what food and drink we desire, going to bed when we want, we are still tied by eating and sleeping patterns. Nobody can truly say they are free, we all follow daily routines, helps us keep some order, make sense of the complex world around us.'

'What's this got to do with betting and systems?'

'Punting is like all those other aspects of life, people have their routines, they'll back a certain jockey whether they're riding well or not, they'll follow a particular horse over a cliff, even though it hasn't won for years. Go against these types and you are already one step ahead of the game.'

Danny found it odd Crabtree still enthused about betting systems and the psychology behind them, yet he didn't want anything to do with the system that proved his crowning glory, the Rule of Lazari.

Had Crabtree and Jeremiah fallen out at the time? Did he regret not taking a share of the future punting profits and their relationship duly soured? Would certainly explain how the media interest soon faded away.

'I understand what you're saying, searching for odds greater than the actual chance of it winning, or getting 'value' as the pros like to say,' Danny said, 'but I still reckon there's something else you're not telling me.'

Crabtree's eyes darkened and deep lines appeared, like contours mapping his face, saying, 'Continue digging up the past and you'll be the one six foot under. Be wise, leave well alone.'

'You threatening me?' Danny asked, though his mind had returned to the calling card left in his kitbag. *Be wise, walk away from this or you will die.* He couldn't recall hearing anyone use the expression 'be wise' before. *Had Crabtree typed the note?*

Crabtree rocked himself from the chair and growled, 'I don't need this anymore, I've done all that was asked of me.'

'But I still got loads to ask–'

'I don't want any more to do with that blasted system.'

Danny felt he'd opened an old wound.

'I've toed the line, done all that's asked of me and yet it never goes, even now,' he replied. 'Don't ever come back, for your own good. Life is short, do not make yours even shorter.'

Danny was taken aback by witnessing the old man flip from Jekyll to Hyde before him. He raised the back of his hand to his brow.

'What?' Crabtree snapped.

'Just a migraine, get them sometimes, stress brings 'em on. Couldn't have a glass of water?'

'And then you must go,' Crabtree said, making no effort to

conceal a prolonged sigh as he shuffled from the room.

Danny guessed the kitchen would be downstairs somewhere, affording him a couple of minutes, given the pace Miles moved at. He paused for a few seconds after Miles had left, ensuring the coast was clear, then kicked into gear. He set about rifling through the drawers of the walnut desk, crammed with loose files and sheets. He stopped to look one of them over. It contained rows of figures with distances down one side ranging from five furlongs to one mile-four.

At first glance, he reckoned they were speed figures for races, an aid for punters to assess the merit of a particular piece of form by the times clocked. He'd often call upon these when he was a form guru. He rooted deeper into the seemingly bottomless pit and came across a file that caught his eye. It was marked in black ink with the word SYSTEMITES. He released the fasteners binding it and out fell loose sheets. They looked like printouts of conversations, with names next to messages or speech text it was hard to tell as he kept furtively checking the half-open door. He'd made out one of the names among a list that rang a bell, Tom Draper.

But then the door flung open to reveal Crabtree stood there, eyes fiery. He wasn't holding a glass of water but a duelling pistol, trained directly at him. Danny dropped the file he was looking at and swallowed hard.

'What the blazes do you think you're doing?' Crabtree asked.

Danny opened his mouth yet the words didn't arrive, caught red-handed. It didn't look good.

'I'll shoot, don't test me, Daniel, I swear as God is my witness. I may be old and frail but it only takes a squeeze of one finger.'

'You wouldn't,' Danny said, though he didn't want to test that theory. Danny reckoned Crabtree bore the round-shouldered haunch of a beaten man; perhaps a lifetime of searching for the secret behind finding winners and, having sold it on, he didn't appear to have anything to show for it. No awards, no certificates or honours, just his fifteen minutes of fame and, Danny guessed, that would now be a faded memory. A waste of such a brilliant mind, he reckoned, anyone would forgive him for becoming bitter towards the winter of his life, but to kill someone at point blank?

Danny raised his palm and said shakily, 'I was only idly looking, didn't see anything, swear I didn't.'

'Don't give me that, you were trying to find something. What was it?' he growled. 'Tell me!'

Crabtree's free hand rose to act as a steadier as the safety catch released with a heart-stopping click. Was this the guy behind the other killings? If so, he couldn't doubt the man was capable of gunning down a defenceless victim. Danny had got sucked into his lair; a honey trap which began with Mike mentioning the Rule of Lazari.

'Think about this, Miles, you'll get life, it's not worth it,' Danny said, running short of bargaining tools. Aware if this twisted old man was dead-set on finishing him off, Danny would have little say in the matter.

'I'm nearing eighty,' Crabtree said. 'The term life doesn't scare me and, in any case, there are mitigating circumstances, you were breaking and entering, you have previous form for this, I shot in self-defence.'

'That wouldn't hold up,' Danny protested, perplexed by how this stranger could know of his teenage misdemeanours.

'With your prints over all my workings, are you so sure Daniel?'

Danny knew Crabtree had a point. 'I'll leave the way I came.'

His blue alert eyes homed in on Crabtree's index finger slowly tightening round the trigger, like a boa constrictor about to finish his prey.

'I warned you, Daniel, don't stick your nose where it doesn't belong, you have this coming,' Crabtree said, gun palpably shaking.

Danny had no clue how he could get out of this alive but he then saw the answer. It was right in front of him. He thrust his weight forward, acting as a snowplough, slewing the mountainous piles of paper and files, sending them into the air like a tickertape parade. Shielded by the floating paper, Danny cleared the desk and, with momentum on his side, barged into Crabtree and swiped the gun from his grasp. He cocked it and shook the cylinder. As the two lead balls fell to the carpet, Danny knew Crabtree hadn't been bluffing about finishing him off.

He wiped his sleeves over the gun's barrel and shaft, last thing he wanted was for Crabtree to plant it beside the body of his next victim and be framed, something similar to the events that had haunted his past when accused of killing his friend and stable-lad Deano. He looked down at Crabtree, grounded and confused. He then tossed the gun to the far end of the room.

Not keen to hang around where he wasn't wanted, Danny left the room and brushed past the housekeeper on the stairs. She was balancing a glass of water, presumably meant for him. Danny said, 'Miles might need that more than me.'

He left the way he came and joined the flow of traffic heading west on the M4, towards the pink winter sunset.

Danny was greatly sobered by recent events as he turned the key to his flat. Although he'd escaped the scene with his life, it felt like a hollow victory. All he had was this word SYSTEMITES and the name Tom Draper. It appeared to be linked to the Rule of Lazari, but how?

He settled at the computer desk and typed an internet search for his newly discovered word. But it didn't throw up any significant matches. Certainly nothing that would link it to Crabtree, Casey or the murdered jockeys.

He sat back and groaned; another wasted journey. At least if Crabtree was after this small set of jockeys dead, perhaps in revenge for a betting plot he'd devised that went wrong, the floored old man now knew Danny was on to him.

With no other leads, he tapped the message button on the answer-machine. 'This is Draper. Help me find the Rule of Lazari.'

'Tom Draper!' Danny said. He knew he'd heard it before. Having thought twice about venturing out that night, his mind was now made up. It could be a trap but he suspected he was living on borrowed time and he felt he had little to lose. Deep down, however, there was another growing force egging him on. Greed. As much as he hated to admit, he was becoming increasingly intrigued by this 'wonder' system. Discovering the formula that grew Lazari's riches would set up Danny and Sara for life; a golden ticket that would lift him from this swamp of debt. It seemed the caller Draper knew exactly where to find the Rule of Lazari and was intent on finding it tonight. Danny didn't want to miss out.

CHAPTER 11

Danny lay tangled among clammy sheets. He skated his hand down his sweated legs and then lay there, eyes wide staring up through the dark at the grey-blue ceiling. A frosty night had been forecast and Sara had turned the central heating up. He made a mental note to do this the night before Silver Belle's next run, save going for a session in the sauna to keep weight down. He'd set his softer mobile alarm for 1.30 a.m. as he didn't want to wake Sara, who was lying alongside, perfectly still, apart from a little finger stroking the pillow. He had planned to get three hours kip before going to the church grounds. He couldn't miss this opportunity to meet the stranger who'd left the message.

But it was no use, the longer he lay there, the more he stewed. He slowly freed himself from the sheets and then struggled on a black t-shirt, wincing as the cotton stroked the remnant bruising on his torso, and then pulled on a sweater and tracksuit bottoms to match. He crept out of the room, Sara remaining like a freeze-frame. He went to the lounge and grabbed his car-keys and a pencil-torch.

He parked up on the outskirts of Llandaff and made the rest on foot, circling the perimeter wall of the church before stopping. His breath formed clouds as he looked both ways before hoisting his weight up and over, landing in a prickly bed of brambles. He set about wading through the foliage before slowing to crouch in the thin veil of the bushes framing the graveyard.

Through the grainy darkness he could make out, amidst the lines of headstones jutting like crooked teeth, a shape, black as soot. Seeing or sensing no sign of life, he flashed the torch against his pullover before stepping out into the cold light of the half-moon. He weaved between the graves and stopped at the edge of the black shape. It was a hole. Beside was a hill of earth and a spade pitched upright.

He powered the torch again and peered in. At the bottom, there looked to be a lead casket, though loose soil was scattered over every surface and Danny couldn't be sure. Its lid propped at a slight angle against one of the walls of earth. *Fuck, these guys are serious.* One of his pals on a stretch inside was sent down for exhuming a body and he suddenly became acutely aware of how it would look if caught right now.

He then directed the beam towards the headstone and ran along the black italic writing on marble.

In memory of Jeremiah Lazari Died 16th March 1998 Aged 67.

No age at all these days, Danny thought. He then recalled the message that drew him here. After the meaning of the Rule of Lazari? Did the owner of the spade believe the Rule was buried with its founder?

He suddenly looked up. A finger of light shone from beyond the side of the church splashing a white circle on a line of ferns bordering the graveyard. The circle grew. Danny felt his stomach tighten. His wide eyes darted in every direction but there was over thirty yards of open space to find cover. Danny reckoned someone willing to exhume a body would most probably go armed. He panicked and lowered himself into the hole. He stood there straddling the open casket, perfectly silent, praying it was a dog walker that couldn't sleep or the vicar disturbed by a digging noise. Hearing footsteps grow ever louder, he knew his prayers weren't answered. He crouched into a ball, knees pressed against his chest, on one side of the coffin, breathing measured.

The grating noise of the spade being pulled from the earth ran right through him. He flinched.

His shoulders fell slightly as he ran through the options left open to him. A heavy shower of earth came pouring down over him. And another. Danny was quick to cover his mouth and nose. He began to contemplate the best way to die: buried alive or shot through the head. He was about to shout up and wave the white flag when an idea struck him. *Nothing like a brush with death to clarify the mind.*

He fished frantically in his jacket and withdrew his mobile. He switched on silent mode and shielded the lit screen as another choking downpour of moist earth covered him. He checked the clock on the phone. 2.34 a.m. He swiftly set an alarm for 2.36 a.m. and flicked the tiny screen on standby. He listened to the almost rhythmic action of the spade scraping the ground, following in a beat by great mounds of earth and stones raining down, then a few seconds where, Danny presumed, the digger had to turn on his heels to face the hill of soil. At that very moment, Danny reckoned they'd be facing away. He waited, monitoring. Scrape, earthy shower, pause, scrape, earthy shower.

Danny leant forward, cranked his arm behind like a pitcher and lobbed the mobile way beyond the mouth of the grave. He prayed it would land softly on the grass somewhere and not crash against one of the many headstones. He waited fearing the digger had seen something. Another face-full of dirt suggested not. Just seconds later, a distant tinny tune rang out. All other noises stopped. Danny heard the spade slice into the turf and footfalls fade away from where he sat under a veil of earth. He got to his feet, shook himself down and faced the weighty coffin lid. Through the gloom, he made out several scratch marks at head-height on the lid. He didn't hang around to examine them closer. Using it as a ramp, he climbed from the grave. Looking across he could see the bent silhouette of a man wearing what looked like a black beanie, presumably trying to track down where the tune came from. Danny wanted to get a mental mug-shot but he was even keener to get out of there and made for the railings framing the grounds. A growl came from behind, 'Aye!'

Danny didn't look around again, fearing his face would be seen. His light and nimble frame cleared the chest-high railings with a leap Silver Belle would've been proud of. Another shot of adrenaline propelled him back to the car in double-quick time and he snaked the quiet streets back to his apartment block.

Danny parked up in the carport and shivered as he twisted the lock to the flat twice. Seeing the lounge empty, he went for a shower in the main bathroom off the hallway. He didn't want to wake Sara by using the en-suite. He then paced to the bedroom, no longer breathing heavily.

'Where've you been?' Sara's muffled voice echoed from the walk-in wardrobe. Danny barely had time to open his mouth when she continued, 'No matter, what about this?'

Her arm appeared draped in a peach-coloured top.

'Yeah, looks fine,' Danny said. 'What are you doing up at this hour?'

'Couldn't sleep,' she said and then asked, 'Better than this?' She emerged into the bedroom with a black blouse, bleary eyed and hair wild. 'Which one: peach or black?'

Danny pointed at the black one.

'You don't like this one then?' she asked, holding up the peach one.

'Didn't say that, just prefer you in black.'

'Because it's slimming?'

Danny couldn't help laugh and said, 'What am I gonna do with you?' Her workmates, or perhaps work colleagues would be more accurate, had clearly done another hatchet job on her confidence and self esteem, he reckoned. 'You're gorgeous with or without them. I'd fancy you in a bin liner. Here,' Danny said, as he reeled her into his athletic arms.

Her face relaxed into a comfortable smile, 'Is this some fetish you've kept from me?' She kissed him and said, 'But not now Danny, got to prepare. And they need taking out in the morning.'

'What?'

'The bins.'

Danny sighed and dropped his weight on the edge of the bed. She hadn't been her usual self in recent weeks, blowing hot and cold, understandable given she'd just lost her job.

'Got up when I heard the door go.' Her head reappeared. 'Have you been running?'

'Like you, couldn't sleep. Just showered to freshen up.'

She disappeared again. 'I can't believe most of this doesn't fit me, I'm sure I've not put on weight since summer.'

'You've not,' Danny was quick to reply.

'Didn't think so, why are they all snug fit at best then?'

'Must've shrunk a bit in the wash,' Danny said, struggling for any other possible sympathetic reason.

'I'm serious Danny,' she said. 'I'll have to join you on one of your runs. Where on earth do you go, seem to have been gone for an age.'

'Oh, stopped off at the 24-hour shop to pick up a bottle of whisky,' Danny said, thinking on his feet.

'Sort of defeats the point, doesn't it?' she asked, now out of the cupboard and laying three skirts on the bed. 'Which one?'

'Oh I dunno, love,' Danny said. 'I'm no Gok Wan. But the blue one matches your eyes, I guess.'

'Thanks Danny,' she replied, 'thought so, that's the one I'd have gone for.'

'What's the special occasion?' Danny asked, fearing it was the wedding of one of her friends that he'd have no option of swerving.

'Got a job interview,' Sara said sternly, as if having to repeat it.

'That's fantastic,' Danny said with clenched voice. 'God, ya should've told me.'

'I did,' she said. 'This afternoon.'

Danny felt bad that he probably hadn't heard, so wrapped up in his own troubles. 'Course, yeah,' he said. 'My brain turns to mush at this hour.' He didn't hang around for any repercussions and went to the lounge, powering up the laptop and pouring three fingers of whisky. *For medical reasons.* It helped quieten the needless worries circling his mind, allowing him to focus on more pressing matters, like who was after him dead.

Perhaps the biggest puzzle was why the killer struck with Simon Thorpe and then waited years before striking again. *Unless it was a copycat killing*, he thought. If it was Tom Draper that was filling in the grave and he was indeed one of the 'Systemites', they certainly meant business in finding it. Perhaps they were behind the murders in their bid to track down this sacred Rule.

He picked up the photo of the Kempton race and shook his head, exasperated. Maybe there would be something in the case surrounding Thorpe on the internet or perhaps on microfilms down the library. He typed in 'Simon Thorpe jockey murder'. The results were disappointing, nothing concrete about the case, possibly because it was still open and police were wary of revealing details of the enquiry. He clicked on an archived newspaper article in the Newbury Bugle dated over five years ago. The headline read: *Father continues fight to find son's killer.*

The photo accompanying it wasn't of Simon Thorpe, though. It was a slim forty-something whose face took Danny straight back to Newbury racetrack car park. *So Mike was Simon Thorpe's father.* Explained the dark rings around his eyes and failing health, slowly rotting away from grief for his son.

Danny relived his encounter with Mike after his unceremonious parting from Silver Belle in the novice chase. He cringed at how badly he'd reacted. *The outcome of the race didn't help*, Danny thought, trying to ease his conscience. He still felt guilty as Mike's motives appeared to lie solely with catching those behind the death of Simon a decade earlier to give him some closure on the whole mess.

Mike probably hoped I could prove the salvation, he thought, and then frowned. Danny knew the killers were after him and perhaps Mike reckoned they could both lay a trap and catch them. He clearly recalled Mike ask him about the Rule of

Lazari. If it wasn't Mike's intention to find this dream formula, then he must reckon it was linked to his son's death in some way. Enough to take the trouble tracking Danny down and, despite taking the abuse in the car park, he still begged him to get in touch. He pulled the card Mike had thrust upon him at the racetrack car park and threaded it between his fingers as he contemplated what to do next.

Perhaps Mike did have the answers, he thought. He lifted the phone from its cradle. Although he wouldn't dream of ringing anyone at this ungodly hour, this was different. The desperation behind Mike's sullen eyes and broken voice suggested he'd be glad Danny made the call, whatever the time or place.

His lips tingled as they touched the syrupy golden liquid swishing in the glass tumbler. He punched the mobile number and waited.

The fifth ring was broken by, 'Hello? Daniel?'

'You were right,' Danny said. 'I did make the call.'

'Please don't hang up,' Mike croaked. 'It's good to hear you.'

There was a silence before Danny broke the ice with, 'I feel your pain, I've been there.'

'You checked me out then,' Mike said.

'I had to make sure who I was dealing with, you understand?'

'No problem,' Mike said. 'I would do the same.'

'My brother died suddenly, murdered,' Danny said. 'They said it would ease in time but it still eats away at me. Have good days and bad.'

Mike said, 'But for me it's just bad days, until I find the fuckers who killed my son. The only thing that gets me up in the morning is the thought of putting them behind bars. Believe me, Daniel, the police better get to them before I do, as I won't be accountable for my actions.' There was a pause. 'At the time, everyone told me how well I was bearing up and admired my strength. But it was all an act, you can't ever get over the loss of your child.' Danny's thoughts shifted briefly to his mum. 'Even after all these years of trying to work it out, no amount of therapy or pills will heal me.'

'I wanna help,' Danny said, 'tell me how?'

'You're being targeted by the same people who killed Simon,' Mike said. 'I initially focussed upon Jeremiah Lazari as my son mentioned his name but when he died, my suspicions moved to his son Lawrence.'

'How did Jeremiah die?' Danny asked; the grooves in the lead casket still fresh in his mind.

'Lost at sea, yachting accident,' Mike said. 'Reports said he was with his business partner, Roland Meyers. Lazari's body was recovered but Meyers' was never found.'

Must've imagined the scratches, Danny thought, *it was dark.*

'Have you heard of the term Systemites?' Danny asked, hoping for more than the web spewed up.

'Not much is known of them. What I can say is that the group dedicate their lives to finding this meticulously crafted equation, as simple as Einstein's theory of relatively $E=mc^2$, yet has still eluded mankind, until now.'

'Like treasure hunters?'

'Yes,' Mike said. 'But the rewards are limitless. Whoever finds the Rule of Lazari will possess a source of renewable wealth for the rest of their life, providing they're able to keep a secret.'

'But what makes them believe the Rule hasn't died with Jeremiah, end of story?' Danny asked.

'They've evidence that the Rule still exists, left by Jeremiah in a place safe enough for it not to be made common knowledge, yet somewhere quite findable. He apparently told those close to him, not long before he died. Rumours and false trails emanated from them, keeping the dream alive, strengthening the belief that the Rule is out there.'

'How do you know all of this?' Danny asked. 'Unless you're one of them.'

'I tried but failed to pass their stringent enrolment procedure and their website is encrypted. They'd obviously got wind of my campaign to find the killers of my son. The rejection only further underlined my beliefs they're behind it all.'

'Have you heard of one called Tom Draper?'

'No,' Mike said, 'I haven't.'

It didn't temper Danny's newfound belief that the shadowy person whose invitation to join and search for the Rule of Lazari just hours before was one of these Systemites. He had to be. But did he find it within Jeremiah's place of rest?

'Where does Jeremiah Lazari's son Lawrence fit into all this? Surely he was left the Rule, seems the obvious thing to do.'

'They weren't on speaking terms when Jeremiah passed away,' Mike said. 'Stress from a struggling business drove a wedge between them, according to my sources.'

'Can I ask a more personal question?' Danny said, softer. 'Did you keep trophies and mementos from Simon's riding career?'

'Couldn't bear getting rid of anything, helps keep his memory fresh and urge me to continue on my quest, despite still reaching dead ends after all these years. The murder of Monty brought it all flooding back.'

'You must be living a nightmare,' Danny said. Losing his dad, regretting having not told him all the things he never realised he wanted to, was bad enough. So many things he wished he'd told him, now too late. *Even the L-word.* Couldn't think let alone say the word love, even after all these years, he was ashamed to admit.

But to lose a son or daughter, out of synch with how nature intended, was unfathomable to Danny. 'Among Simon's racing stuff, do you have a black and white photo in a silver frame, it's an action shot of a race at Kempton in 1996. There're six horses in focus and a lake in the background.'

'I vaguely recall the one, I'll need to get up and have a rummage.'

'Call me back a.s.a.p. on this number,' Danny said. He put the phone down and waited. The distant bell from the clock-tower above City Hall chimed four times.

While he waited for the reply, Danny logged into the

Weatherby's website and made an entry in a re-opened Grade 2 novice chase for Silver Belle at Lingfield on Saturday, an essential prep race given the unsettling turn of events at Newbury racetrack.

Hardly worth going back to bed, he thought, as the phone rang. 'Got it?'

'Yes,' came down the line. 'Why pick out this?'

'Your son came third that day, I came second, Monty was first.'

'I vaguely recall the race,' he said. 'Was Simon's first after a break through injury.'

'I think it holds secrets that could solve this,' Danny said.

'What do you mean?'

'Not long ago, I was threatened, the attacker told me not to go the way of the others. Scared the shit out of me, he did. So I paid a visit to the jockey of the fourth, Casey Jones, who was none too pleased to see me turn up on his doorstep, ushered me out the back way where I was met by a car, pulling up beside me bold as brass. Couldn't see who was inside.'

'Because of the mirrored windows?'

'Yeah. How'd you know that?'

'I was bundled into that very same car,' Mike said. 'And it was Lawrence Lazari in the driver's seat.'

Danny's eyebrows arched. He said, 'Looks like we're both marked men.'

'I'm afraid so.'

'I'd better pay this Lawrence a visit,' Danny said. 'Before he comes calling for me. Stay one step ahead.'

He suddenly felt like he'd revealed too much. After all, he couldn't be sure this Mike guy hadn't become one of the Systemites, or working in collusion with Lawrence and was luring Danny into paying Lawrence a visit, fall into his trap. He therefore stopped short of telling him when he would go, possibly catching Lawrence off-guard with the element of surprise. 'Here, your phone wouldn't be tapped.'

'Highly unlikely,' Mike replied, 'not had a break-in and haven't let any stranger into my house recently, and don't intend to, neither.'

'I'd better go,' Danny said, 'I would give you my mobile number but haven't got one at the moment, gonna get a replacement shortly. Just use this landline for now and keep me updated if you discover anything new.'

'And you the same,' Mike replied.

They hung up and Danny finished off the dregs of his whisky.

The moment that haunted his memories that night wasn't being showered by dirt in Jeremiah's grave, but the scratches on the coffin lid as he climbed from the grave. What made them? Was it Draper seeing if the Rule was concealed within the lid? Or had Jeremiah Lazari been buried alive? Danny shuddered at the mere thought: his worst nightmare. If so, who would do such a thing? Sounded like Lawrence had fallen out with his father Jeremiah, but to do that to his own flesh and blood? He'd either have to be mentally unhinged or pure evil. There was an obvious way to find out.

CHAPTER 12

Danny took a running jump and managed, at the third attempt, to garner enough purchase to grip the top of the seven-foot red-brick wall blocking his path to the Lazari estate. He hoisted his light frame up and sat, legs straddling, while he checked the drop the other side, no more than eight feet. He lowered himself before dropping the rest for a comfortable landing. He was then confronted by dark and dense woodland. He felt for his handheld digital recorder concealed within an inside pocket in his black jacket.

He wanted to leave here with some hard evidence. With no way of knowing how far this stretched, he thought it safer to follow the curvature of the wall until reaching open ground. It wasn't long before he was met by daylight and a wide gravel driveway. He was now the right side of the tall iron gates, within enemy lines.

He swerved crunching his way along the winding driveway and crept along the grass verge instead, all the way to a colossal house. *Chateau Lazari*. Almost as big as one of those stately National Trust homes he'd been dragged around as a kid. However, it wasn't the grandeur of the house that caught his eye but the car parked nearest the front porch, a navy blue Jag with those familiar reflective windows.

Initial instinct told him to turn on his heel and get out of there, while he still had the chance. He now had conclusive proof that Lawrence was involved in this and was possibly the mastermind behind the whole operation. But he knew raising the alarm with the police would do little good. After all, what had he to go on - a car following him, that's all. He couldn't link the Jag to the killings or the thug that beat him senseless outside his apartment. He had to face his fears. Shying away would only serve to put his life in even graver danger than it was.

He emptied his lungs as he pressed the doorbell and waited. A minute or so and the heavy iron-studded door creaked opened. He was met by a plump woman, mid-fifties, bleached hair crowning a round, friendly face. She wore a blue cotton smock overhanging loose-fit tracksuit bottoms and she cradled a basket of cleaning stuff.

'It's Daniel Rawlings,' he said. 'Lawrence is expecting me.' He took the risk that (a) Lawrence was in and (b) he would be eager to confront Danny, seeing as he seemed so keen to follow him leaving Casey's.

'He shouldn't be long,' she said. 'This way.'

That was easy, Danny thought, *didn't even need to flash some ID.*

'Do you live here, in staff quarters?'

She laughed, 'No, Mr Lazari doesn't like company that much you see, I do my rounds and then leave. Suits us both fine that does.'

'Looks old,' Danny said, eyes drinking in the opulent surroundings.

'I beg your pardon,' she said and gave him a look.

Danny added, 'The house.'

'Oh, sixteenth century they say, the oldest bits anyhow,' she said, stopping to move a wooden rack containing an assortment of umbrellas and walking sticks in the hallway. 'Legend has it, the place is haunted. Must say, I've heard noises, but think I'd be moaning and groaning at that age.'

It was Danny's turn to smile.

'Listen to me harping on, need this place spotless. Mr Lazari won't be happy,' she said, before lowering to a whisper. 'Though, between you and me, he never is.'

'I'll leave you to it,' Danny said.

'Right you are, dear. Wait down there if you would,' she said, pointing to an open door revealing one end of what looked like a billiard table. 'Like I said, he shouldn't be two ticks.'

He made his way along the hallway, though it was more like a gallery. Hung from the oak panelling on both sides was a series of grand oils painted in a similar style and bathed in pools of soft light from wall lamps. Would no doubt make the *Antiques Roadshow* experts drool, he reckoned. The line of paintings fell short on one wall, as if there was one missing from the collection.

With no immediate sign of Lawrence, Danny entered the billiard room and past time idly checking out a scattering of antiquities. His brother Rick, who'd been an auctioneer, would've had a field day here. He looked up at the tall oil paintings there, presumably of members from the Lazari family-line. There was also an array of hunting rifles showcased in a glass cabinet. He picked up a porcelain vase before carefully returning it and then began running his fingers down a sun-blanched tapestry, the texture of hessian, hung from the far wall.

'Don't touch that,' a voice growled. 'It's worth more than you will ever be.'

Charmed I'm sure, Danny thought. He turned and was confronted by a tall, thin man, propped by a cane. His wiry greying hair swept to the right.

'Lawrence Lazari,' the man said, stood with military bearing. 'And who are you and what is your purpose? My time is money, you understand.'

Like father like son, Danny reckoned, suspecting it was no compliment in this case.

'And you're clearly short of a bob or two,' Danny joked, casting an eye over at the gallery of oils. Lawrence's stern expression remained fixed. 'Dante Rossetti, fine examples of early pre-Raphaelite. My father was an avid collector.'

'The one that got away,' Danny said, eyes drawn to the gap at the end of the hallway.

'Again, who are you and what do you want?' Lawrence asked, clearly in no mood for small-talk.

'Don't give me that, you know who I am,' Danny said. 'And we've things to clear up.'

'What *things*?'

'I know the truth behind the murdered jockeys Monty and Simon, and there's a link to the Rule of Lazari.'

Lawrence loomed closer. Danny held his ground. *No way was he being harried by this sponger made good by his father's hard graft, handed everything on a silver plate.*

'Where did you hear this nonsense, the internet no doubt.'

'From a reliable source,' Danny said. 'Simon's father.'

'You just don't know when to leave alone,' Lawrence snapped. 'Poor misguided fools, both of you, the blind leading the blind.'

He raised his cane and jabbed Danny's right shoulder.

'Eh!' Danny growled, grabbing the wooden shaft. 'You deny it?'

'There's nothing to deny. Keep something from the public, which we had to given its sensitive nature, and the rumour mill starts to turn.'

'But what if those jockeys somehow discovered the formula,' Danny said. 'They'd need dealing with, wouldn't they?'

'This is your final warning, Daniel,' Lawrence growled.

'Or what?' He waited for an answer. 'Go on, say it!'

Lawrence's cane ran its way across Danny's chest. Its progress was halted before Danny had chance to back off. Lawrence prodded at the obstruction and hearing a metallic thud, he then smiled and said, 'Or I'll ask you to leave.'

'I'll carry on until this is out there, get justice for the dead. That'll wipe the smile off ya face.'

'You disgust me,' Lawrence said. 'Do-gooders, delving into others' business, yet you know nothing. Your type is worth nothing, not fit to wipe the shit from my arse.'

'You need help with that do you?'

Lawrence's eyes widened as he stepped forward, faces now inches apart. Danny held his ground. That was until Lawrence hacked up and blew a ball of phlegm at his face. Danny saw red and lunged forward, swiping the cane from Lawrence's grasp and gripping it behind his head, primed to whip it down with an arcing blow that would break skin. Yet he stopped himself, just a split second before delivering the first blow. Lawrence cowered behind his weak arms.

Danny looked down and hissed, 'You won't get away with this.'

The subsequent silence was broken by the distant creaks and groans, as if the old house was talking to him, perhaps warning him to get out while he could.

Danny ran a sleeve over his face and quickly simmered down from the altercation, coolly adding, 'I'll see myself out.'

He slid the cane across the green baize and breezed past Lawrence, who called upon the billiard table as a steadier and shouted, 'That's the last mistake you'll ever make.'

'Let's hope so,' Danny called back.

CHAPTER 13

Danny pushed his spine against the firm back of the computer chair as he opened his emails. With Christmas out of the way and the season gathering pace, it was all systems go in his bid to revive the ailing career of Silver Belle. Sara was curled up on the sofa lost in the latest Grisham novel, taking a break from enveloping copies of her CV, ready to be posted out first thing tomorrow.

There were three spam emails and one from the credit card company warning his latest payment was overdue though he'd glossed over those. It was the message sent at 2.23 p.m. that grabbed him. It was from Mike. How'd he find my email address? *Suppose being a private investigator had its advantages.* The message simply read:

FYEO
Hi Danny
My contacts managed to dig up this nugget (see attached file). It's a record of bets placed by Jeremiah Lazari in the weeks leading to Simon's death. Can't reveal source as it's a sensitive document. Give it the once over, I'll call when I've got more.
Speak soon
Mike.

Danny clicked the file open. It was a list of horses' names with recorded bets beside each, complete with dates and times. Where the hell did he get this from? It scrolled over three pages, so Danny printed it off to take in the wider picture.

Some of those runners were shaded on the printout, as if a marker had been used on the original document. Were these the winners? He logged on to the racing database and he soon discovered that most of the runners had won their respective races, including Elusive Dreamer ridden by Monty McCann in the Kempton event in the photo.

It certainly didn't smack of a typical betting scam, Danny reckoned, as it was far easier to make money from getting an individual horse beaten than to orchestrate a guaranteed winner as there are always other runners to potentially put a spanner in the works and spoil the plot.

So if it wasn't a betting scam, what was it? *Money laundering perhaps*, Danny pondered. He grabbed a pen from a glass pot on the desk and set about etching out a chart with the names down one side and the pillars that underpin form analysis highlighted by Crabtree along the other. He began charting each runner's preferences regarding going, distance, track and so on. *No obvious link*.

He set about looking deeper into the form of each of the twelve horses under the spotlight. He checked each runner for race-fitness, their age and sex, and also checked for patterns within each of their form figures, seeing if any were strong at a particular time of year. There were eight colts and four fillies in the list, ranging from two to five years old. *Nothing there to work with*.

Recalling the sheet of figures on Crabtree's desk, Danny then pored over speed ratings to see whether they'd clocked fast times. He sought to find the missing link – a pattern to make sense of why they were highlighted in the first place. He couldn't see any trend that could possibly form the basis of a betting system, other than all without exception were gambled on, odds shortening from the opening show. He moved on to their trainers and jockeys. Although three were ridden by Simon Thorpe and two Monty McCann, the others were ridden by different jockeys, including Casey Jones.

This was giving him nothing but a sickly headache. But he

had to plough on. Looking for some inspiration, he fished for the photo of the Kempton race.

He thought perhaps the more he looked at it, something would leap out at him.

Armed only with the fact each of the runners were subject to market confidence, he typed an internet search: 'betting investigation Kempton 1996'

Sara sighed and put the book facedown. 'What you up to?'

'Just doing some form study.'

'That Crane is using you.'

'Tell me about it,' Danny replied distantly, looking over the results of his search.

'You're paid to look after the horses and help out,' she said, 'not run the whole yard.'

'Fat chance of that,' Danny said, 'with Crane bedridden 'n all.'

'You eaten?'

'Gonna skip this one,' Danny said. 'Weighed myself earlier, hovering just under ten stone. If Silver Belle's gonna scrape into one of the Cheltenham handicaps, she'll be at the foot of the weights and don't want to jeopardise her chances by carrying a few pounds over.'

'Don't mind me tucking into some Black Forest Gateau?'

'No,' he said, smiling.

'An hour's workout doesn't half work up a hunger,' she said, arm lost in the fridge. 'Famished.'

Danny glanced down at her green sports bag slumped next to the armchair – the one she used for her weekly evening dance class.

He'd clicked on archived articles documenting the recorded bets collated by the Press Association in the ring at Kempton that year. Danny scanned down the search engine results. He hovered the cursor over a report for the day this photo was snapped. His attention was drawn to a £20,000 bet placed on Elusive Dreamer at one of the rails bookies though it didn't mention which one. It was a striking bet for a typically quiet

121

midweek card. Jeremiah clearly knew what he was doing. The bet came in at 3/1, netting him a cool £60,000 plus his stake.

Not many of the bookies could lay such a hefty wager and survive. Danny recalled Crabtree suggesting the Rule of Lazari sounded the death knell of some notable bookmakers. Was this hype or myth, or perhaps it was the real deal after all.

He changed the search to: 'southern on-course bookmaker bankrupt.'

The same few names kept cropping up among the results. It became obvious to Danny that three bookies sold their pitches after having their licences revoked within a month of the Kempton result and one of them was Heathcote and Son. Merely reading the name jogged his memory. He could recall a blue bookies' board with that name painted in yellow italics. He went to a headline that caught his eye: 'Bookie Heathcote dies.'

They didn't get to him 'n all, Danny thought. It was a piece in the *Racing Furlong* website dated June 25th, 1996. Danny read:

The body of Wiltshire-based rails bookie Eddy Heathcote was found by his son Lionel yesterday morning. The popular bookie was forced to file for bankruptcy after reportedly laying a string of winning bets. He was found hanged in a park near their family home. Assistant in the firm Lionel paid tribute to his father in a statement, 'It is with great sadness that I have to announce the untimely death of my father, Eddy. He was a very popular and proud member of the bookmaking community and we want him to be remembered this way. It's an extremely difficult time for the family and we wish to be left to grieve in peace.'

The recent downturn in fortunes for Heathcote Snr., who had owned several pitches at the smaller West Country jumping tracks like Taunton and Newton Abbot, led to his enforced departure from the betting ring. There has been speculation this may have contributed to his father's apparent suicide. The Heathcote name will return as a fixture at the southern tracks of England and Wales when Lionel reportedly takes out a bookies' permit sometime in the future.

Danny sat back, eyes returning to the scrolling printout. Mike hadn't called and he checked the answerphone. Nothing.

CHAPTER 14

With the Cheltenham Festival looming large, Danny was desperate to get a serious workout under Silver Belle's belt. The lack of definition around her ribcage told him she was carrying some condition and would need to shed a few kilos to hit her optimum racing weight on the big day. When she lined up for her main target at Cheltenham next month, she'd need to be sharp as a tack and no amount of work on the gallops could replace the benefit of a competitive race. He learnt this the hard way from his days as a form analyst. He could often dismiss runners on their seasonal return as they were entitled to need the run though, but this wasn't always the case with the bigger yards in more recent times, equipped with state-of-the-art gadgetry like trotting machines to intensify work-rates, and solariums and swimming pools to help improve blood circulation, suppleness and well-being.

All right for some, Danny thought, kneading the small of his back. No such luxuries at Crane's outfit, though the rolling gallops were a saving grace.

Danny was well-versed in what it took to get a horse to a boil on the day of the big race. It was often a tricky balancing act, getting the horse sufficiently race-sharp yet fresh enough to produce a personal best performance on the day. He hoped the Grade 2 prep race lined up for Silver Belle would put her spot on. But what concerned him presently was choosing the mare's best engagement from the fixture list for the four-day festival at Cheltenham. His tired eyes stung as he pored over the entry restrictions, some allowing only four-year-olds, others five years and over. There were races for mares only, juvenile hurdlers, even a marathon race covering the cross country course, with its mix of slopes, hills and obstacles, in the middle of the track.

Although he had unflinching faith in her latent talent, the prospect of winning a Championship race or a Grade 1 race at Cheltenham would be no more than a pipe-dream, as the very best from Britain, Ireland, France and beyond gravitated there to do battle. It never paid to be greedy in this game, so he reckoned it best to swerve them and aim her for one of the valuable handicaps for novice chasers at the meeting, given the mare's current lenient official rating.

He opted for the *Listed Clayborne Novice Handicap Chase* on the opening day's card. It was worth over £120,000 to the winner.

Would solve a lot of problems, he thought. Having lacked the speed for the minimum two miles and failed to see out three miles as a hurdler, Danny was confident she'd find the two-miles five-furlongs a happy medium. Meanwhile, he was nervously hoping for a big run from her on Saturday, not least because she needed a rise in her official rating to even qualify for the fiercely competitive Cheltenham target.

Sara's head appeared from behind the door. 'You ready?'

'Two minutes.'

'Call it a day, Danny. Do it in the morning,' she said, yawning. 'Come to bed, will you?'

Danny glanced over his shoulder, but she'd left. The computer's clock shone 1.23 a.m.

He composed and sent an email noting the British Horseracing Authority of Silver Belle's intended entry at Cheltenham. Despite ailing health, Roger Crane was still the name above the door at Samuel House and he sent the email via the boss' registered email account to ensure it didn't bounce.

'Job done,' he whispered, before retiring to join Sara in bed.

Merely the thought of partnering Silver Belle for her key prep race this weekend gave him a rush, like Christmas morning as a kid.

Danny felt renewed hope having pressed the send button to the BHA, buoyed by the prospect of being his own boss, the future in his own hands. Something he'd always dreamt of.

Sara was folding away some fresh linen in the top drawer.

'Come here,' he said, reeling her into his powerful arms.

He kissed her passionately on the lips. She parted from the embrace. 'What's brought this on?' she said softly.

'Just occurred to me,' Danny said, 'what's really important.'

'You better believe it,' she said, smiling and dropped the remaining sheet as he pulled her close and then cradled her supple cheeks with both hands. A great intensity filled both their eyes, glistening in the dim light from the bedside lamp. Their lips touched again, eyes now shut. She rested her arms on his tight shoulders and slid her hands over his cropped hair. He lifted her t-shirt up over her head and she mirrored the action, revealing his honed torso complete with battle scars. A sweet scented cloud of perfume filled the air as he ran his hands over her feminine curves and soft silky skin. 'Danny,' she uttered, breathy.

His eyes took in her nakedness. The pair fell back onto the soft mattress. He tenderly explored her with his pliant tongue. She groaned with pleasure as he entered her. Steadily at first and as the sense of anticipation rose, his thrusts grew more rapid.

A tremor of desire shook her voice as she whispered, 'I want you so bad, Danny. Now more than ever, I need you.'

Instinct made Sara wrap her legs around. He rolled to one side, taking her along with him. Now on top, she ground her body against his, craving more. Her choppy breath made her shapely breasts heave. *This felt better than the first time they'd made love.*

With the last shreds of self-control, she bit her lip as if halting the urge to cry out. As a joyous release of tension left his body, he forgot the worries he'd been shouldering. She sighed with satisfaction as she removed herself from him and settled alongside, breathless. Her face radiated warmth as she smiled.

CHAPTER 15

Danny straightened, eyes wide, fearing he'd heard a dull thudding from the hallway, or had he merely dreamt it. *There it was again.*

Sara was lying perfectly still. A clap of thunder wouldn't have stirred her from that slumber. Danny picked up the alarm clock and tried to focus. 6.32 a.m.

Whoever it was in the hallway had bypassed buzzing the videophone from the foyer nine floors below. Who in their right mind would call at this hour?

Not good news, Danny thought. Was the ponytail thug back to finish the job? Was it the police investigating the exhumation of Jeremiah Lazari? He was tempted to lay low and press the pillow against his face, hoping it would go away. Perhaps he'd heard it through the walls of next door's flat. But the thud returned, louder this time. They needed getting rid of before Sara woke and asked questions.

He slowly lifted himself from the sunken mattress, pulled on clothes lying dishevelled on the floor, and crept into the hallway, pressing one side of his face against the fisheye.

A fifty-ish man stood the other side checking his watch. The banging was replaced by the man's cut-glass accent permeating through the wood, 'Mr Rawlings, I really need to speak with you. I know you're in, your car is parked up and you've not left. Please would you open? We need to discuss something.'

Was this the man behind the killings of Simon Thorpe and Monty McCann and was he about to add Danny to the list?

'Who are you?'

There was a pause, as if they were conversing via satellite. 'I think you know.'

'I'm not going the same way as the others.'

'What others?' the man said. 'Daniel, let me in and I'll explain. I'm here on my own.'

Danny knew the stranger would most likely return and next time with muscle to back him up, *no point in delaying the inevitable*. Although seemingly harmless, Danny knew appearances can be deceptive. He left for the kitchen and removed a seven-inch blade from a knife block, praying Sara was still out cold. He slipped it carefully down his combats, so the handle wrested on the belt strap and draped his t-shirt loosely over. He returned to the front door and turned the lock. Chest out and shoulders back in a fighting pose, like a strutting peacock, he was confronted by an immaculately dressed man in a black clean-cut suit with short grey-brown hair, scalp reflecting the hallway spotlights.

'At ease, Daniel, can I come in?'

Danny stepped out into the communal hallway and looked both ways, all quiet. He appeared to be a man of his word.

The man stepped into the apartment. 'This way?' he said, inviting himself into the lounge.

Danny felt the shape of the concealed knife, primed to strike if trapped.

'Are you the ringleader? The one making my life a misery, my nerves are shot.'

'I own the company,' the man replied.

'Got ID to prove it?'

The man withdrew a driving licence. A poorly lit portrait photo of the face before him was beside the name Jacob Tate. He said, 'No business card.'

Danny asked, 'So you'll know about the Rule of Lazari?'

'You've lost me.'

'Do you work for Lawrence?'

'I work for myself,' Jacob replied sternly. 'The words cross and wires spring to mind.'

Danny wasn't so convinced. 'And what about that ape you sent round? Left his mark he did.'

Jacob raised his eyebrows. 'I'm afraid he doesn't know his own strength sometimes.'

'Tell me about it,' Danny remarked. 'What's this all about?'

'I'm here to work through some financial issues, come to an arrangement. I sent a personal letter some weeks ago informing you of the situation and, as you say, you've already been given notice,' he said calmly. 'And yet, you've not paid the sum owed.'

'What sum?'

'Don't play the innocent, Daniel. It was in the letter, hand delivered to your postal box to ensure receipt.'

'It wasn't stamped then.'

Jacob shook his head.

'I get fliers, unmarked letters from estate agents wanting to flog the apartment, sales leaflets, it's all hand-delivered junk. They must slip them in when the concierge is on a fag break. No longer open them.'

'Likely story, Daniel, but it doesn't change the fact that the ten-grand debt you accrued with the credit-bookmakers Target Bet was sold on to my company and the interest is accumulating as we speak, so it's in *your* interest to pay up, now.'

'But the firm went bust,' Danny said. 'The debts were wiped. Case closed.'

'I'm afraid the law doesn't see it that way. Don't take liberties, Daniel, otherwise you'll see a different side to me, one that you wish you hadn't seen.' The man settled on the couch. Danny gave anxious glances towards the lounge door. If Sara entered hearing the voices, or fancied an early snack or glass of water, he had no feasible answer for why this stranger had visited or why Danny had let him in.

'So what's the damage?' Danny asked, fearing the answer.

'£12,500 if you include the £500 charge for this personal visit.'

'You're having a laugh,' Danny said. But the seated man wasn't even smiling.

'If you do not play ball, we have, shall we say, more persuasive ways to make you cough up the money due.'

'See what the police have to say,' Danny said. 'This ain't right.'

'You'll find the law's on our side.'

'Could do you for harassment,' Danny said, holding his side. 'Got proof an' all.'

'That could have been done by anyone,' Jacob said. 'You have two months to find the money, plus interest at two hundred per cent.'

The man stood and neared, not much taller than Danny, but stockier. He now noticed the white trace of a scar running from his right eyebrow down the side of his face. 'Default,' he growled, 'and you'll want to be dead once I've finished with you.'

'I'll find the money,' Danny said, wanting him out of there. 'But not in full . . . instalments. Until an investment I've made pays dividends.' Sensing the man wasn't sold on the idea, he added, 'And I can give you a tip.'

The man picked up one of the gold-framed photos of their wedding day on the shelf beside the plasma screen. 'She's pretty.'

'Leave her out of this,' Danny said, voice clenched. Keen to steer it back to the debt, he repeated, 'I can give you free tips.'

Jacob returned the photo and said, 'What kind of tip?'

'A horse,' Danny said. 'Got proper inside info, it's a dead cert.'

Jacob laughed. 'Do you think I would honestly take a racing tip as part payment from someone who'd racked up the debt gambling in the first place. What do you take me for?'

'But I own and train this one, can't get any closer to the horse's mouth. Entered for a big prize at Cheltenham soon enough. If she goes in, I'm good for the lot, promise on my life.'

Jacob's eyes flitted from the plasma screen to the running

machine to the music system. Danny suspected he was totting up their value for when the bailiffs came knocking.

'Two months, clear?' Jacob said, brushing Danny on his way out.

Danny nodded, relieved at the stay of execution.

'Oh and Daniel, make sure you put the knife back,' Jacob continued, glancing over at the wooden block by the sink with one empty slit. 'You wouldn't want to sit down where it is.'

Danny shut the door and punched the wall out of rage, skinning his knuckles. Fuck! Where am I gonna get over twelve grand from? *Credit rating's fucked.* It just served to pile on the pressure. He didn't just want Silver Belle to deliver the goods, he now needed her to.

He returned to the lounge. It turned out he was never being hunted by those after the Rule of Lazari in the first place. That was, until he went to Casey, unwittingly putting himself in the firing line.

Having a rare morning off, Danny was determined to get back to sleep. But he was still lying there wide awake when Sara stirred into life.

Later that morning, he felt in need of some fresh air and went down to Raymond Barton's bookies, see who was there.

He caught a glimpse of Stony, who was back on the fruit machines. *Will he ever learn?*

Stony looked up. 'How's tricks?'

'Could be better, just been harassed by an unwelcome visitor, asking for money he was.'

'I haven't told no one,' Stony said, raising his hand from the flashing SPIN button on the machine.

'I know you didn't,' Danny said, recalling the ponytailed debt collector leaving the betting shop empty-handed when he'd visited months back.

'The knuckle-scraper that asked you for my name wasn't the ringleader, just the chimp,' Danny said, 'It was this Mr Big of the set-up that came round, bent my ear. He'd been sold an old debt of mine and it was pay-time.'

'Get down Citizen's Advice I would,' Stony said. 'They'd have a word. These guys can't get heavy-handed, not these days.'

'Wouldn't be any good, they don't work by telephone or fixed address, always one step ahead of the law. Couldn't risk reporting them, value my limbs too much.'

'I dunno, Danny, you don't make it easy for yourself.'

'Keeps me on my toes, I guess,' Danny said.

'See from the entries you're on board that nag Silver Belle.'

'No tea for me tonight, touch and go whether I'll carry a few pounds overweight. Makes all the difference against those classy types,' Danny said. 'And what do you mean 'nag'?'

'Wasted too much of my hard-earned on that dodge-pot to know better,' Stony said.

'Not without a chance tomorrow, though,' Danny said. 'Working all right at home, just a matter of getting her into a rhythm early, her confidence will grow from there.'

'See she's forecast to be an outsider.'

'Where?'

'On teletext, 25/1. Worth a few quid?'

'Wouldn't go that far, Stony, this is her toughest task to date. Reckon 25s is about right for her this time. She'll do well to beat the Grade 2 rivals, save your money for when she goes to Cheltenham next time.'

CHAPTER 16

Danny stretched his legs in the car park of the service station at Junction 13 to break up the four-hour trip down the M4 to Lingfield racetrack. It was grey and cold but the much-needed rain hadn't materialised.

On arrival, the public car park was near-full. *Doubt many will be having money on my mount*, Danny thought, trying to ease the pressure. Although he never doubted his skills in the saddle on the Flat, he was still a relatively new-boy over the jumps, with only a handful of rides. He wanted to get the mare round in one piece and pick up some prize-money into the bargain.

He led Silver Belle from the trailer as Kelly stepped aside. She was best behaved in his hands. Kelly knew this and held back.

Danny was nervously crunching away on a mint, keep energy levels up.

'You bought them for her,' Kelly said, taking hold of the reins. 'She'll need a treat after the race.'

Danny patted his jacket pocket. 'I've saved a couple.'

The tiny mare was taken off to the stabling area in preparation for the feature event on the card at this leafy Surrey track, while he made for the jockeys' room.

With time in hand, he got permission from the clerk of the course to run a lap of the track, sweat off a few pounds to ensure he made the correct weight and also check first-hand the state of the ground, rather than rely on the official's judgement.

Twenty minutes before the feature, he got kitted out in his new green and brown silks. There was a slight fraying on his right elbow where he'd met the ground at Newbury but they were pristine in every other way. As he left for the paddock area, he scooped a clump of earth from a nearby flowerbed and rubbed it into the body of his silks, a good luck ritual breaking them in. He wasn't normally superstitious but he needed all the luck that was going.

He got a leg up from Kelly in the parade ring and soon found himself at the start. The hot favourite Jackdaw was strutting like a puissance. He looked a picture and he seemed to know it.

Danny ran over the race plan in his head. He'd mapped it all out countless times lying in bed and running over it again was merely a way to put a lid on his growing nerves.

After the aborted run at Newbury, Danny's senses were heightened and his eyes darted between the other runners milling at the start and the scenery surrounding the track.

The tape rose and they were away for the third race – the Grade 2 feature on the card. Used to more forceful riding tactics, Silver Belle had been conditioned to go hell-for-leather from the get-go and, with Danny reining back, her grey head swished this way and that, eagerly trying to get to the front. Danny held firm as the half-tonne mare tried to pull his arms off, fighting at the leash.

He was the backmarker, where he wanted, sat a couple of lengths off the main group of rivals, as the field cleared the first, an open ditch. By the third fence, she'd settled down but it left him wondering whether he'd done the right thing. How much energy had her early exuberance taken out of her? He'd find the answer soon enough. Perhaps Crane was right all along with his race-tactics and the reason for Silver Belle's string of failures was more down to her lack of ability. He banished those thoughts as the fourth fence came upon them. He got in short and brushed the top, losing some momentum. Great clumps of turf were carved up into the air as the small field continued their progress down the back stretch.

133

The runners kept up a good clip turning the corner near the three-mile start and were then faced with the home-run for the first time. Danny's arms tensed as he witnessed one of the joint leaders plough through the birch, firing his jockey into the soft turf. He took evasive action, pulling down a sharp left on the reins and swerving the threshing legs of the fallen rival.

Human instinct led him to glance back, see if they were both okay. The horse was already up walking gingerly away from the scene while the jockey was uncurling himself, like a contortionist emerging from a box. His attention quickly returned to what lay ahead, annoyed that he'd let his emotions rule his head. *No time for thinking of others*, he reasoned, it was a battle out there with no love lost and Silver Belle deserved nothing less.

Even though they met the next three regulation fences on a good stride, the quality of the market leaders, spearheaded by the class-act Jackdaw, was beginning to show and Danny administered a few sharp reminders to help keep her interested as they cornered into the finishing straight. Sitting about eight lengths off the battling trio up front, Danny asked Silver Belle for full effort in a vain attempt to close the gap, claw back the deficit. He got lower and pushed hard, but she lacked the race-sharpness and the class of those in front and could only summon the energy to plug on at the one pace. He took heart from fluent jumps at the third and second last fences as the grandstand grew larger, despite her heavy legs and breathing. Clambering over the last, he knew the cause was lost and unduly punishing her would only dampen her spirit. He eased Silver Belle down yards from the line, finishing a gallant fourth of the seven who'd set out.

The speakers bellowed, 'First number 3 Jackdaw 4/6 favourite, second number 5 Stonemason 7/1 and third number 1 Robotic 5/1.'

With no funds left, Danny was well aware of the £2,532 prize for crossing the line in fourth, a decent sum for finishing out of the frame. Not a bad day's work and would pay for her upkeep and entry fees in the lead up to Cheltenham, and also service his credit cards in the meantime but he'd be kidding himself if it was anywhere near enough to get himself out of the debt he was in.

He hoped the spin would raise both her fitness and confidence levels to boot. He ran his hand down her mane as they walked back to the parade ring.

'Don't forget to weigh in,' was the first thing Kelly said. 'Don't want you missing out on the loot, given all the work you've put in.'

'Didn't disgrace herself,' Danny remarked as they were led in behind those who'd finished in the frame. 'Can't complain 'bout that.'

'She's done you proud,' she said. 'And you didn't look out of place there either, couldn't tell the difference between your riding style and Jack Walters on the winner.'

Danny was flattered; Walters held the current jump jockeys' title. 'Cheers, Kelly,' he replied, grinning, 'but I suspect my action's a bit more agricultural than his. Still feeling my way in the winter game.'

'Nonsense,' she said. He dismounted and loosened Silver Belle's breast girth. 'You'll get your revenge at Prestbury Park, no worries.'

'Wish I had your faith,' Danny replied, though he'd be lying if he said he wasn't encouraged by her improved display just now. The more patient tactics appeared to rekindle some of her competitive edge against stronger types and he hoped it would spark a revival in time for Cheltenham.

CHAPTER 17

Danny dropped his car keys in a dish on the hall-stand. He pushed a button next to a red light flashing on the answer-machine. He began to listen while stretching his stiffening arms.

'You have one message. . . Danny, it's Mike, can't talk long, I'm on to something big,' the voice was clipped, breathy. 'I think . . .' When it lowered to little more than a whisper, Danny rushed forward and twisted the volume dial. 'I've unearthed something, going to the police, think I'm being followed. Just take a closer look at the photo, there's a link we missed, easily done as it's black and whi-' The line went dead, just a low bleep, like a heart monitor flat-lining. 'You have no more messages.'

Danny punched Mike's number on the memory dial and waited. 'I'm sorry but the person you have called is unavailable. Please try again later.'

He didn't know any of Mike's friends or colleagues to contact and raise the alarm. The only name he had was his late son, Simon Thorpe. It suddenly occurred to him how little he knew of the man. It would be futile calling the police. He didn't know what had happened to him. Perhaps it was merely a bad reception and he'd got cut off.

He replayed the message, making a mental note of the time it was made. 7.21 p.m.

He returned to the printout of data sent by Mike and sighed. The results spanned merely five weeks. Why choose this period? If the Rule of Lazari was boosting the Lazari fortunes over years, it seemed odd to Danny that results were kept for just a short spell. *Such a small sample just didn't make sense,* Danny thought, *where were all the other results?* Why hadn't they kept those? As a work-watcher on the gallops for the betting syndicate, he had to prove himself over a month trial period. Perhaps these were the initial results of the system compiled by Crabtree for Jeremiah to look over. Any system had the potential to yield profits in the short-term but it was the long term that invariably proved the stumbling block.

As a punter, there were good days, weeks, even months, but the only way to keep ahead of the game was to find a strategy that could give you the edge all year round.

He was about to toss the sheet down out of frustration when something caught his eye. It appeared to be a watermark of what looked like a symbol of a crown within a circle, though he couldn't be sure as it was so faint. The symbol sparked some familiarity in Danny, though he couldn't place where he'd seen it before. He turned back to the runners and ran his hand over his scalp. Something suddenly occurred to him. He craned forward and picked up the framed Kempton photo pushed to the back of the computer desk, against the wall. Before Mike got cut off, he said, 'there's a link we missed, easily done as it's black and white.'

Danny's fingers skated across the glass. *The secret perhaps lies in the colours. The colours. That's it! The jockeys' silks.*

Danny went to the internet *Racing Post* form-base and called up that specific race. Monty won the race in green and red striped silks and white cap. Danny was on the second wearing black silks with a white disc on both body and cap. He moved on to the third, ridden by Simon, whose colours were the same as Thorpe's, apart from a blue cap. Casey Jones came in fourth wearing the same green and red silks, though his cap was red. They were all in the same ownership. Danny called up the form files for each runner and, while they were trained by different yards. They were all owned by Jeremiah Lazari.

What threw Danny off the scent was the fact Thorpe was largely based at a yard in Ireland. He was on a retainer for

Lazari and must've ridden in the race before going on to better fare at Sandown the following day.

He studied the form comments beside each runner. Danny remembered it was a particularly rough race and he was hemmed in on the rail, short of room at a critical stage. Seemed like Lazari's three runners deployed team tactics to ensure the winner Elusive Dreamer got the job done and, according to the printout, netted £60,000 in one recorded bet alone. *God knows what else he'd got on in the off-course bookies,* Danny thought.

He pressed his back against the leather swivel computer chair, lost in thought. Jeremiah must've set this race up. *Crafty bastard,* Danny thought, *that's where Lawrence gets it from.*

But if the horses on Mike's email were indeed the picks thrown up by the Rule of Lazari, why would he need to take out the added assurance of framing the race? What self-respecting 'wonder' system needs a helping hand from insider jockey tactics? And was it Lazari who placed that hefty recorded bet? There was only one way to know for sure, visit the betting ring.

CHAPTER 18

The next day, a smooth trip down the M4 saw Danny arrive a good hour before the opener at Chepstow. He left Kelly to keep an eye on My Noble Lord, telling her he had some business to sort out. He thought it best to seek out Lionel Heathcote before the busy afternoon trading began. A man warmed by a fleece and a deerstalker was busying himself erecting a board with the name Heathcote. Many of the bookies introduced their children when they were old enough to take bets and process them on laptops behind each pitch. It was all computerised these days, with printout receipts rather than the colourful cardboard tickets of the past. Lionel had learnt the ropes when his dad was alive and, over a decade on, he'd clearly avoided the pitfalls that had finished his father.

It was a relief to see the man was still in this risky business as many would have come and gone in the decade since his father's death. 'Lionel Heathcote?'

'Who's asking?' he replied, slightly hoarse as if under the weather.

'Danny Rawlings.'

Heathcote continued busying himself unpacking his stall and slotting leads into the side of a laptop. 'Weren't you a jockey back in the day?'

'Yeah,' Danny said.

'Thought so, never forget a name, me.'

'I need to chat with you about something to do with your father.'

Lionel's brow lowered. 'If it's to do with unpaid debts or bills, it was all sorted through the courts years back.'

'Nothing to do with that,' Danny said, showing his palm. 'Something I need to know, off the record.'

Lionel ran a fingerless glove under his nose and said, 'Five minutes, that's all. Gav, finish setting that up, I won't be long.'

The pair walked to the bar within the grandstand and Danny treated the slim thirty-something to a coffee. As he paid for them at the till, his fingers pinched the breast pocket of his jacket. He returned to where Lionel sat, deerstalker gone.

'It's about your father. He took on some big players in the ring, shortly before the business went under,' he said. 'I need to know who placed the bets, was there one face you can remember and could put a name to?'

'Why do you ask?'

Danny said, 'Think they were up to no good.'

Lawrence paused and blew the steam from the coffee warming his hands. 'Yeah, it was Jeremiah Lazari.'

Got him, Danny thought. 'You singled him out, above all the other full-time punters, he must've been well known?' Danny asked, surprised by Lionel's instant recall.

'He caused a big stir, only for a short while mind you, back then. There was a buzz, not one I'd seen before at any of the smaller tracks, when his ugly mug showed up in the ring. It was squeaky bum time for even the most battle-hardened of us bookies when he stepped up, with that suitcase of his.'

'How many bets did your father lay with him?'

'Four or five. A lot of the others gave him the cold shoulder, they'd marked his card. There were a handful of 'faces' that you'd think twice about doing business with, often party to inside info, they knew more than us. Best option was to limit the size of bet they could get on or refuse the bet point blank. What can we do, we work to such fine margins that we have to be wary, like casinos on the lookout for card counters.'

'But your dad took him on.'

'Yeah.' Lionel's sorrowful eyes sought the Formica surface

of the table. 'I told him to decline them, but he saw the suitcase full of readies and, like a rabbit in the headlights, took the risk. He knew what he was doing and what was at stake. Years of prudently playing the percentages and margins to balance the books, all gone up in smoke with one bet.'

'Did he have a pitch at Kempton?'

'Years back, yeah.'

'1996?'

'Yeah, around that time.'

'Can you remember laying a horse called Elusive Dreamer to Lazari or one of his associates?'

'If memory serves me, my dad accepted a huge bet on that one. I'm sure that was the final nail . . .'

He stopped as if completing the saying would strike too close to the truth and the heart. Eddy Heathcote was dead within the week.

'Why have you come to me about this?'

'Heard your father went out of business at the time and put two and two together. How much did Jeremiah bet?'

'I'd have to check the ledgers but it was a serious play.'

'And it was definitely Jeremiah Lazari?'

'In person. Remember it like yesterday. I nearly stepped in and stopped it, but I didn't.' His eyes grew colder and more distant. 'But that's life, full of 'what ifs', no more so than in this game. All's fair in love and betting, aye. It was my father's choice to take the bet on and just so happens it came in on this occasion. Like I said, all's fair and that.'

'Except I don't think it was fair.'

Heathcote cast him a glare. 'What are you getting at?'

'I think Lazari was fixing races at the time and that Kempton race was among them.'

'I don't want to know,' Lionel butted in. 'Couldn't take it if my dad hung himself 'cos of foul play, if that's what you're saying. You see, he died doing what he loved, that's what helped get me through that nightmare, he loved the cut and thrust of occasionally taking on some of the big punters. In my eyes, he took a bet fair and square and bowed out gracefully.'

'You're probably right,' Danny said, sparing Lionel's feelings and memories. Last thing he wanted was to open up old wounds.

'One more thing,' Danny said, 'How long was Jeremiah a 'face' on the scene?'

'Not long at all,' Heathcote said.

'Really?' Danny said. 'Are we talking months? Years?'

'Two months, may be three,' Heathcote said, 'Sorry I can't be more accurate, memory a bit blurred at the edges now.'

'No, that's enough,' Danny said, distantly. 'And this brief period was around the Kempton race.'

'Yep,' Heathcote said, tossing his empty plastic cup in a nearby bin. 'He vanished soon after he'd burst on to the scene. Like many of them, except he left on a winning note. Lot of the bookies were left scratching their heads, but they didn't complain. It was like a boxer that's got his rival against the ropes and then just backs off, for no reason.'

Danny asked, 'You've got no clue why? Was he struggling to get bets on?'

'That was the rumour buzzin' round. Look, if that's it, I'd better get back, Gav will be seriously pissed off.'

'That's it.' He'd got what he was after. The horses on the printout were indeed some sort of betting ring or scam. 'Get back to your pitch, missing out on serious money talking to a paranoid fool like me.'

Heathcote didn't need to be told twice and left promptly. Danny winced downing the dregs of his lukewarm tea and removed the micro-digital recorder from the breast pocket of his jacket. He pressed stop and returned to the stabling area to help out Kelly. Having watched Rhys come home a respectable fifth on My Noble Lord, he left the track three races before the end of the afternoon card, avoiding the worst of the traffic.

It was dark and cold as he slotted his Golf into the reserved parking space on the second tier of the secure under-croft parking area. His phone vibrated – a text. He made a pained expression as he looked down at it, fearing the debt collectors had a change of heart. However, what he saw on that tiny screen was a whole lot worse, it made his blood chill. 'One word to police, she dies.'

Danny froze. Thoughts spun back to the moment Jacob Tate displayed interest in their wedding photo. But he soon quashed them when he looked at the phone number. It matched his old mobile. *Had the bastard at the graveyard kidnapped Sara?*

CHAPTER 19

Danny rushed from the carport, through the secure doors. The lift was apparently stuck on ground floor, presumably locked by removal men struggling to cram in heavy furniture. The turnaround in these places was frightening, many let by city workers on short term contracts. It was impossible to get to know your neighbours though that was sometimes a good thing. He couldn't stand still and started to charge up the stairwell, two at a time. He fumbled his key in the door and stepped into the cool, echoing hallway. He flicked on the inset spotlights, splashing light on the beech laminate and whitewash walls. He checked his watch. Sara was normally there, relaxing with a wine or some chocolates by now. He paused for a moment, fingers resting on the door-handle, hoping the text was just an empty threat or some callous spam, or virus. He burst into the room and sensed instantly there was no life there. Everything still, deathly quiet. He checked the kitchen. There was a large pot of stew simmering on a low heat on one of the electric plates on the hob. That gave him hope. Perhaps she'd gone to the bedroom or the en-suite bathroom. She'd never leave something on the cooker. She was always worrying about causing a fire. Always nagging him to turn off TVs, unplug toasters. He paced to the spare bedroom, nothing. And then, last chance saloon, he stepped into the main bedroom. The curtains were drawn. No one had been here since they'd both left that morning.

He checked his mobile again, 'One word to police, she dies.'

He paused and blinked at the tiny screen, see if there was some mistake. He dropped to his knees in front of the toilet bowl and now knew the true meaning of 'worried sick' as he retched forward. Having relieved his stomach of the burger and chips he'd devoured on track, he kicked into gear, mind sharpened.

He tried her mobile. He heard its tinny tune sound from the hallway. She'd left it behind.

Back in the lounge, he checked her contact book on the desk and ran his finger down the list of her best friends, picking out those names he'd recalled her mention and those he'd met at some dim and distant party. He half expected her to skip into the lounge in her jimjams, smiling. But then his thoughts would darken.

The apartment was still with everything in its place. There was no sign of any burglary that had gone wrong. There was no evidence of any struggle whatsoever. He glanced over at the cooker again. He began to shake as he checked each room again, going over the same ground, more frenzied this time. An eerie stillness befell the place, as if he were on the Marie Celeste.

He returned to the lounge and turned off the stew. Thinking perhaps he was being too hasty, he sat down and drew a calming breath. He waited, watching the clock-hands slowly turn. An hour had passed, though it seemed like an eternity. But it was no good as his worst fears kept haunting him, he couldn't keep still. He checked his mobile. No new messages. He dialled his old number but got no reply.

He'd turn the place over if needed. He began pulling drawers out of cupboards, dragging clothes from their hangers, slewing bookshelves clear, desperate for even the slightest clue of where or why she'd left the flat earlier that day. Her credit and debit cards were still there. He wasn't sure whether that was a good or bad thing. There was no sign of her keys. He went to the door and examined the lock; still in perfect working order. He went to the bedroom and, in one of the drawers beneath the bed, folded sheets hid her diary. That had been a no-go area for Danny; everyone needs a private place to work the day's events and troubles through. His was in the van on those interminably long journeys back from the racetrack.

He felt bad for looking but these were desperate times and he reasoned a betrayal of her trust was okay, just this once. She was probably visiting a friend and Danny rarely mixed with her yoga buddies, or those from dance class. Having been lost in his job at all hours, he wouldn't even know who most of them were he was ashamed to admit. If she was enticed away, she must've known them, as there were no obvious signs of a break-in.

He flicked through the pages, every available inch of white covered in blue ink, picking up every fifth word or so.

This is hopeless, Danny thought, and then skipped a great chunk, concentrating on entries for the past fortnight. Most of them concerned mundane day-to-day matters: arguments and tiffs with her colleagues or boss, worry about nearing the overdraft limit again, aspirations about the future. She hadn't let on how strongly she yearned for a change of scenery and lifestyle, a fresh start. He stopped at the entry for February 23:

Danny seems bullish about Silver Belle's chances. Hope he's right. God knows we need a change of luck. Saw a lovely farmhouse just outside of Penarth, got stabling area and every-thing. Dream on! And I'm late.

He ploughed on until an unusually brief entry stopped him in his tracks.

February 27:
P! Not told Danny, find right time.

Danny knew from his betting days, whenever he needed to remind himself what he'd bet on or the stake, he'd use a short-hand so Sara wouldn't discover his shady habit. With this in mind, her diary entry took on new meaning and struck him with a hammer-blow. He flopped back on the soft duvet, staring up at the white ceiling. How could he be sure?

He straightened and opened the top drawer of the cabinet on her bedside. Danny knew it was chocked full of what he called 'women's stuff'. His hands burrowed deep into the drawer, past pills and potions and house magazines and make-up and foundation puffers, mirrors, notepads and eyeliner sticks. And there it was, right at the bottom – a pregnancy test, stained blue. Sara was pregnant. P!

It all added up: her mood swings, night sweats and sudden lack of interest in a pet. Signing off the entry on February 23 with the word 'late', Danny guessed she meant her period.

He flopped back again, cushioned by the cool mattress. He felt a peculiar mix of elation, heightened concern for her safety and disappointment that she couldn't face telling him the news. It was now March 7th. Why had she held back? Had I been that much of a bastard?

His mind rewound to conversations they'd had, picking over miniscule looks and flippant comments to find the reason. He cringed as he recalled repeatedly protesting he didn't want pets and even put a limit on the plants she could display, saying they take up too much cost, time and space, and they'd be 'a right pain when we wanna go on holiday.'

'Chance would be a fine thing!' she'd reply. She had the canny knack of having the last word.

He so wished he hadn't given off that impression, or she'd read that much into those throwaway remarks. He meant nothing by them, certainly not regards having kids.

With her gone, he felt his true feelings and thoughts filter through. Like a drunk having a moment of clarity, it had suddenly become obvious to him that there was nothing he wanted more than to have Sara's child. But she wasn't here to tell her. He couldn't bear this.

Having exhausted all avenues of enquiry, impulses led him to reach for the phone and, sat on the edge of her side of the bed, his finger hovered over the nine-button on the dial. But then he ran over the words in the threatening text 'One word to police, she dies.' He was well-versed in assessing risk and reward but these stakes were too high to cope with. He returned the phone.

He could feel pressure pushing in on his skull. The walls felt as if they were closing in, crushing him. He could hear each stuttering breath as his lungs fought for air and a pain throbbed somewhere behind his eyes. He had to get out, do something. Fight or flight.

He strode down Queen's Street, sidestepping faceless shoppers. He swerved a group of Japanese tourists taking snaps of the famous animal wall of the castle, topped with carvings of everything from cheetahs to monkeys. He briefly glanced over the bridge at the River Taff just beyond the Arms Park rugby pitch, now dwarfed by the Millennium Stadium. Sparkling white beads lit the slowly meandering grey-brown waters. He was in no mood to slow and admire the setting. He turned and passed iron gates marking the entrance to Bute Park. The open green spaces helped ease the closed, confined feeling of the bustling city centre. He'd never had the misfortune of a panic attack but he now had a better idea of what it was like.

Passing joggers were merely brightly coloured blurs as he became lost in his reverie. And then, his new mobile vibrated. Danny delved for it in his jacket pocket. There was another text message, again sent from his old phone number.

'Meet outside St. Teilo's church, Thursday 1.00 a.m. and await further instruction.
1) Do NOT talk about Sara, go about your business as normal.
2) Do NOT talk to police
3) Follow orders.
Fail to do so, she dies.'

Danny punched his old number but was met by the recorded message, 'I'm sorry the person you have phoned is not available'. That's a fucking understatement, Danny thought. He felt helpless, completely at their mercy. He couldn't do anything; only wait for Thursday morning to come.

CHAPTER 20

Danny found it hard to muster the energy or enthusiasm to send Silver Belle over the schooling fences. But he needed something to sidetrack his mind from the fact Sara was missing and he was no closer to finding her. And the mare needed to iron out her still occasionally erratic jumping. Like a mourner, he wanted to keep busy, pretend things were okay, until the rendezvous at St. Teilo's that night. He'd fall apart otherwise. Preparing Silver Belle for her big day at Cheltenham had been his pet project over the winter and he didn't want those months of sweat and toil at all hours to go wasted.

It was still dark as Danny arrived at the yard. The headlights glinted off the driving rain as he pulled into Samuel House. The patter on the car's roof was like music to his ears. With Cheltenham looming large and his mount crying out for a testing surface, a downpour sweeping east across Britain would hit the track a few hours later. Relying on inaccurate weather reports, the clerk of the course had adopted a policy of watering this past week, fearing the ground would dry and make it dangerous for the jumpers. This would deter runners and, in turn, affect ticket sales.

With an extra drenching, the track will surely be riding soft, Danny hoped. *Thank God for weathermen, they're worse at predicting than Stony.* He skirted the farmhouse and paced to the stables. He flicked on the light in Silver Belle's box. She was already awake, seemingly unsettle by the crackle on the corrugated roof and the rush of water channelling into drains. Danny tacked her up.

A square of light on the other side of the courtyard told him that Kelly was already at work in the box occupied by My Noble Lord, probably checking him over after the Chepstow exertions. He saw a glimpse of her slim silhouette, striking against the yellow glow as she appeared to be changing the gelding's feed. Danny led Silver Belle out and, not wanting to disturb the other inmates, he raised his arm to acknowledge her. She waved back.

Minutes later, the rain had been swept away by a brisk easterly wind. They made the short canter to the training ground. He suddenly felt a tingle of anxiety. He wasn't sure why. Perhaps it was the fact it was their final serious workout before the big day and just the one mistake now could leave its mark mentally come the race when they'd be tackling the fences at full racing speed and peak confidence was paramount. A perfect preparation was essential, as he knew there'd be at least a dozen rivals primed to the minute to take advantage of any hiccups.

With no one within earshot, Danny said, 'You know what to do girl, we've done this time and time again, should be second nature by now.' She pricked her ears from the sound of his voice. He often talked to her, when he knew they were alone. He sometimes found it easier than he did with friends and family as he knew he wouldn't get any grief from her for saying the wrong thing.

The thick cloud cover was breaking off in the west and stars were dissolving in the lightening sky. Danny frowned.

He steered Silver Belle to face the line of fences and kicked her lightly in the belly to wake her up and get her mind on the job. She soon reached half-speed and continued to accelerate into the first fence which she met with clinical accuracy brushing over the birch. *Low and efficient*, Danny beamed, *just perfect*. But there were two more to clear before he could rest easy. Four strides out she began to stutter into the fence but, unlike her early days, another forceful shake of the reins made her mind up and she took it on with relish, floating through the crisp morning air with an eerie weightlessness, much to the delight of her rider.

'One more,' Danny whispered, 'just one more.' The fence grew larger and, as if feeding off each others confidence, they left the ground on a perfect stride and landed the other side running. Danny surprised himself by whooping. *What a confidence booster*, he thought, *all systems go now*. His moment's relief was tempered by thoughts returning to Sara. Such a dark cloud could only clear once he knew she was safe and well. With no hard proof as to who had taken her, he was stuck in some kind of hellish purgatory, as if in suspended animation. With the finishing touches made to Silver Belle's build-up complete, he returned to the stables.

'All right, Kelly,' he said, eyes smiling.

'It went well then,' she said.

'Like a dream,' Danny replied.

'Coffee?' she said.

'No, buzzing enough as it is,' Danny said though he wasn't deep down. He didn't want Kelly asking awkward questions about Sara. 'I'll join you for an orange juice or somethin'.'

Kelly left it to Danny to remove the tack from Silver Belle and make sure she was okay. He approached the side of Samuel House and entered the communal area where the stable lads and lasses were allowed. He placed his helmet beside the welcome mat. Racket was bouncing around and yapping as Danny struggled to tug off his muddied boots, thinking it was a game.

Kelly was finishing up the washing and Danny was stood just behind staring out of the window down at the gallops where Rhys was now working one of the young hurdlers. She turned and seemed startled by his presence.

'You gave me a start,' she said, before laughing.

'Sorry,' Danny said. 'Didn't mean to creep up on ya like that, wouldn't guess I used to be a cat burglar. Miles away were you?'

'Wish I was,' she said. 'Won't have enough saved for a holiday this year.'

Her shiny black hair was so striking against her soft white skin. The silhouette of her shapely curves was showcased by the morning light streaming through the kitchen window.

She'd be a catch for some lucky fella, Danny thought distantly. She wore the same perfume as Sara.

'You okay?' she asked.

'Yeah,' Danny said. 'Why do ya ask?'

'Oh, nothing, you've just seemed a bit flat recently.'

'Nothing I can't sort,' Danny said, lacking conviction.

'What's the rest of the day hold for you?' she asked.

'Not a lot,' Danny sighed. 'Yard's got no runners today, thank God. Couldn't manage a day on the road.'

'You?'

'Don't know, might hit the town later once I've finished grooming.'

'Yourself or the horses, cos I'd say you look all right to me.'

She smiled and her hand ran through her glossy hair. 'Danny, me and some friends are going for a few drinks in town later, thought you might join us, if you've no other plans, of course,' she said, colour back in her cheeks. Her hazel eyes widened, unblinking. 'What do you say? Sara can come along if you're worried about . . . I'll leave it with you.'

'Bit awkward, Sara's gone away for a few days. Wouldn't look good if I was out gallivanting in town.'

Kelly suddenly leant forward and kissed Danny on the lips, hand cradling the back of his head. Danny didn't react, caught off guard eyes shut, a mix of shock and pleasure momentarily overriding a wave of guilt from wrongdoing. *Didn't see this coming!*

For a beat, he was lost in the moment. *Not enjoying this, not enjoying this.* He couldn't deny it felt good, for those few seconds. But he wouldn't, or perhaps couldn't, get Sara's image out of his head. He was first to withdraw from their brief interlocking embrace. 'What was that?'

'You didn't enjoy it?'

'No, *what* was that?

'I hated seeing you sad and I . . . I don't know, I thought you felt, kind of the same way.'

'But . . . ,' Danny started but couldn't find the words.

'While the cat's away,' she said, running her hand down his forearm. The brush of skin on skin sent a tingle down his back. He was flattered by this unexpected attention and affection in his hour of need. Kelly had clearly picked up on the painful loneliness that'd suddenly surfaced since Sara's disappearance and she'd made it briefly subside. But he knew it wasn't the answer, far from it. After all, he feared the 'cat' might be lying dead in a ditch somewhere. 'I don't know what signals I was giving off Kelly, but I swear you misread 'em big time.'

'I'm sorry, I. . .'

'What were you thinking?'

'But I've seen the way you look at me,' she said. 'Don't say you don't feel the same.'

'Whatever looks I made, believe me, I wasn't asking for all this.'

Her eyes glistened. He knew he'd been too harsh on her, overstepped the mark, like she'd just done.

He'd forgotten no one knew the wider picture, not even the police.

'It's not your fault,' Danny said. Perhaps it was his, he reasoned. He was never any good at reading the signs, like a foreign language to him. Out clubbing, seeing a girl eyeing him up, his mates would egg him on, saying 'get in there Danny, it's on a plate.' But Danny was never so sure. No way was he going to crash and burn and be a laughing stock.

She frowned, seemingly unconvinced by his change of heart. He continued, 'Another time, another life, different circumstances, I'd jump at the chance. Not every day a young and beautiful girl is interested and, believe me, I'm flattered, well, extremely flattered, but I'm meant to be with Sara, we're married, I love her. You understand?'

'Yeah, sure,' she said, blinking.

'You find me irresistible, couldn't escape my charm. I mean, what female couldn't,' he added.

She mirrored his smile and said, 'I'm sorry.'

'Stop saying that. It's done, we move on.'

'What will you do?'

'Nothing, she's gone away for a few days, meeting an old friend,' he said, mindful Kelly would only nag him to go to the police.

Kelly left the room, seemingly struggling to shrug off the embarrassment, and passed Rhys on his way in. He couldn't shrug off a smirk.

Danny immediately suspected something. 'Were you lurking?'

'You dark horse, get in there,' Rhys said, without full conviction, leading Danny to suspect his pal might be hiding a secret affection for her.

'I'm married and in love,' Danny said, dampening Rhys' youthful exuberance. He'd never uttered the L-word in front of any of his mates.

Danny didn't want to linger at the stable, avoid any potentially awkward moments with Kelly so soon after their misunderstanding. He drove back to Cardiff.

That evening, he ordered a curry for one though his appetite had also vanished. Would soon be back into the old destructive habits, he feared, if Sara wasn't around; back on junk food, drinking too much, slacking at work.

Fed up with channel-hopping, trying to find something half-decent to watch, he decided to retire early to bed, see if he could surprise himself by managing to catch up on some much-needed shuteye. After all, he was set to return to Llandaff by 1 a.m., meet the call of the message he'd received by text in the park.

His nerves were fraying at the mere thought of whom or what he might find when he got there. The not knowing was the worst part. He was normally a sound sleeper but since his troubles started, he couldn't remember the last decent night he'd had. He set both alarms to ensure he didn't oversleep.

Trying to drift off, he used reverse psychology, telling himself to stay awake. Every time he did this, the more he felt the accumulation of recent sleep deprivation hit home. He soon felt himself fading away to a more comfortable place.

His body clock woke him with a start. He rolled over, half awake, about to say sorry for crossing into Sara's half of the bed when his skin merely touched cool, smooth sheets. He bolted upright, as if struck by a stun-gun. His wide eyes looked down at the alarm clock, heart thumping. For a frightening beat, he feared he'd overslept and they would've carried out their threat. The alarm clock read 12.23 a.m. Danny blew hard and jumped into action, fired on by a rush of adrenaline.

CHAPTER 21

Danny shifted his weight between black leather trainers as he waited, bathed in the cold light of the phone-box outside church grounds in Llandaff. He could see his rapid breaths form cloud patterns as they dissolved into the night air. *This better not be some hoax.* But he knew Sara's disappearance wasn't public knowledge. Only Danny and the person who'd sent the text message knew she'd disappeared. The threats therefore had to be genuine. He expected the phone in the booth to ring and order him to go someplace else less open and public. It was now just gone 1 a.m. and, with the streets eerily dead, he prayed no one would walk by when the call came.

Spotting a shadowy figure slowly come into focus, Danny bit his lower lip. *Don't ring*, he thought, *please don't ring now.* The man neared, head bowed, mostly concealed by a woollen hat pulled down over his ears. He leant slightly to the right to counter the weight of what looked like a tool bag in his left hand. As he passed, the man whispered, 'Daniel, follow me.'

Danny did as he was told, not saying a word.

The pair paced along the leafy avenue of this fashionable suburb of Cardiff. The distant yap of a dog broke the silence. As they neared a bus stop, dimly lit by a single strip-light, the man said. 'In there.'

They stepped under the glass-walled shelter. He lowered his beige bag to the ground; it made clunking sounds of metal on metal. He said, 'Explain what we've come here to do.'

Bathed in the flickering light from behind frosted glass,

Danny got a better view of the man's wanly skin, slightly pocked and bristly. His eyes were glazed as if he'd been badly hurt in the past, or was it merely tiredness. Either way, Danny could relate.

He could see there was nothing left behind those glassy eyes, the shutters were locked down and he'd long since given up hope finding the key. He got a good look at the man's face, absorbing every feature to give him a chance of picking him out in an ID parade if it was needed to nail him later on. But his appearance was ordinary in just about every way, the sort of bloke who could lose himself in a crowd: average height, build and looks. Brown eyes with, what little Danny could see, hair that matched. But it wasn't his fairly unremarkable appearance that caught Danny's eye. It was his headwear, a black beanie. His mind was sent straight back to the night at the graveyard. The man before him didn't appear to possess the will or desire to take a risk getting a mere parking fine let alone daring to exhume a body from a grave plot in the middle of the night. However, thinking back, his average build matched that of the silhouette he could make out in the grainy light the other night. And the text that led Danny there was from his old phone. The same one he'd used as a decoy in the graveyard. It had to be the gravedigger, calling himself Draper on the text.

'We're going to break into the church,' the man said.

'What, tonight? Now?'

'Yes.'

Danny mind was log-jammed with concerns. Travelling back home in a taxi having just been released from spending six months at Her Majesty's Pleasure as a teen, he recalled the defining moment promising his mother that he'd turned over a new leaf. 'No more, Mum. Gonna make you proud.' He remembered she just turned and forced a smile, as if unconvinced. But he was placed with a yard at Lambourn within months and had lived up to that word ever since.

'Is that where she is?' Danny asked, thoughts still firmly on Sara.

'An oil painting, in the chapel annex beneath the clock tower.'

'A picture, in the spire?' Danny said.

'Yeah, but we can only gain access via the main building.'

'It's for you?'

'Not exactly,' Draper replied. 'I'm only after what's on the back of the canvas.'

'But the painting itself must be worth a fair bit.'

'Probably,' Draper said. 'This is where you come in. I know you have experience in B&E.'

'That was years back, though. Seen the light now.' Danny tried to figure out who could have 'informed' this stranger. The kids he'd been led astray by back then, according to the local press, had either got into drugs and were six feet under or went on to more serious crime and were doing time. And then he hit on something. He asked, 'Who's this painting by?'

'Why should that interest you? This is my job, follow orders and you'll be rewarded.'

'I'm Danny Rawlings,' he said, nothing to lose.

'I know,' the man said.

'And you're Tom Draper,' Danny said.

'Good, pleasantries over, now let's get down to business.'

'Got to be able to trust you, if we're going in there, I need to know more about you.' Danny asked again, 'Who's the painting by?' He had a pretty good idea the answer but he needed to hear it from Draper's lips.

'It's a Rossetti,' Draper said. 'Dante Gabriel Rossetti, alright?'

He flashed back to the visit he'd made to the Lazari estate. It was Lawrence behind it, recalling the gallery of Rossettis missing the 'one that got away'.

Getting others to risk all to complete his precious set of paintings. The coward's way out. Lawrence knew of his criminal past and had clearly passed it on. He gripped Draper by the arm. 'Who're you working for?'

'Myself,' Draper said, trying to shake himself free.

Like hell, Danny thought. 'You're lying.' *No way this weak and feeble man could be the mastermind behind it all.* 'It's Lawrence Lazari, isn't it?'

Draper didn't reply. He didn't need to; his mask had peeled off, revealing a guilty frown.

He was about to threaten Draper further, bully the whereabouts of Sara out of him, when he reined himself back, nagged by those conditions for her safe release in the text message:

1) *Do NOT talk about Sara.*
2) *Do NOT talk to police*
3) *Follow orders.*

'Here's the floor plan and tools are in there,' Draper said, pointing at the shoulder bag.

Danny unfurled the plans. He glanced over them. 'I'm guessing there's an alarm?'

'If you want what you're after, it will pay to follow my command and keep quiet,' Draper replied.

Nothing in the text message to say questions couldn't be asked, Danny thought. 'Were you at the graveyard the other night?'

'No.'

'What's on the back of this Rossetti then?'

'That's my business.'

Danny cast another line, hoping for a stronger bite. 'The Rule of Lazari perhaps?'

Draper's lips parted slightly and his dead eyes now showed a glimmer of life.

Danny sensed he'd registered a chord somewhere. He wanted to connect with this guy, get him on his side, like a hostage befriending their taker. What could possibly urge Draper to exhume a body and prepared to break into a church all for the sake of a betting system?

Drawing on past experiences, Danny suspected he knew. He took a punt and said, 'You're a failed gambler, looking for salvation.'

Draper's lips parted another degree and his Adam's apple dipped like a yo-yo. Danny took a cautionary step back as Draper's hand burrowed into his suede jacket. Had he said too much? When he saw it was merely a wallet Draper produced, he stepped forward again. He looked on as Draper rifled through its contents, sifting a wad of receipts and credit stubs. His eyes lit up as he pulled out a small colour photo and he smiled warmly as he showed it to Danny.

'She's pretty,' Danny said.

Draper nodded. 'Her name is Siobhan.'

'She has a nice smile, friendly, welcoming,' Danny said, looking down at the brunette. Draper ground his jaw. Was he fighting back tears?

'She's no longer with you?'

'She left,' Draper said, voice cracking. 'Promised I'd quit betting, but let her down time and again. The promises meant nothing in the end. Home was repossessed, she then packed her bags and I suffered a breakdown, losing my job.'

'I'm sorry,' Danny said. 'Really I am.' The revelation resonated uncomfortably close with him and made him pine for Sara yet more. This sorry lost soul could be him if he didn't find her in time.

Draper wiped his streaming nose and said, 'I'm doing this for her.'

Danny handed back the slightly tethered photo. 'Even if you find this Rule, it's not the answer.' Draper remained silent. 'She's gone, move on, get help. You've got a problem and this Holy Grail of betting systems will only feed your addiction.' Draper was now wiping his eyes.

Danny just shook his head and shrugged his shoulders. He had no more answers.

There was a pause, Danny lost in thought and Draper presumably lost in memories of happier times.

'Penny for them,' Draper said.

'What?' Danny asked, though he'd heard and was buying time.

Draper added, 'Your thoughts.'

'I just want Sara back and if this is what it takes, bring it on.'

'You will, but we must complete this job, we're against the clock.'

'We'll force a side door – the heavier main entrance is fastened by stronger bolts, and more of them. Once in, we go to the chapel annex. There's a trip laser beam at knee height. Break the beam, the photocell in the doorframe will activate a siren and we're done. We'll need to be careful lifting the masterpiece over this, as there's no way we can turn it off, clear? There's a water mister in there to locate its level.'

Danny nodded, 'How do ya know all this?'

'It pays to do research, my contacts know their stuff.'

Draper leant forward. He blinked a few times, as if to stop his watery eyes spilling over. 'It's time.'

Danny felt his throat tighten. Although in no way religious, he felt a growing unease about entering unlawfully a house of God. He feared his brother Rick would be turning in his grave at what was about to take place. Danny hoped he'd understand. This wasn't about greed; he was driven into this purely by fear for Sara.

He felt the shape and weight of the clunking tool bag, lying slumped on the ground. It was years since he'd last done this, and that was mostly small two-up two-down mining cottages in the valleys, nothing remotely on this scale. He feared he'd just waded out of his depth but he knew if this guy could help get Sara back he had no choice but to carry on. They were swallowed by the night.

Danny removed the pencil torch as they approached a small door to the side of the building.

'Force the lock,' Draper whispered.

Danny drew a calming breath. In the dead of night, mere footsteps echoed like claps of thunder. He grimaced as he hammered a chisel, with a sharpened edge at the end of the blade, so it was prised between the door frame and the ancient stone wall. The wood began to give and splinter, as he continued to beat at the mushroom end of the metal shaft. But it was proving stubborn, with the door showing no hint of budging. He didn't want to force it and jam the lock.

And then they both turned, attentions gripped by a square of light from one of the houses overlooking the church boundary. Danny looked up, praying there wouldn't be an enquiring silhouette looking down on them. But he was relieved to see the window was frosted.

'Someone going for a piss,' Danny whispered. If they'd spotted something, turning on a light was the last thing they'd do, Danny reckoned, making it harder for them to see us and easier for us to see them.

Draper then knelt and fished deep in the tool bag. He removed a thick strip of wire and offered it to Danny, who gave a look and sighed. *Why the hell wasn't this given to me first off?*

He began fashioning a hook shape and went about picking the weighty iron lock. His free hand pressed against the thickly varnished wood, feeling for a slight vibration from the mechanism turning. He continued to manipulate the curled wire with imperceptible twists, expertly feeling his way. Click. Danny froze. His free hand pushed the door. As it creaked open, he looked over his shoulder and raised his thumb to Draper. It was like a void inside, deepest space, forcing Danny to flick on his torch. Its slender beam hit the flagstone floor.

Danny shadowed Draper as they skirted what looked like the dark shape of pews, row after row of them. He kept the torch pointing downwards. Lifting the beam to one of the many towering stained-glass windows would risk blowing their cover. He was led by Draper to a door at the far end of the nave, alongside an altar and pulpit.

Danny fell to the floor and placed the torch beam pointing at an angle sufficient to light the area, yet away from the doorway, aware that even a beam of light could be enough to break the infra-red laser and trigger an alarm. He shook the can and sprayed, its clouds of water vapour glittered against the light of the torch. He started at ground level and continued to press down on the can until he stopped as a piercing green line of light about a foot above the floor told him enough. He got to his knees and continued to spray, covering every inch of the door mouth. Danny turned and lifted his index finger and mouthed the word 'one.'

He then picked up the torch and both stepped over the beam in an exaggerated manner. Danny looked around the small windowless room. The far wall was masked by a large plinth holding the painting.

Draper held back and handed the tool bag, pointing to the artwork, as if to say 'over to you.' Danny ran his torch over the structure and the oil painting of what looked like a biblical scene in vibrant colours, similar to those he'd witnessed at Lawrence's house. He began scaling the skeletal steel frame and motioned for the bolt cutter, setting about weakening the metal arms connecting the steel casing around the canvas with the wall.

'We're gonna have to take the casing with the canvas,' Danny whispered over to Draper, who kept lookout at the door leading on to the nave. After an agonizing spell as he worked at cracking the joints and releasing the Rossetti oil, it suddenly broke free from the back wall. Danny steadied it and growled, 'Come and get the other side.'

Draper rushed from his lookout post and reached up. 'Lift on three,' Danny ordered, 'one, two, three.'

The pair shakily prised it away from the wall and, clear of the frame, wasting no time lowering the canvas complete with cumbersome steel casing, to the carpeted floor of the chapel.

Danny and Draper shifted it from the chapel annex on counts of three. Danny's arms ached, but he was sure they'd feel even worse when he awoke the next day. They took the strain raising it a safe distance above the laser beam and had made it a third of the way down the aisle. Danny was about to ask where Draper had parked the getaway van when the side door by which they'd entered swung open.

'Wind,' Draper said, seeing Danny's face crease.

Danny shook his head. 'I pushed it closed.'

'The lock's fucked,' Draper said. 'Loose on its latch, now let's get this outta here.'

Danny wasn't so sure and ducked for cover, shielded by the canvas. Tom remained rooted to the spot, like a deer in the headlamps, and called into the blackness, 'It's you!'

Shit, Danny thought, no way he'd be able to explain his way out of this.

'What are you doing?' Draper then asked. One by one, his words echoed around the chamber.

A crack of gunfire then bounced off the ancient stone walls as Draper slumped to the ground. Danny's stomach also hit the floor as he glanced across, fearing the worst. Yet Draper wasn't hit, he'd merely dropped his weight to dodge the bullet. Perhaps, then, it was Draper who'd fired the shot, Danny hoped. He growled, 'Didn't know you were armed.'

'I'm not,' Draper said. 'They're after this.' His eyes glanced towards the steel casing they sheltered behind.

'We can use it as a shield then,' Danny said, 'On three, we back up, drag this with us.'

'It's way too heavy,' Draper whined.

Footsteps began slapping the stone floor, louder with each step.

'Do it or we'll die!' Danny growled, desperation firing his voice.

Danny tensed his arms and said, 'One, two, three.'

They heaved it inches from the ground and walked backwards from where they came, arms and legs taking the strain. The footsteps sounded closer and closer, though. Moving in for the kill. Danny looked over his shoulder and could make out what looked like a door frame to their right. 'Through there.'

'But the painting, my Rule!' Draper cried.

'Fuck that,' Danny cried. Another piercing shot, this time striking one corner of the canvas. Danny flexed his stinging hand from the jolting impact. He looked down at the indentation where the bullet had lodged into the steel. He pointed between two pews and said, 'Keep low.'

The pair dived for cover from behind the painting and scrambled on all fours behind the heavy wooden seating, knees skating over the cool stone floor. Danny knew it wasn't the exit but anywhere was better than in the line of fire.

Draper pushed his weight to swing the door open and Danny piled in after him. As Danny slammed it, he caught the briefest glimpse of two shadowy figures; their interest had switched to inspecting the damage on the artwork. *That's what they were after.* Draper was right.

CHAPTER 22

The pair clambered up the stone spiral staircase. The echo of gunfire still rang in Danny's ears as he led the way up the cool, dank stairwell. He barged his way past a door at the top of the winding steps. His eyes had long since adjusted to the darkness and he could make the outline of oak struts and sloping walls. They'd reached the belfry. Two shuddering chimes from the church bells housed in the clock tower beyond the sloping wall off to his right confirmed his suspicions.

Fearing the armed assailants would follow them to finish the job off, Danny powered up his pocket torch and was the first to venture onto the ancient oak rafters. He pensively moved deeper into the room, amidst a nest of wooden pillars and supports. He looked back and splashed light on Draper, who remained standing near the doorway, his ghostly face scarred by eyes a fiery mix of terror and rage. The stark light glinted off something in his hand. Danny's eyes narrowed. It was a knife, serrated six-inch blade shimmering.

'It won't be no use,' Danny shouted back. 'Guns trump knives any day.'

'I won't be using it on them.'

'Whoa,' Danny cried, 'it's them and us now, if we've a chance of getting outta this alive.'

Draper loomed closer. He'd changed, no longer receptive to anything Danny was saying, as if possessed by darker forces.

Danny backed off, deeper into the wooden chamber, stepping over the struts and swerving the support pillars. He

166

swept the torch-beam and paused, absorbing the mental image of what lay ahead and then flicked off the torch that was revealing his whereabouts.

With the image of the room still freshly imprinted on his photographic mind, he negotiated the wooden obstructions. And then, he felt something hold him back. Danny ran his hand over a waist-high tape. He flashed light down. It was red and white chevrons, saying *Danger: Keep Out*.

He felt the greater threat was behind him, so he ducked under and ploughed on. He then recalled the church roof appeal he'd donated to. Fine rain along with the faintest blue light seeped through holes in the slate-tiled roof. Danny had read in the local rag that many of them had been blown off during last year's storm and it seemed only a few had been crudely replaced by temporary wooden boards.

Danny trod gingerly onwards, mindful of the knife-wielding Draper in pursuit. Why had his accomplice suddenly turned? Perhaps he thought Danny had tipped others off and set this whole thing up? He might be safe here as Draper would be in two minds whether to risk the beams most probably riddled with wet rot beyond the cordon. He could take refuge in this section, shielded by one of the plethora of thick pillars, until the gunmen below left with what they came for and Draper simmered down.

He lowered to the floor, easing the burden on the decaying wood by distributing his weight over the wet rafters. He felt them bow ever so slightly as he lay flat, perfectly still. He sensed they'd also warped over the years and the slender gaps between each beam afforded him a view of the nave below. He could make out the movements of shadowy figures, both in black. They were shifting something.

Must be the work of art, he fumed. They'd stepped in to grab the spoils after the hard work had been done removing it from the chapel. Perhaps that's what riled Draper so much. Was he part of this elaborate plan? Maybe it was his role to kill Danny – the only witness to the crime – before joining his accomplices below. And foremost in his thoughts, where was Sara?

Maybe Danny had been used for his skills and would now be disposed of in case he ran to the police. He didn't want to hang about to find out. They'd now moved out of vision from where Danny had his face pressed against the cold, sodden wood. He glanced up to see if Draper was within range. The darkness was impenetrable. No shadowy movements, or shapes or sounds. *Draper must've turned to scarper while he could.*

His eyes returned to the gap. It seemed like they'd got what they'd come for and the coast was now clear. All he had to do was negotiate his way back through the belfry and he could disappear into the cold night air, pretend this never happened. Perhaps he'd done enough to secure the release of Sara and could wait for the next message detailing instructions for her safe return. He sure felt he'd been through the wringer.

His breathing quickened as he saw the figures below re-emerge into eye-line. This time, instead of the painting, they cradled what looked like large canisters. It was hard to make out their actions in the dimly lit chamber below. Hearing a loud splash of liquid on stone, Danny shuddered. The floor now glistened as they continued to empty the large cans, the contents sloshing between the legs of the wooden pews.

One then left while the other continued to shake the can in a sweeping motion, like a sprinkler system, until empty. Danny looked on in horror as the figure retreated and then flicked an arching dot of light on to the newly formed lake, igniting it into a fireball so bright Danny had to back away and blink his eyes. The blinding flash of the explosion of flames below burnt onto his retinas in swirling patterns of white, orange and yellow. He had to get out, quick, before the whole place went up in smoke. He pushed himself up. The strengthening roar beneath his feet was a continual reminder he was against the clock.

Preparing to leave, he thought things couldn't get any worse, but then he flicked on the torch. Stood the other side of the sagging cordon was the haunting figure of Draper. 'Look Tom, I'm not sure whose side you're on or what the hell this is all about but we've got to work together, if we're gonna get out of here alive, yeah?'

'You set me up,' Draper snapped, icy. 'You employed *them* to take the painting off me with the Rule of Lazari on its back. I would've shared the rewards of the system but no, you greedy fucker, you wanted it all.'

'I was never after the Rule,' Danny protested. 'I was like you but I don't bet no more. You were free to take it. For fuck's sakes, they shot at me as well.'

'No they didn't, not one bullet was aimed at us.'

Danny said, 'They were after the painting in one piece.'

'But how did they know it was tonight?' Draper snapped.

'I could ask the same of you.'

Danny could imagine the apocalyptic scene below as he felt the heat through the rafters. The beams creaked and moaned, like the bows of a galleon, as the saturated wood began to expand.

'You gotta trust me,' Danny said firmly.

'Trust you!' Draper said. 'Years of searching for the Rule and I was this close to finding it, until you betray me.'

Draper pulled off his beanie. His forehead glistened in the light of the torch. He ripped the cordon and pushed it away. Danny suspected Draper had been on the precipice of another breakdown and all this had sent him over the edge.

'But it's our last chance to both get out of here alive, please,' Danny begged.

'My wife has gone, my dreams are dead, why should I carry on?'

'At least, let me go.'

'I'm afraid it's too late for that, Daniel.'

Danny cried, 'Don't do this. You're not thinking straight!'

He wasn't sure if it was to his advantage keeping the torch on, or to attempt passing Draper in darkness and risk being caught by a lucky swipe of the blade. He dropped the torch, it pointed away from the pair, giving off enough light to make out the shape of Draper as he continued to edge forward. Danny crouched to adopt the stance of a sumo wrestler. Low centre of gravity, arms out, hands like crab pincers, ready to grapple the deranged man seemingly intent on doing them both damage.

'I'm no traitor, Tom, it's not too late. I can get the painting back, just you see. We can both be rich, don't think this is the end.'

'I think we both know it is, otherwise you wouldn't be humouring me,' Tom replied. His voice was empty, almost robotic, as if he was prepared to die here and now. Danny wasn't and his light frame leapt forward, grabbing Draper's wrist and squeezing with all his might. Draper grunted and let slip the blade which dropped like an arrow to stick in the softened wood. Danny grappled him to the floor. Draper threw a wild punch which caught him on the temple. Danny returned the gesture. The roar below sounded like a blacksmith's furnace and rivulets of smoke escaped the cracks as the pair rolled on the beams, bowing slightly from their combined weight, as each struggled to gain the upper hand. A loud snap beneath them and they briefly stopped fighting, acutely aware of something greater that could kill them both.

'Give up, Tom,' Danny growled, now pinning him down.

Draper smiled, 'Don't be afraid of death, it comes to us all.'

'But just not yet,' Danny shouted, releasing himself from their interlocking limbs. Another portentous snap. As if in slow motion, Danny witnessed the two thick struts supporting Draper vanish, taking the stricken man silently with them, no time to scream.

The wood, stressed and weakened by water damage and old age, literally crumbled beneath, unable to bear his weight. Danny rushed forward. He first saw white fingers clinging to the edge of a surviving beam. He edged forward and could see them supporting Draper, who looked up, eyes white with terror, the like Danny had never seen before and hoped he'd never see again. Sweat leaked from Tom's furrowed brow as he desperately clung on for his life. Towering flames licked at his dancing feet as he mouthed 'help', eyes intense, like a madman.

Danny squinted down between billowing plumes of choking smoke. Instinct led him to kneel and reel him to safety. But he sensed the wood on which he stood begin to tremble. Without the support of a beam alongside, Danny feared they'd all collapse like dominoes. It was under strain from Danny's weight above and the scorching heat rising from below. He caught increasingly brief glimpses of Draper as great clouds of smoke were funnelled through the gap.

Danny knew the floor would give any second. Why should he risk all for someone who wanted him dead and, in any case, had a death-wish himself? He was about to turn and leave when Draper cried something to change Danny's plan. 'I die, she dies.'

Did he in fact kidnap Sara? If so, he was the only one to know where she was being held captive. He couldn't afford not to save him.

Danny carefully lowered himself down and straightened his arm. Eyes shut from the gritty smoke, he felt Draper's smouldering suede jacket but he wasn't sure whether the rest of him was attached or had been devoured by the raging fires. When Draper let go of the beam and Danny took the strain, he knew the answer as Draper felt like a dead weight. Danny felt his body shift forward. He feared being hauled over the edge as well. He leant back, away from the waves of burning heat forcing through the gap. Straining every sinew of his strong arms, he managed to hoist Draper's head above the fiery parapet. His face and neck were red-raw, small parts of his skin melted away.

'Help me here,' Danny growled, as he felt Draper's weight slipping back down. 'You're not gonna die, you selfish bastard.'

Danny held his breath as the choking smoke shrouded where he sat on the edge of the precipice. One last heave, that's all he had left. Three...two..one. An almighty growl escaped his lips and Draper's head again appeared into view, eyes open this time. 'Grab the side!'

Draper did as he was told, though barely conscious, as if drugged.

Once Draper's weight was safely on the remaining boards, Danny flopped back. The smoke was thinner there and he quickly supplied his thumping heart and aching limbs with some much-needed oxygen. He tried to ignore the rumbling wood beneath his skull. One last lungful. He sat up and looked across at Draper, who'd now come round and rasped between choking coughs, 'My ankle. I can't move, my ankle!'

'You'd better not be lying about Sara,' Danny said, standing. He grabbed Draper by the arm of his charred jacket and hoisted him over his shoulder in a fireman's lift, while ensuring his feet were placed on different beams to halve the load borne by each.

Danny flexed his knees, testing the weight. He had to hope his calf muscles, built up from years in the saddle, would support them both as he attempted to clear the two-beam gap left by the decaying floor. Danny knew he'd drop like a stone to certain death from a standing start and stepped back two paces. He growled like a weightlifter psyching up to clean and jerk a personal best. The wall of smoke pumping through the gap made it a jump into the unknown, a leap of faith that the boards the other side were still in place.

Danny strode forward and pushed with his stronger lead leg. The pair disappeared and emerged the other side, landing in a heap. Momentum sent Draper tumbling forward to some place safe beyond the floored cordon, leaving Danny still very much in the danger area. Before he had time to clamber to his feet, the beam that had taken the brunt of the impact started to groan and then fell from beneath him. And now it was Danny scrambling desperately for his life. He'd reacted quickly enough for his upper body to remain in the belfry, but his legs hung over the edge. 'Help, Tom!' he choked, lungs feeling like they were about to burst and watery eyes red with grit.

His legs felt like they were melting, possibly engulfed by the flames, as he desperately pushed his torso forward. His fingernails dug into the damp wood, gaining some purchase. He knew if he could manage to gain enough momentum to swing one of his legs up on to the beam, the other would follow. Yet he froze, like a climber stuck on an icy slope, petrified any movement would send him over the edge, devoured by the fireball below. But he could barely feel his legs now and he knew if he was going to risk all, it had to be then. He tensed his hands, acting like crampons. 'Tom!' he cried one last time. Nothing. His accomplice had either been injured in the fall or escaped.

He heard the distant wail of sirens. Too late for me, he feared. With the last ounce of energy left in him, Danny swung his left leg up sufficiently for the toecap of his singed trainers to meet the top edge of the beam. No way was he going to lose his footing and he pushed it over. In a single swinging motion he raised his other leg up and thrust his weight forward, grabbing at the wood and skinning his fingertips. He'd done it. Although clear of the gap, he still wasn't safe and wasted no time scrambling his way beyond the cordon. He ran his hand down both legs to assess the damage. First thought was one of relief they were still there. His combats had partly disintegrated and parts of his legs stung to the touch, particularly his left shin but not half as badly as he feared.

He spat some of the muck collecting in his mouth. It came out as stringy and grey. He then set about feeling his way back to the stairwell, past the assault course of beams and struts. There was still no sign of Draper. Danny thought he must've made a break for it, *clearly not so keen on dying after all.*

That was until, yards from the door they'd stumbled through just minutes earlier, he tripped over a shapeless mound on the floor. There wasn't anything there before, he reckoned. He struggled to his feet and went back. The smoke had yet to fill this far along the belfry and he could make out Draper's bedraggled jacket. He was lying there, groaning, 'My ankle.'

He must've collapsed in a heap having struggled to fight his way through the darkness.

With the words 'I die, she dies' still prominent in his thoughts, he bent down and dragged Draper by his arms, like a sack of coal. He shook the door open from its frame. It was stiff to budge, the wood having expanded from the heat rising. He began to stagger down the spiral staircase, bouncing off the curved wall like a drunk, dragging Draper in tow, yelping after every bumping step.

Halfway down, he almost cried when he heard the loud clumping footsteps coming the other way to meet them. The last memory he had was a yellow helmet topping a large Perspex eye-shield, reflecting his face, blackened by smoke. The man handed him an oxygen mask. He felt his legs go, almost as if his mind had given permission to shut down, like a computer switching to stand-by. The fireman was there to cushion his fall.

CHAPTER 23

He blinked his stinging eyes open and stared up at the white-washed ceiling, mind cranking into gear.

'Daniel,' his mum's voice came from his right. 'The drugs must be wearing off. Daniel, can you hear me?'

Danny opened his mouth. It felt as dry as his eyes. 'What happened?' he croaked.

'You blacked out, my love,' she said. 'What a blessed relief. I'm so proud of you, rescuing that young man from the church like that.'

Propped by pillows and attached to a drip, Danny looked over. 'Feel sick with tiredness.'

'That'll be the painkillers. They'll soon wear off. Doctors say you were very lucky, your lungs passed the X-rays with flying colours. Could've been a different story if you weren't fit and young.'

The blurry edges sharpened, as did his thoughts. But for one blissful moment he believed Sara's disappearance was just some bad dream and she would enter the private ward arms opened invitingly. The fact she wasn't there with his mum during visiting hours brought it back home to him. 'Sara?'

'I couldn't get her by phone, I left a message on the answer-machine at your flat, so hopefully she'll arrive soon. You just rest your head. Think of yourself for now, we all need you better.'

'I can't, Mum, I've got to get going.'

'Nonsense, the doctor's recommend a day's rest before you

leave. I've brought the local papers along, treating you as a hero, rescuing that lad. You'll soon be right as rain.'

Danny reached for the paper. A headline on a strip down the right side read: *Hero saves friend from church blaze*. Friend?

'He said the pair of you were forced up to the belfry by armed robbers and was trapped when the church was set alight,' she said. 'The thieves were trying to destroy all evidence, including you both as witnesses. Is nothing sacred anymore?'

Danny sat perfectly still, trying to soak all of this up. Draper had clearly set the story for the both of them and it made sense to toe the line. Last thing he wanted was the police on his back when Sara was still missing.

'Where's Tom Draper?'

'He's being treated for third-degree burns in a private room just down the way,' his mum replied.

'He's here!'

'He requested an armed policeman to guard the corridor, not sure why that would be, perhaps if the robbers came back . . . it doesn't bear thinking about. Perhaps you could go and visit him when you're on your feet. He'd like that, I'm sure.'

'Perhaps I will,' Danny said.

'I brought grapes, newspapers and a few odds and sods from the hospital newsagents, didn't have much selection, went for a music and a car mag. And there's a case with some of your old clothes you'd left in my house. Hope they still fit. Is that all right?'

'Yeah, I'm about the same weight these days,' Danny sighed, still groggy. 'Put the reading stuff there and I'll look at 'em later.'

'Tea-time visiting hour's almost up,' she said. 'I'm going to have to leave you in a mo. But I'll be back first thing in time for the doctor's rounds, see if you're up to leaving. Oh, it's such a relief, been praying all hours, and my friends at the Christian group.'

Danny forced a smile as she kissed him on the forehead. He gazed at the clock as the door to his private ward clicked shut. *Time seems to grind to a halt in these places.*

Feel fine in my head, he reckoned, *perhaps a little weak and unsteady, but I can walk that off.* He rocked himself from the bed, took a moment for the wooziness to subside, and pushed on slippers left neatly bedside, presumably by his mother. He carefully detached the drip, shuffled to the door and poked his head round. Like his mum said, a man in black stood facing away, blocking one end. Closer, an unattended cleaner's trolley was stood to one side, clearly midway doing the rounds.

Wearing a backless gown, Danny moved quietly along the corridor, mindful not to alert the guard some thirty yards away. Circular glass lights above were mirrored in the shiny linoleum on which he limped gingerly. He glanced through the windows either side as he progressed, until he spotted Tom lying alone in a single room, eyes open and distant. He stopped and slowly pressed down on the door handle, glancing across to where the policeman remained motionless, clearly not expecting the threat to appear from within the hospital ward.

Tom lay under a single sheet. One forearm was swathed in bandages and his neck had blistered in small patches. He groaned.

Danny said, 'Good to see you too, Tom.'

'What do you want?'

'We have unfinished business,' Danny said.

'Do we?' Tom said.

'Aside from the fact I saved you and then you leave me for dead in that hell-hole Tom, if that really is your name,' Danny croaked past aching glands and throat like sandpaper. 'Makes it easy to see you're capable of leaving Sara for dead.'

'Never even met her,' Tom replied, maintaining eye-contact. 'I've told police and press the story, we were innocently caught up in an armed robbery. Got them both off our backs,' he croaked. 'In my eyes, we're quits now.'

'That doesn't concern me,' Danny said, looming in close. He picked up a plastic cup brimming with water and sat on Tom's hand clamping it down. He peeled away the top of the bandages.

'Shall we test how effective morphine really is?'

Tom cried in pain, 'What the fuck . . ' Danny tilted the cup to tipping point above skin like the surface of Mars.

'Now, let's talk business.'

'You can't do this,' Draper cried. 'One pull of this and the guard will have you on the floor in seconds and I can change my side of the story you know.' Danny glanced over at Draper's free hand primed to tug on an orange plastic triangle on the end of a cord hanging from the ceiling.

'First off, you wouldn't dare change the story, not now it's out there, you'd be in as much shit as me. Secondly, tell me why the hero of the hour, who went out on a limb to save you would then go and try to harm you. They'd laugh it off. Even if they listened, I think they'd interested in knowing who'd exhumed Jeremiah's body. So go ahead and squeal to the police, they'll soon be on to you.'

Draper's eyes narrowed, face puce. 'Just get off me, it's fucking painful.'

Danny got to his feet and glanced across at the window looking onto the corridor. He hoped the cleaner was a slow worker. 'Where is she?'

'Who?'

'Don't test me, Draper, cos I'm this close to finishing you off right here.'

'I honestly don't know who you mean.'

'Sara, you know the one, my wife, missing nearly a week,' he said. A bolt of pain pierced his chest, even the mere thought of her suffering made him wince.

'I don't know,' Draper said. 'Honestly, I've never met her.'

'You're lying,' Danny said.

'Prove it.'

'I follow orders in a text from her captors and you magically turn up. And in the fire, you shout up 'I die, she dies.' The text read, 'One word to police, she dies.' See the similarity. It all adds up. You sent that text, you kidnapped Sara! Whatever sick fuck of a game you've been playing, it's over.' He felt his blood pressure soar as he spat between gritted teeth, 'Where . . . is . . . she?'

'I . . . I knew she was missing, that's all,' Draper said, unsettled. 'My grip was about to give, I felt my feet burning and didn't want the rest of me going the same way. Survival instinct took over, can you blame me for a white lie, last roll of the dice. Would be cinders if I hadn't, you should be proud, a life saver, you'll get a medal for this.'

'The only life I'm concerned about is Sara's,' Danny said. 'All right then, if you didn't take her, tell me who did?'

'Couldn't say,' Draper said.

'There's a shock.'

'Can you leave me rest and mend, we'll finish this another time.'

'No,' Danny growled. 'We're finishing this now. If you don't tell me, you'll need a 24-hour armed guard from this day on!'

Draper's chapped lips remained pressed together.

'You knew them, didn't you,' Danny said.

'What?'

'Those who took that bloody painting and your precious Rule of Lazari.'

'No,' Draper.

'Come on Tom, you fucking said, 'it's you,' when they arrived. Do you usually say that to complete strangers?'

Draper shut his eyes, probably wishing Danny would go away.

Threats weren't working, so he tried a softer approach. He was sure there was a heart in Draper somewhere.

'She's pregnant,' Danny said.

Draper opened his eyes.

'If you have one shred of human compassion you'd help, think of Siobhan and the hurt you felt when she was no longer there.'

'Pregnant,' Draper said, turning to gaze distantly out of the window. 'If I'd–'

'Whoever set up our meeting at the church also tried gunning us both down, before nicking the piece from under our noses and then torching the place, left us to fry they did.' Draper remained silent, as if sobered by the revelations. 'And your loyalty and trust still lies with these monsters. You owe 'em nothing Tom, apart from revenge.' Danny put the cup down, feeling he'd made some headway. 'Just tell me who they are and where I can find them, I'll do the rest.'

Draper's eye-line turned to his bedraggled suede coat hanging over a visitor's chair in the corner. 'Inside pocket.'

Danny paced feelingly over to the khaki jacket and pulled out a card. It read: systemites Siobhan cantona7

'It's a forum we use, those of us trying to find the Rule of Lazari. It's at systemites.co.uk. Siobhan is my username, cantona7 the password. Glory, glory Man Utd.' He forced a smile.

'I'd done a search for it but came up with no results,' Danny said, perplexed.

'It's encrypted, so that only those chosen can come on board. The moderator on the forum had gotten wind that Lazari had left the formula for the Rule on the back of the canvas, proper inside info. I guess we'll never know now, with it being in others' hands. But it's out there somewhere, I know it. Licence to print money, they say.'

One born every minute, Danny thought. 'But why the fuck did you dig up Lazari's remains?'

Draper sighed. 'A misunderstanding, I second-guessed the leader of the forum. I was told the Rule might've gone to the grave with the multi-millionaire. I took this as read, thinking the Rule was buried with him in the lead casket.'

'But you found nothing?'

Draper shook his head.

'You've been used,' Danny said.

'But it's out there, I have to find it to win my fortune and get Siobhan back.'

Danny shook his head in dismay. He now felt sorry for the guy, more misguided than evil.

'Perhaps,' Danny said, wanting to spare his feelings. 'Who knew you were going to the church last night?'

Draper steadied the cup to his lips and tilted ever-so-slightly. 'Only you and Dante.'

'Who's he?'

'The leader of the forum.'

'And only he knew, no other member.'

'We discussed it off-forum, sending private messages.'

'Is Dante his real name, or a username.'

'Username I guess, presumably a tribute to his favourite artist Dante Gabriel Rossetti.'

Danny winced as he swallowed hard, picturing Lawrence's collection of Rossettis. 'Fucking hell,' escaped Danny's lips. *Lawrence was Dante, had to be.*

So it was Lawrence he'd witnessed splash fuel across the nave of the church and set it ablaze. All for the sake of the painting. How could he stoop so low? Inherited his father's ruthless, obsessive streak no doubt.

'And you say Dante posts regularly on this forum.'

'He runs it.'

'I'm afraid you were being used. It was purely the painting he was after not the Rule.'

'What?'

'You were being ordered about by this ringleader to meet his needs, not yours. And Dante doesn't need to seek the Rule, he's the son of Jeremiah Lazari.'

Lines appeared on Draper's grazed brow. 'I don't believe you.'

'It's the truth whether you want to believe it or not. The guy you recognized in the church is Jeremiah Lazari's son, Lawrence.'

Tom's eyes welled.

'Don't be ashamed, I got sucked into it an' all. I guess if you want something bad enough, you'll go to any lengths and judgement flies out of the window. Mine certainly did.'

Danny heard a loud clatter echo down the corridor, a

warning signal for him to leave, sharpish. 'Gotta go,' he said, standing.

'Danny, I honestly didn't know they'd gone that far. If I had. . .'

'I know.'

'If you need any help, they say I'll be okay to leave tomorrow. Burns are shallow. They need the bed apparently. Just call me, my number's on the other side. I want to help.'

Danny clenched the card in his hand and slipped back to his own bed. He changed into snug-fitting clothes he didn't even recognize, clearly stuff from his mum's house he'd left behind once moving out as a teenager. He pulled on a thick navy and white sweatshirt over tight stonewashed denim jeans; something out of a Wham video. He masked grogginess as he discharged himself from hospital grounds not a minute too soon and used his debit card to ride a train back to Cardiff. He felt the details on the card Draper had given him may be his last hope of tracking down Sara. He feared it was too little too late.

CHAPTER 24

Danny booted up and went online. He typed in the web-address on the back of Tom's card. www.thesystemites.co.uk.

The screen went blank and a grey box appeared stating *Restricted Access. Please fill log-in details.* Danny's eyes flitted between the card and the screen as he typed in the codes: username Siobhan and password cantona7. When nothing happened, Danny feared the laptop had crashed, or that Tom was leading him on another wild goose chase. But then the white screen turned black. Large white writing at the top of the page scrolled *The Rule of Lazari is out there. . . .*

At the foot of the screen, there was a row marked: members online. Siobhan was the only name currently active. He was in.

He began feverishly skimming over the forum messages, sorted chronologically. Longing to find the merest trace of evidence, however small, that Sara was alive and well.

Danny slowed as he came across the entry:

Dante: *New blood has emerged. His name is Daniel Rawlings. Acting suspiciously. He knows too much. Needs sorting.*

Must've been the day I visited Casey Jones, Danny reckoned, that's what kicked off all this mess.

Dante: *New blood is too close, scare tactics needed.*
Siobhan: *What in mind?*
Dante: *Just a reminder what he can expect if delving any deeper.*

183

Siobhan: *Agreed. What needs doing?*
Dante: *Leave a note making it clear he is not wanted. Will be riding at Newbury in two days time. I'll send a pm to your email box with wording. I have another surprise for him. Remember, we have come too far for the Rule to be taken from us.*

More like he suspects I'm on to him, Danny reckoned. He clicked on Draper's private messages tray and a note had indeed been left by Dante, simply the words: *Be wise, walk away from this or you will die.*

So Draper wrote and left the calling card in his kit bag that day, though this Dante was clearly the driving force behind it all.

But why would Lawrence, aka Dante, be playing sadistic games with these people. For the fun of it?

Dante was bullying the other members. It seemed to Danny that they were obeying his orders under a climate of fear that they may be next.

Danny scrolled down and came across this entry.

Dante: *Daniel may pay you a visit, Miles. Toe the party line, tell him nothing more.*
Arkle: *Very well, though I didn't bargain on this when I came on board. Thought my part had been played!*
Dante: *You were paid handsomely, Miles.*

Danny recalled the visit to Crabtree that following day. He swallowed hard and read on.

Arkle: *He knows more than we fear. Caught him reading a transcript print-off from this forum.*

He recalled the cat named Arkle fleeing Crabtree's Cheltenham home. *So Crabtree was lending a hand in all this*, Danny thought. He was distracted by the name Dante flash up next to Siobhan low on the page. Lawrence was lurking.

Danny read on.

Dante: *I hear from a reliable source that Lazari may well have died with the Rule.*
Siobhan: *I get you.*

This is where Tom's imagination must've shifted into overdrive, Danny reckoned. Whether through desperation or madness, he went in search of Jeremiah Lazari's resting place.

The following day's entry went:

Siobhan: *I have an item that might interest you.*
Dante: *Go on.*
Siobhan: *Will send pm.*

Danny suspected the item was his phone and had been passed on to Lawrence, who sent the texts revealing Sara's capture.

Dante: *New blood is playing a dangerous game. We can fight fire with fire!*

The entry was made just hours after Danny had threatened Lawrence at his estate. Like a photo left to slosh in a developing tray, the picture began to emerge. He needed to search the Lazari estate, while there was at least a chance Sara was still alive.

He clicked on the username Dante.

Danny's finger skated over the keypad and ran the cursor over the button: Enter a message. He clicked and a pop-up window titled Siobhan appeared. Danny began to type in the entry box, under the guise of Siobhan, 'Dante, we need to meet.'

Moments later, Dante replied with, 'Why?'

He needed a strong enough incentive to entice Lawrence away from his lair.

'I now know your identity and why you asked me to take the Rossetti,' Danny typed.

'You are mistaken,' came the reply.

'Don't lie, I saw you. The secret is out.' Danny paused, thinking of what Tom would say. He needed to draw Lawrence to a place conveniently close to his estate in Wiltshire.

'What do you want?'

'Let's meet at service station at Junction 13 on M4 to discuss this further,' Danny wrote. It was a regular stop-off for him to refuel en route to the racetracks in the South East.

Danny waited. No reply. Had he inadvertently raised Lawrence's suspicions and his cover was blown?

But then the message popped up, 'Meet at quiet time, 2 a.m.'

'See you there,' Danny typed and then logged off, before Lawrence had time to change his mind.

CHAPTER 25

Danny needed help breaking into Lawrence's estate. It was long odds-on it'd be alarmed, possibly with guard dogs roaming.

He sent a text to Draper's phone asking if he was up for exposing the man that'd used him so cruelly. Draper replied within the hour, and they arranged to meet at the village of Everleigh at 2 a.m. that night and make their way from there.

He hoped Lawrence believed it was actually Draper on the forum, leaving the house free for him to search for at least clues as to Sara's whereabouts and proof he was the callous killer Danny believed he was.

He ran over the layout of the house in his mind, picking out possible weak points of entry imprinted on his photographic memory.

It then suddenly occurred to him that if things went wrong and he didn't return, no one would be any the wiser to what he'd already learnt about Lawrence. If he were to die tomorrow, there was no guarantee the info would get to the police and that sobered him. It wasn't the fear of dying that left him unsettled, it was the unbearable thought that Sara would most probably be left to perish.

He removed the digital recorder he'd taken when talking to Heathcote at Chepstow from his jacket, and the printout of horses sent by Mike. He also printed off internet search results for the Rule of Lazari and the Rossetti painting. He penned down the link between the owner Jeremiah Lazari and the jockeys. He then saved the threatening text messages sent to his mobile. He noted this down for whoever in authority was investigating in case he didn't make it back alive. Who to leave it with?

He could trust Stony but he didn't want him to bear the responsibility, similarly with young Rhys. He mulled other names over and then glanced at his watch. Perhaps James would be willing. He removed the watch and punched the engraved number on its back into his phone. 'Hello?'

'James, it's Danny. I need a favour.'

'Of course, but what?'

'My wife's gone missing, abducted,' Danny said. He filled his lungs as if a weight pressing down on his chest was lifted, releasing the burden of a secret that until now he hadn't revealed to anyone.

'What on earth are you talking about, Daniel?'

'It's a long story. But I need your help.'

'Have you gone to the police or reported her missing?'

'Can't risk it,' Danny said. 'They said she'll die if I do.'

'But how can I help?'

'I've put together some things about those involved. I reckon it's this guy called Lawrence, son of Jeremiah. I'm going there tonight, see if she's there.'

'You poor soul, this is terrible,' James said. 'How will you protect yourself?'

'Won't be armed,' Danny said. 'Done more break-ins than I care to remember, never even took a knife back then. I'll be fine, spotted hunting rifles in a display cabinet if it gets desperate. But I've laid a decoy, so the house should be empty.'

'How can I help?' James said.

'If something happens, I need you to go to the authorities with the info I've managed to collect.'

'Of course I will, but are you sure this is the best course of action?'

'Got no other option,' Danny said. 'If she's being held there, I'll sure as hell find her.'

James said, 'If you leave it with, say, your concierge, I'll be only too glad to help out if the worst happens.'

Danny paused. 'Okay, I'll leave instructions with the concierge for you to collect a Manila envelope and post it to the police.'

'Will do,' James replied.

'Wish me luck,' Danny said.

'Be safe.'

Night fell and Danny thought it best to at least try to get an hour's kip. Despite setting two alarms for 12.15 a.m., he couldn't trust them implicitly and struggled to settle, coming off worst in a fight with the sheets. The more he tried to slow his breathing and skirt around thoughts of what lay ahead, the more his anxiety grew. With no distractions, the still of night put his worries under the spotlight. He eventually resigned to get up and prepare. His fingertips reached for the ceiling and he cracked his neck and spine, occasional aftershocks of a crashing fall he'd suffered at Ascot years back.

He applied a fresh coating of the skin cream that was left on his bedside cabinet at the hospital and pulled on his jockey's gloves, cut from thin black leather, and his coat to match. He grabbed his keys from a shelf beneath the hallway mirror and his toolbag. *All set*, he thought, *here goes.*

The motorway was quiet at this hour, with deserted stretches. Danny put his foot down and drew alongside the village green at East Everleigh with time to spare.

Yet Draper emerged from the blackness, tugging on his now familiar beanie hat as he approached the passenger door of the Golf.

Draper groaned as he sat beside Danny. 'Bearing up?'

'My legs sting like hell, even with the morphine and dousing it with some cream they gave me,' Draper said, 'but I'll live. You?'

'The pain's dulled,' Danny said. 'I need you to act as lookout. Agreed?'

'Whatever it takes,' Draper said. He'd mellowed. 'How can you be sure Lawrence won't be there?'

'Can't,' Danny said, shifting the car into gear. 'But I'm guessing he's taken the bait.'

Danny left his car parked near the wall circling the Lazari estate. He gave a leg-up to Draper, who fell with a thud and a groan the other side. Danny joined him.

Draper then held back, acting as lookout where grass met with the gravel driveway, ready to call out if disturbed.

Danny could see a security box flashing high above. He flicked on his torch and made out wires sprouting from its top. They were tacked along the wall, just below guttering. He wrestled past thick shrubbery and then tested his weight on the first metal strut holding a drainpipe to the brickwork. He began his ascent, the cast iron pipe holding strong, until he met the guttering. He pulled wire-cutters from his pocket and deftly sliced the top wire, disarming the system. He slid effortlessly back to earth and then set about prising open one of the many ground-floor leaded windows. He forced it ajar and, with a furtive glance left and right, he scrambled his way inside. His eyes struggled to adapt to the dark as he went to power the torch.

It was quiet and eerily still, just as Danny hoped. He negotiated the dining table and chairs and made for the main hallway. He could find his bearings from there. Venturing deeper between corridors and rooms in this labyrinth, he began to call Sara. He was tentative at first, mindful that Lawrence might have bluffed falling for Danny's message left under Draper's username. As desperation soon took hold, he found himself belting out her name. 'Sara!'

She must be here, he reckoned, somewhere in this maze. He half expected to turn and see the tall willowy silhouette of Lawrence in the doorway, cradling one of those hunting rifles he'd seen in the billiard room. He could hear each breath and the wooden floors groaned from every footfall, as he frantically carved his way through the house, not caring for anything but finding Sara safe and well. The rooms were exquisitely furnished, like those he'd caught glimpses of, casually flicking through one of her home and style magazines.

He found a rhythm as he went about systematically

sweeping the building: swing door open, briefly peer head round. 'Sara?'

He didn't care about disguising the fact he'd broken in, the snapped security wires would tell Lawrence enough.

Fearing she was cowering in a corner somewhere, not sure who was calling her name, he began shouting, 'Sara, it's Danny! Sara!'

Not hearing her voice come from the black was getting to him as his search became frenzied, turning over tables, cushions and pulling away curtains.

If he's laid a finger on her, Danny fumed, *fucking recluse better not be some perv.*

Like a minesweeper, he'd cleared the first floor. Nothing.

He soon found himself back where he'd started in the hallway on ground level, none the wiser, having exhaustively scoured every nook and cranny. She wasn't here. He glanced at the front door but he just couldn't leave, not empty-handed. He'd come this far. The slightest sign or impression she'd been here at some point, anything. The messages on the forum were damning evidence but he began to question whether they were real, whether this was all one elaborate joke, albeit an unthinkably sick one.

With Tom on lookout, he afforded himself another five minutes searching time. He ran the torch-beam along the paintings. The gallery was now completed by the painting taken from the church. The tear in the bottom right-hand corner where the bullet had sliced through the canvas was proof of this.

Lawrence had clearly left Danny and Tom stranded, engulfed by flames. His mind returned to that fateful night. Through the gap in the beams, he was sure there were two figures that ignited the petrol in the nave below. Was it one of the other forum members promised a share of the future rewards from Lazari's racing system.

Mind alert, something then occurred to him. While talking to Lawrence in the billiard room, he picked up a porcelain vase.

Lawrence didn't bat an eyelid. But when he got within touching distance of the worn tapestry on the far wall Danny recalled the man nearly bit his head off. It was slightly dishevelled and had no place being there, lowering the tone. The words of the housekeeper also came flooding back, the place is haunted, 'I've heard noises in these walls.'

He rushed along the galleried hallway and made a beeline for the lightly tethered material. With no care or thought, he yanked at the drape. And again. It came away in his hands, falling to the wooden floor in a silent tangle.

Danny kicked it aside, convinced the answer was hidden beyond the wood panels facing him. He began tapping the wall, a dull thud each time. And then, he stopped, eyes lit up as if straying across some lost Inca temple. He tapped again in exactly the same spot. The thud was higher pitched and echoed. Danny glanced up and down the guilty panel, fingers feeling the joins. He then began to push, putting all his weight behind. It wouldn't budge. He stood back and began kicking at the wood. His boot made only slight indents. He looked around for a lever or button but there was nothing. He thought about calling Tom in, perhaps the strength of two would do it. He circled the room, applying pressure on anything that protruded or might look out of place. He pulled at the shafts of snooker cues in a rack on the wall and looked behind paintings, lifted vases. Nothing.

His eyes darted from one corner of the room to the other. He suddenly noticed one of the wall lights on the wall near the hollow panel hadn't flicked on like the others. He yanked down on the wall-light and watched the panel release from the others.

He looked around the billiard room and his eyes settled back on the cue rack. He removed the cue with the thickest butt and weighed it in his palm.

An exhilarating rush at discovering an opening was replaced by apprehension of what he might find. It had been days since Sara's disappearance and he couldn't banish his worst fears. He moved towards the loose panel. Snooker cue gripped in his right hand, he felt his way like a blind man along a corridor until, after a half-dozen pensive steps, his progress was halted by another door. With no handle, he pushed his weight forward and he fell into what looked like a self-contained room, with fold-down bed in one corner and kitchen units and a sink in the other. Like a studio flat he'd viewed when property hunting in Cardiff Bay years back.

A large skylight punctured the ceiling, letting in some silver light from the moon and stars. Danny flicked on a desk lamp. Peach wallpaper covered the walls, with a gallery of framed photos mounted next to the kitchen. Danny went to take a closer look, snooker cue now by his side. His eyes scanned over the pictures. It was like a catalogue of the success stories of the Lazari family. One of them was the black and white shot of the Kempton race. Must be the nerve centre where Lawrence planned it all, Danny reckoned; a place to hide evidence away from the prying eyes of the authorities.

He returned to the desk and, with sleeve tugged down over his hand, pulled the drawers open. They were bare. *Clearly got rid of any evidence after the authorities came snooping.* But he was aware this place was also an ideal hideout to keep someone captive. He smelt the air for traces of Sara's scent, her favourite perfume, anything that could prove she'd been there. But it was the smell of carpet cleaning fluid that caught the back of his throat.

'Sara?' he called. Perhaps she was trapped behind one of these walls, or beyond the only other door leading off the room, next to the gallery of photos. He peered into the dark room and flicked on a light. He stood braced, cue held in front. His grip eased when he saw it was a compact shower and toilet, no sign of life.

He began to believe she'd been held here until the night of the church robbery and, once he'd carried out Lawrence's ill-doings, she no longer served any purpose and was disposed of. Entirely possible, he feared, as Lawrence was behind the other killings. Perhaps that explains the chemically smell, covering his tracks.

He didn't venture further down that dark path. He quickly tapped each wall. It was a long-shot, but he thought there may be more hidden secrets in these old walls. All of them were solid, though. He'd seen enough and returned to the billiard room in the main wing of the house, hope of finding her fading fast. He rested his weight against the billiard table, hands gripping the baulk cushion. He'd discovered Lawrence's lair where he'd most probably held her captive, yet he was too late. He gripped the cushion tighter and then slammed his fist down on the polished oak rail, though he felt nothing.

On hearing the distant clap of a door, Danny looked up. Must be Draper coming in from the cold, wondering what the hold-up was. But then he realised the only way in without a key was via the open window. So who was it? Couldn't be the housemaid, he thought, not at this ungodly hour. It left only one option – Lawrence Lazari, returning from Newbury having realised he'd been tricked.

The footfalls echoing down the galleried hallway grew louder with every step.

Danny's furtive eyes flicked across to where the hunting rifles were stacked in the glass case. They'd been removed.

He had no time to even duck from view when a figure emerged from the shadows, towards Danny, clearly aware of and not intimidated by his presence.

As the slight figure came into the guttering light, Danny felt his jaw drop and his vice-like grip on the cushion return. 'James?'

'What the . . . where's Lawrence?' Danny asked.

'I've sent him to Newbury overnight, like you suggested.'

'I don't. . . you're lying,' Danny said. 'Why would Lawrence listen to you?'

'Why shouldn't he? He is my loyal son after all.'

'What?' Danny said, buying a few seconds to take it in. 'Jeremiah?'

The man before him didn't reply, lips stretching into a knowing grin.

'You faked your death.'

Danny's eyes flicked across the room for a means of escape, but he couldn't retreat to the dead-end that was the secret hideout and Jeremiah blocked the only other door. He thought about barging past this frail old man. When he removed a gun from his jacket pocket, Danny thought better of it. 'Don't even think about it, Danny. Your luck has finally run out. I've been watching you closely on your one-man crusade and now it has to end.'

'I've got all the proof I need,' Danny said, 'Kill me, the truth will out.'

'That reminds me, I must collect that envelope up from the concierge you'd so kindly made for me.'

Danny was running out of hands to play. 'Others know.'

'You are the only one still standing.'

'But Mike Thorpe,' Danny said.

'You are the only one.'

Danny's worst fears for Mike's safety had been realized. 'You fucking psycho.'

'Did him a favour, put him out of his misery, he kept persisting in interfering, like you have. I warned him but he was so intent on avenging his son's death, like a dog with a bone, one that needed putting down. Once I'd got wind that he'd unearthed the link, connecting the race-fixes with the trial period requested by the tax authorities, I had to contain him.'

Danny cast his mind back to the printout of bets over a five-week period. They were a trial period, as he suspected, but not for Crabtree to prove the system's worth to Jeremiah. He then recalled the faint watermark of a crown in a circle. That's where he'd seen the symbol, on his tax forms. It was Customs and Excise property. 'So a tax fraud was behind all this?'

'The business was on its knees by the mid-nineties, cheaper foreign imports and spiralling costs made it impossible to compete. I'd invested everything I had in that business and thirty years of my life to build it up into a world leader, no way was I going to let it collapse like others had. Drastic measures were needed and, knowing profits from betting were exempt from tax, with the Government getting the revenue from an operations tax on the bookies' profits, I could siphon off millions to offshore accounts, saying it was winnings from the legendary Rule of Lazari.'

'And you roped in Miles Crabtree, the world's leading form guru, to put his name to it,' Danny said, 'help add authenticity.'

'Had to if they were to believe me,' Jeremiah said. 'I'd laundered the best part of £80 million when the tax authorities launched an enquiry, requesting proof of bets and receipts. Asking awkward questions, ones I couldn't answer. With no way of locating the money, they also asked for hard evidence the betting system worked. Under threat of prosecution and a lengthy sentence, I needed to ensure results went my way.'

'By getting your jockeys to adopt race-tactics to frame races.'

'And they agreed to this for the month trial,' Jeremiah said, 'enticed by a handsome pot at the end. It was the tensest month of my life, as the racing authorities were also on my back.'

'But why kill them?'

'Simon Thorpe, like his meddling father, got cold feet. He couldn't take the pressure of lying in interviews before both the tax office and the BHA. All he had to do was toe the line, say the Rule of Lazari existed and he wasn't riding to orders. But no, he had no balls and threatened to reveal all. It's then I stepped in to resolve the matter.'

Danny swallowed. 'And Monty?'

'The recorded bets made me nearly half a million over that brief period and, with the help of the best team of lawyers and accountants money can buy, the tax office closed the investigation as they held insufficient evidence to prosecute. That was until, ten years on, Mike Thorpe, out to avenge his son's death, pressured his old colleagues in the Customs to reopen the case. Suffering a bout of depression, Monty was too fragile to deal with it all rearing its ugly head again and I couldn't trust he'd remain loyal, now no longer working in my colours. Mike effectively signed the death warrant of Monty. Shame, I had liked the guy, rode some good winners for me.'

Danny said, 'But Casey was prepared to toe the party line.'

'And he was rewarded handsomely with a share from the offshore account.'

'But if the business was on its knees, how could you put aside so much?' Danny asked.

'It was company turnover,' Jeremiah said. 'Not profit. Sales remained good, but rising costs of production meant profit margins were squeezed, particularly with the advent of China on the world market.'

Danny said, 'But there was no need to go on a rampage, it's as if you got a kick from finishing others off.'

'It becomes addictive, exerting power over others. Power that I'd forgone since going into hiding in there.' His eyes flicked to the open wall panel before settling back on Danny. 'When the business was flourishing in the eighties, I had hundreds working for me, under the rule of Lazari. I couldn't bear losing this,' Jeremiah said.

'So you go on a killing spree to make you feel better.'

'Faking your death isn't as restricting as you might think,' Jeremiah said. 'Being wiped off every register and database, I was free to go about my business. Providing I wasn't caught in the act, I could go on.'

'Sick fuck.'

'I'm only doing this for my son, so he doesn't go bankrupt or get embroiled in another fraud enquiry. That would bring disgrace on the Lazari name.'

'Disgrace!' Danny cried. 'Bit late for that.'

Jeremiah shrugged his shoulders, gun still held firm.

'Why form an online community?' Danny asked, stalling for more time.

'I didn't,' Jeremiah replied. 'It was already there. I merely jumped on board to check what was being said about the betting rule I'd concocted.'

'And?'

'Seems like people are only too willing to believe. Soon realised I could manipulate these poor deluded fools to my own end. I took control of the forum, made it encrypted and used them to carry out those deeds which proved difficult for someone 'beyond the grave'.'

'Poor fools like Draper.'

'Ah yes, after a lifetime of losing, he was obsessed with this ticket out of it.'

'How the fuck did you get away with it all?'

'Quite easily, Daniel, amazing what you can get away with when, in the eyes of the law, you don't exist. For Christ sake, the government has no clue how many illegal immigrants there are living here, fat chance they'd catch me.'

'Explains the prints on the gun.'

'Made no odds to me, I'd led a clean life prior to vanishing off the radar. They held no prints of mine in the database. I knew Lawrence would be a suspect and untraceable prints would put the police off the scent.'

There was a pause as Danny tried desperately to think of another question, playing on Jeremiah's pride at getting away with it all these years. His hand left the cushion and ran along the rails beneath the pocket, hoping there was a billiard ball there, but it was empty.

'Hands where I can see them,' Jeremiah said.

A gust of wind blew hard outside. Danny could hear his heart thud like a battle-drum. 'What's so precious about that bloody painting?'

'I couldn't rest until the set was complete. But no price could persuade the church to part with arguably Rossetti's finest work. I'm not used to being refused. It became an obsession, the one thing money couldn't buy. No longer was it something I wanted, it was something I needed.'

'And you roped me and Draper to do the dirty.'

'Unlike other professionals I could call upon, I trusted you wouldn't vanish into the night with the valuable masterpiece, with Sara's life at stake.'

'And you enticed Draper along as a helping hand, saying the Rule was written on the canvas.'

'I was dismayed when I learned of your Houdini-like escape. However, given where we're at right now, it appears the near miss has merely bought you a day extra.'

'You can't be Jeremiah. I looked inside your coffin, there were remains,' Danny said.

'A dead body was in my coffin, it just wasn't mine. It was my sleeping partner in the business, Roland Meyers. I came clean about the scam, thinking he'd be delighted by my ingenuity, saving his investment, but he panicked and, fearing the authorities were closing the net and he'd be among the catch, he wanted out, so I granted his wish.'

'What did you do?'

'I drugged him,' Jeremiah said in a matter of fact way. 'Slowly drifted off into a coma and that was that. The funeral director was bribed and he was buried below my headstone.'

Danny recalled the scratch marks on the casket's lid. 'You sure he was dead?'

Jeremiah smiled. 'You know, thinking about it, I couldn't be certain. That bastard was going to betray me, simply dying wasn't enough. He needed to suffer, like I was. Sometimes, Daniel, it really doesn't pay to be honest.' He was talking with relish, as if he was finally allowed to reveal some good news, having kept it a secret for too long.

'How could you possibly get away with the funeral on such a high-profile stage,' Danny said, still struggling to make sense of the revelation. 'Lawrence arranged it all, did a splendid job by all accounts, wish I could've been there, really do.'

Danny was becoming acutely aware of the ease with which these answers were coming, without any great concern that he might pass them on. He felt the prospects of getting out of this alive were diminishing by the minute. 'But if you believed I knew too much, why did you spare me and not the others who threatened to blab?'

'Don't flatter yourself. Danny Rawlings was the next name on the list, I paid for a hit man to finish you that day at

Newbury. He had you in his sights and you were fast nearing within range, only for you to put a spanner in the works by ejecting before the second fence, alongside the wooded copse where my man took cover.' A smile spread like wildfire across his gaunt face. 'I recall the papers described your unseating a dramatic turn of events in a small piece, hidden away. If only they knew what might've been, it would've made the front pages.'

The shadowy outline of Tom silently emerged in the doorway. He came armed with a gun and was framed by a soft corona of light from the gallery behind but Danny's eyes didn't waiver from Jeremiah. He wanted to keep Lazari talking at least until he spilt the beans about Sara and her whereabouts. 'Got to hand it to you Jeremiah, you've masterminded quite something here.'

'Like a ghost, I could manipulate and do as I pleased. And flattery will get you nowhere.'

'What about Mrs Lazari?' Danny asked, ensuring Draper was fully aware of who they were dealing with.

'My wife had an affair.'

'And I suppose you killed her too.'

'She was too close to me.' At least he has some compassion, Danny thought, quashed by what Lazari said next. 'I couldn't risk killing her as the finger of suspicion would point at me, as I was still 'alive' at the time.'

'And where is Sara?' Danny asked, tone darkening. 'It's the least you owe me, for fuck's sakes.'

'You like pushing your luck, don't you. Remember, I hold the power here.' His gaze met the gun in hand before settling back on Danny. 'Sara will not like that side of you.'

Danny growled, 'So she's alive. Where is she? You sick fuck, where is she?' He stepped forward.

The snooker table light was enough for Danny to make out Draper's hands tighten around a gun as he crept forward now just ten or so feet from the back of Lazari. Danny glared at Draper beyond Lazari's shoulder. 'Don't!' Danny cried to Draper, echoing down the hallway.

Lazari smiled. His gaze still relaxed on Danny, refusing to turn. 'Don't take me for a fool, Daniel. The oldest trick in the book.'

A shuddering crack echoed down the hallway. Lazari's eyes fell lifeless as he dropped to the floor, limp like a pile of washing. He lay there in a growing slick of blood, glistening like resin. They both stared at the fallen man, waiting for the other to speak.

Tom's hand went to cover his mouth. 'Oh my God, what have I done?'

'You read my mind,' Danny said. 'He was the only one who knew where Sara is.'

'I only came in from the cold,' Tom whimpered, now on his knees, repeating, 'What have I done?'

'Pull yourself together man,' Danny said. 'It's not like he didn't have it coming. He confessed to the killings and played on your gambling habit.'

'What do you mean?' Draper asked, now shaking.

'The Rule of Lazari never existed,' Danny said. 'Made up to cover some tax fraud.'

'I don't understand.'

'Just consider this payback for the years he stole from your life, searching for the Rule that never was. Like I said, had it coming.'

'But what are we going to do?' Tom pleaded.

'I'll take that as the royal *we*, cos I didn't pull the trigger.'

'But you're here,' Tom replied waving the gun. 'Assisted murder.'

'I'll give you assisted murder all right,' Danny said. 'And where the fuck did ya get that thing?'

'From some guy down my bookie's, forty quid.'

'Put it down, before you do any more damage. All I care about is getting Sara back and you may've killed off my last hope. What the fuck were you thinking?' He spat the words out as if they were poison.

'I'm s-sorry,' Tom said. 'How can we make this right?'

Danny rushed forward and started fishing in Lazari's numerous pockets.

'What are you doing?' Tom cried, backing away from the body to cower in the corner near the door. 'They'll get your prints.'

'We're out in the middle of nowhere in the house of a recluse, no one will have heard the gunshot and even if someone did, they'd put it down to a farmer or huntsman. Doubt the police will ever see the body.'

'But?'

'Like Jeremiah said, he doesn't exist no more. In the eyes of the law, he's already dead. Wiped from all records. Looks like he was right about something, shame he's not around to see it.'

'But his son, Lawrence. He'll want justice . . . or revenge.'

'Think, Tom,' Danny snapped. 'He can hardly go to the police and tell them his dad miraculously was found alive and was then murdered in his own home. For one thing, it would open the floodgates in the tax fraud.'

'So what do we do?'

'Nothing,' Danny said. 'Just leave the way we came. Lawrence will return from his wasted trip to Newbury and have to sort this out. Clean up the mess. He's obviously involved in the money scam, having Jeremiah lodging in the secret part of the house back there for over a decade. No wonder he was a recluse, wouldn't want many visitors snooping around. Might well have been the mastermind behind the faked death and he was living in the lap of luxury at the expense of mugs like me paying tax like a good boy. Payback time.'

Draper didn't reply, as if body and mind had gone into shock mode. Danny found himself surprised by how calm and collected he was, glancing over at Draper, whose facial burns had become more pronounced set against his whitening complexion.

Danny suddenly stopped searching Jeremiah's waistcoat pocket and withdrew a pocket comb and a piece of paper, the size of a small business card. He read a code comprising a mix of letters and numbers.

'What the fuck does this mean?' Danny asked himself, more of a plea for his mind to process quicker. He wasn't sure when Lawrence would be back and whether he'd be armed.

Further thoughts escaped his lips, 'A code . . but for what? A safe, a deposit box. Think Danny . . . think!'

Danny eyes darted from wall to wall. *Nothing obvious in the billiard room.* He stepped over Jeremiah and his eyes scoured the Rossettis. *Doubt he'd put anything behind those, risk damaging them.*

But when he reached the end of the gallery, he was about to turn when he noticed the final painting just didn't seem to belong with the others in both style or size. He prised his fingers behind the gilded frame and ran them up and down. Click. His eyes lit up as he felt a catch release and the picture swing towards him, revealing the face of a steel safe set into the wall. He quickly set about keying in the code, occasionally glancing back down the hallway, checking Tom hadn't done anything else stupid. He tugged on the safe handle. It was shut tight. He typed it in again but the result was the same. *Shit!*

He didn't risk another try, fearing it may trip an alarm.

'Tom,' Danny shouted back down the hallway. 'Tom!'

Tom's plump silhouette came into the light. 'We gotta go. Lawrence could be back anytime.'

'Okay,' Tom replied.

He checked his watch and, realising whom had gifted it to him, he ripped it away from his wrist in a fit of rage. *Don't want any reminders of that fucker.* He slammed it down, smashing against the marble floor in bits. Danny crouched and examined one of the pieces lying among the tiny cogs and watch face. He knew immediately what it was – a tracking device. He'd seen them on a techie programme he once idly watched. Fucking 'ell, Danny said. 'That's how he knew where I was.'

'Whatever it is?' Draper said. 'Either take it with us or leave it.'

'Gonna leave it,' Danny said. 'Where did ya get that?'

'What?'

Danny pointed at Draper's wrist. 'Someone gave it to me.'

'That someone wouldn't be lying dead over there?'

'Yeah,' Draper said. 'Do you reckon I should get rid of it, could be possible evidence.'

'Something like that,' Danny said. Now wasn't the time to go into it. The pair hastily left.

CHAPTER 26

After a day of fretting that dragged along at funereal pace, it was time for the Listed chase on the opening card of the four-day Cheltenham Festival. He'd notified the police of Sara's disappearance and the relevant missing person's unit, both saying they'd monitor the situation and put the word out. With heavy heart, he'd made a conscious decision to take Silver Belle along and see how the race developed though his appetite for success was no longer there. After a winter of careful nurturing and schooling the mare, it would be a waste not to at least have a go. *It's what Sara would've wanted*, Danny thought. *Listen to me, talking as if she was already . . . gone.*

But it was hard for him to summon the energy needed to ride in the biggest jumps race of his life. It wasn't only to settle debts hanging over him but to set up a new life for the two of them, or make that three.

Danny arrived at Samuel House at 8.20 a.m. He was early as he knew traffic would be bumper-to-bumper around the racetrack on the opening day, with race-goers arriving from all parts of the country and beyond, gravitating towards a card that boasted the Champion Hurdle as its feature. Danny knew it was good for racing, but not so good for his travel arrangements.

Rhys was pulling on his trainers in the communal kitchen when Danny entered. 'All set.'

'Just about,' Danny replied. 'Where's Kelly?'

'I said I'd give her a ride,' Rhys said and winked.

Danny smiled. 'One track mind.'

Rhys stood and scooped the *Racing Post* from the pine table.

'Is Roger going?' Danny asked.

'Said he'd be watching it on the box,' Rhys said. 'Probably a good thing, wouldn't want any more aggro on track if they lose.'

'All the best,' Danny said.

'And you,' Rhys replied. 'That Silver Belle ain't an easy ride you know.'

'See the mind games have started already,' Danny said, smiling. 'Just cos you're on the second fave.'

'Catch ya later,' Rhys said, shutting the door behind.

Danny's smile quickly evaporated, stood there alone, dark thoughts returning. He coughed a few times, lungs still aching. He was glad he didn't have to pass the racecourse doctor.

He sighed and returned to the horsebox. He patted his jacket pocket to check he'd brought Silver Belle's favourite mints. He wanted to be alerted of any roadworks en route, or tailbacks, so switched on the van's GPS system and began to type in the map reference for Cheltenham racecourse at Prestbury Park. He stopped as it suddenly struck him. He put the van in neutral and hands feverishly went about searching all his pockets one by one. He withdrew the blood splattered paper found on Jeremiah. He hurriedly typed in the code and it threw up a rural location somewhere in Wiltshire countryside.

Could this be where he'd left her? He used the van's lighter to ignite the paper, aware of its possible incriminating nature. He then slipped on his riding gloves to protect his red-raw fingers.

'We're taking a detour,' he shouted back to Silver Belle in the box behind his headrest as he shifted into gear and pulled away.

He snaked the country lanes, following orders from the female voice on the GPS unit, and pulled up on a muddy verge alongside a metal gate. It was apparently the nearest he could possibly get to the grid reference entered, as the road was about to fan away in the opposite direction. Yet the GPS system was still reading over two miles to go, due west. Beyond the swing-gate was a roughshod field climbing as far as Danny could see.

He backed out Silver Belle from the trailer and put the tack on. He slipped his boots into the irons and set about the steady incline on fallowed farmland. A trot grew to an easy canter as he felt a growing sense of urgency, fearing the worst.

The mare was keen, primed for race-day. But he was also acutely aware it only took a loose stone or shrapnel to bruise a foot, rendering her out of action for weeks. He therefore tried to contain her eagerness by keeping her on a tight rein.

He came across a dip where an irrigation ditch dissected the land. Danny kicked Silver Belle on the approach to where the ground fell away and she flew the gap, clearing with yards to spare. Another incline and the pair had crested the rise. Her ears pricked, looking around, seemingly relishing the workout, fresh air and change of scenery.

Danny reined her in again and took in the sprawling patch-work of fields glowing earthy tones in the morning sun, dissolving into the hazy horizon. He felt the mild warmth stroke his neck, the first hint of spring. He dismounted, easing her burden, and looked out on the awe-inspiring vista, scouring the sweeping landscape for any landmarks, farm buildings or wooded outcrops; anything that could possibly provide shelter.

After hurried sweeps left and right, he couldn't see anywhere that could possibly sustain life. He didn't let his mind think the unthinkable; that she could be lying dead in one of the fields he looked down on, or buried at that grid reference. His alert eyes again crossed the panorama, this time slower, zooming in on any tiny detail, however insignificant. He knew this was the highest point, a perfect lookout. Once setting out, he needed to be sure of where he wanted to go. *Getting lost in the fields below would lose valuable time*, he thought, something he had little of.

Seeing a stone building he'd at first missed, Danny remounted and shook the reins, setting out on the downhill journey. The pair pulled up alongside the stone and flint hut he'd spotted from afar, probably once used for storing farm equipment, feed or hay. Slates were missing from the roof, much of the rendering had gone and the windows were boarded.

He jumped off Silver Belle and tied her to a haytrough, upturned and rusty. He noticed a weatherworn name plate on its base. It read: *Property of Lazari Estate.*

'Hello. . . hello!' Danny shouted.

All he heard was distant birdsong. He tried rattling the wooden door, weather-beaten yet jammed tight. So he began kicking, again and again. 'Sara! Sara! It's me, Danny.'

He drew upon strength he never knew he possessed, fuelled by the thought of Sara beyond the door. But was she there or just her body or had she been moved on?

Feeling the rotten door begin to give, he delivered one more telling blow with the heel of his boot, forcing it free from the hinges. He peered inside, eyes adjusting to the dark. Streams of daylight leaking through gaps in the roof splashed over the stone floor, littered with straw and a steel bucket.

Danny spotted in one corner what looked like a pile of stained sheeting. He rushed forward and pulled at the plastic awning. Sara, ashen-faced, frail and dishevelled, lay crouched foetal-like, back supported by the damp wall. The smell of urine and faeces hung heavy. She blinked her eyes open and forced the ghost of a smile. Danny crouched and gathered her limp body in his arms, holding her tight, repeating in a calming doctor's voice, 'It's all right, it's over now.'

'Thank God you're alive,' she whispered faintly against his ear.

'It should be me saying that,' Danny said, slightly perplexed by her concern. *Always thinking of others*, he thought, tightening his hold. 'Need someone to laugh at my jokes.'

She laughed, little more than a wheeze.

'See.'

They embraced for what seemed like an eternity. Danny didn't want to let her go. 'Are you okay? The bastard didn't do anything . . . you know,' he said awkwardly, fearing the answer.

'No,' she said, teary. 'Thank God. Starving, though.'

Danny sighed.

'Where is he?' she asked, as if suddenly woken from a nightmare.

'You won't be seeing him again,' he assured, removing Silver Belle's mints from his jacket pocket. 'Down a few of these, you'll need the energy.'

'Take a few deep breaths,' Danny said, punching buttons on his mobile. 'No chance of any signal, not out here. We're gonna have to make it back to the road ourselves.'

'I can't, not by foot,' she said. 'But I don't want you to leave me, I can't be alone.'

'Silver Belle's outside,' Danny said. 'You'll be okay on her back, we'll go steady all the way.'

'How can you be sure he's not around here, lurking somewhere.'

Danny wasn't keen to reveal that Lazari was dead and he'd been at the scene. He replied, 'You'll have to trust me, love, you're safe now.'

She said, 'Managed to collect rainwater in that.' Danny glanced over at the bucket bathed in a laser-beam of sunlight. 'But this didn't make it easy.'

She raised her right wrist, shackled with an iron clasp at the end of a chain bolted to a metal plate on the stone floor.

Danny went out and returned with a piece of sharp flint and set about weakening the rusty iron fastening, the metal cracked after several arcing blows. Danny asked, 'Sure you're okay?'

'Yes,' she said, 'but don't think I could walk too far, feel woozy in the head.'

Danny had no intention of leaving her to get help. He couldn't possibly let that happen, not with Lawrence Lazari still loose and possibly after revenge. He acted as a crutch, carefully steadying her and then supporting her out of those putrid, dank surroundings. She shut her eyes stepping into the light. It was there, against the stark daylight, Danny realised how ashen her skin had become but he didn't say anything for fear of alarming her unduly.

Danny tried his phone again but, as he suspected, there weren't any bars on its display out here. He then untied Silver Belle and mounted, hoisting Sara to straddle the mare behind him, arms locking weakly round his waist. They slowly retraced a path back to the horsebox. He checked the time as he got off Silver Belle and closed the gate. 11.10 a.m.

In all the commotion, he'd completely blanked out the afternoon's big race he'd spent most of the winter preparing for.

'We'll be at Salisbury General in no time,' he said, wrapping a Samuel House-embossed fleece around Sara fetched from the van and eased her into the passenger seat.

'There's some chocolate in the glove compartment.'

She reached in and unwrapped the bar.

'I told you not to let anyone in,' Danny said. He wasn't blaming her but he had to know the sequence of events to keep his own sanity. Find out whether he could have done any more to prevent all of this?

'I didn't,' she said.

'But the locks weren't forced.'

'That's because I'd left and locked up in a hurry,' she said. 'Got a text message from your mobile, telling me to meet you at Sophia Gardens, it was urgent you said and would only take twenty minutes, so I left a stew simmering, grabbed my coat and went.' There was a pause. 'At least it's got my weight down.'

Danny glanced across and saw her muster a Mona Lisa grin. He wished he hadn't asked, feeling a wave of guilt from not having owned up to parting with his phone on that night at the graveyard. She'd gone ballistic when he'd carelessly misplaced his watch, a birthday present, at the racetrack and he couldn't face the same reaction about his phone.

He recalled one of the entries on the Systemites forum a day after: Draper telling Jeremiah Lazari that he was in possession of something that will be of some use. If only Draper hadn't found the phone, Danny thought. *Should've cancelled the account there and then. What was I thinking!*

'It wasn't me,' he said mournfully.

'How was I supposed to know? It was your number that came up on the screen,' she said, voice still scratchy, occasionally breaking up. 'I arrived and was bundled into the back of a car. My hands were bound until they tingled and tape covered my eyes. I was petrified.'

Danny couldn't bear hearing this but he knew it would help her recovery if she recounted those experiences, however harrowing.

'They needn't have, I recognized the man's voice right away,' she said. 'There's no way you would guess who it was.'

I think I could, Danny thought, preparing to put on his shocked face.

'Your friend James.'

'Jesus, no,' Danny said, feigning surprise.

'At least he'd said he was your friend when he'd popped round to our flat but you were out racing somewhere,' she said. 'Didn't let him up.'

'I'll choose my friends better in future,' he said, voice trailing off.

'I feel queasy.'

He glanced across. She was now cradling her head. 'Do ya want me to stop?'

'No,' she said. 'Quicker they see me the better.'

'Don't talk any more,' Danny said. 'Save your energy, you can tell me everything once they've found you a bed, get you hydrated again.'

'But there's another thing, more important, before I get checked over, Danny . . . there's something I haven't-' She paused.

'I know,' Danny said. 'It's the best news ever.' He turned.

'I was going to tell-'

'I know you were,' Danny said. 'My fault, never gave you a good time to. Let's get you to the hospital, check you both out.' He fired up the engine and pulled away. He cranked up the gears and continued, 'I was too blinkered by my work, you always said I was an obsessive but I realise now, it's what I want, this is what we both want.'

'Of course,' she said softly, eyes now shut. 'What sort of animal would do this?'

Danny didn't reply; there was no need. The animal was now dead.

Her hand left her cheek and rested on his hand clasping the gear-stick. His mood suddenly lightened. *She was safe now, that's what mattered.* The horses in carriage began whinnying as he shifted up the gears.

She said, 'Why did you bring the horses?'

'Oh, no reason,' Danny replied sheepishly.

'What's the date?'

'March 12th.'

'But it's the big day,' she said. 'You're going to miss it.'

'Doesn't matter.'

'Like hell it doesn't,' she fumed. She'd witness second-hand every high and low Danny had endured with the mare as he attempted to keep her sound and prime her for this season finale. It seemed like she was secretly looking forward to it as much as he had been.

'You've got to go. You've worked towards this all winter and can't miss it, I won't allow it.'

Danny looked across. 'I can't leave you.'

'You said yourself, this could be the making of us, get our own place in the country,' she said, voice still weak. 'I'd love that, get my pets as well.'

'But I'm not happy about this.'

'Danny! I haven't the strength to argue,' she said. 'God knows, we need the money, if there's even the slightest hope, you've got to go.'

'If you're okay with it,' Danny said, already psyching himself back up for the afternoon's task.

'If she can carry both of us up a hill, she must be a cert.'

Danny smiled. 'Rest now.'

He detoured to Salisbury Hospital and collared a junior

212

doctor to take Sara under his wing and noted down the number of the ward nurse. Before being wheeled off for observation, she said, 'Give 'em hell, Danny.'

Danny kissed her and rushed back to the horsebox, checking his watch. 11.49 a.m.

'This is gonna be tight,' he muttered, knowing he had to get to Cheltenham, meet Kelly, get changed and weighed out all by fifteen minutes prior to the 2.00 race. He'd cut it fine many times as a Flat jockey, but they were at minor meetings where the traffic around the track was light. He knew from going to the Cheltenham Festival as a punter that it was bedlam in the area during the lead-up to the first race.

He soon found that tingly sense of anticipation return.

CHAPTER 27

Danny buttoned his silks, still flapping loose over his white britches. He carved a path through the racing fans, respectfully parting like the red sea, once catching sight of his colourful attire. He'd yet to tie the colours to his cap as he past the security guard at the entrance to the parade ring. *Glad there's no dress code*, he thought.

Being the owner and effectively the trainer, he could skip the traditional meet and greet with connections on the grassy centre. He stood on the tips of his riding boots, scanning the sixteen horses being paraded for the crowds packed against the railing. Silver Belle was the only grey in the field and she stood out like a beacon.

'What kept you?' Kelly asked, frowning. 'The bell's just gone for them to get mounted. Wasn't sure what the hell to do?'

'I'm here now.'

'I didn't have time to wash her down, legs were mucky,' Kelly said. 'Did you give her a morning workout after all?'

'Something like that,' Danny replied, inspecting Silver Belle's mud-spattered legs. The mare seemed sound and in remarkably rude health given the morning detour.

Kelly gave Danny a leg up. He tied the silk cap taut and threaded his whip through while adjusting his feet in the stirrups.

The runners were led out in Indian file along an offshoot threading between the main grandstand and the Guinness enclosures. He barely had time to soak in the palpable buzz charged by the packed crowds either side. Probably a good thing, the nerves might well have got the better of him otherwise.

Kelly's hand left the bridle as Danny let out a few inches of rein and the pair galloped steadily to post on the far side. The extended two-mile four-furlong start meant they had to cover well over a circuit of the track and were set to line-up away from the grandstand. There was rawness about the place, a breathtaking aura, larger than life. A grimy quilt of cloud unfurled over the dark shoulders of Cleeve Hill.

Having underachieved on the racetrack, the official BHA handicapper had dropped Silver Belle to a rating of 116, meaning she'd scrape in to the race near the bottom of the weights. Having met the hotpot Jackdaw on level weights last time, he was effectively eight pounds better off in this bid to exact revenge in this handicap. Jackdaw was still very much the punters' favourite on his bid for a five-timer and the giant LCD display in the Silver Ring showed this, with the gelding the current 5/2 favourite. Silver Belle was fourth in the betting at 12/1.

Danny's attentions turned to the starter who'd begun to climb his podium and turned the mare to point the right direction, behind most of the milling runners.

'Jockeys, lead them in!' the starter shouted, above the growing crackle of anticipation from the hoards of racegoers the other side of Prestbury Park. 'Turn at the back, won't be delaying any longer.'

Danny straightened Silver Belle, who was understandably buzzy; this was all new to her. The tape flicked up.

The runners devoured the ground on the cavalry charge to the first fence which came upon them all too soon and, like a shoal of leaping salmon, they streamed over in unison, a fine exhibition of jumping from such an inexperienced bunch of novices. Silver Belle cleared the second like one of the brush fences on the training ground. It was now Danny that was buzzing.

He found himself penned in towards the rear, scraping paint on the inner and tracking one of the outsiders – a notoriously bad jumper – but Danny had no room to negotiate his way out of the pocket. From his punting days, he used to despair at jockeys playing a dangerous game buried among the main pack where a clipped hoof or a slight drift off a true line could prove costly. But he knew Silver Belle was a flighty mare who needed settling, switched off behind rivals. Otherwise, she'd pull far too freely and her tank would empty on the stiff climb for home.

The third fence came upon them and, as if helplessly witnessing an horrific car crash unfolding right before his eyes, time seemed to slow as the runner in front parted the birch, a real howler of a mistake that left the gelding with no chance of finding a leg the other side, firing the partnership into the hallowed turf.

Instinct urged Danny to shield his face and shut his eyes but he barely had time to desperately yank down hard-right on the rein. As a result, Silver Belle landed awkwardly on her lead leg, off balance. Yet her light frame and nimble legs managed to deftly sidestep her stricken rival. He recognized the fallen jockey as Ridley Moore but he had no time or inclination to glance back and check if he'd got to his feet. In the heat of battle, winning was the only thing on his mind.

Neither had he time to admire how quickly he'd reacted. Something was missing. Having burnt fingers numbed by creams and leather gloves, he needed to look down to discover he no longer held a whip. It must've escaped his hand when sidestepping Ridley and was nestled in the thick grass beneath the drop side of the last fence. Not only had he lost his main method of correcting his mount if she began to hang off a straight path, he knew Silver Belle had a lazy streak and could hold a bit back for herself. Without a few persuasive slaps to go about her work, there was no way he'd pass this classy field, Danny reckoned, any realistic hope of plundering the prize was gone.

The early hampering also served to light up the mare. She needed further restraining as she pulled at the leash to go faster. She'd tended to run in snatches on occasions in the past – one minute struggling to go the pace, the next too keen for her own good - but Danny had thought she'd lost that quirk with experience and age.

The upcoming plain fence was opposite the grandstands and a visceral roar boomed from the crowd as the field negotiated the tricky fence like old pros. Danny was still looking on from the rear, happy to bide his time while the others forced a generous pace up front. The finish line second time around was the only place where dreams are won and lost. Silver Belle's name had yet to be mentioned by the commentators blaring from the speakers dotted around the track.

Danny could see the bottle-green cap worn by Rhys bobbing several places ahead. The upcoming fence and open ditch were met on a downhill stretch along the back straight of the second circuit and Silver Belle had now found a rhythm, blissfully unaware of Danny's predicament. He was trying to conserve energy as he knew he'd need to use brute strength from the saddle to get her home ahead, carry her there if he had to.

They popped over the next efficiently, shadowing the main pack. Her big ears began to revolve like satellite dishes. She was clearly taking everything in, even enjoying it, certainly more than Danny was at that moment. But there was still a long way to go and he made a concerted effort to stay in the here and now.

The following regulation fence saw Silver Belle jump another like a buck yet land too steeply the other side this time. She put her landing gear out and, had she not been a diminutive, lightly framed mare, she might well have buckled on impact but Danny sat back and flexed his arm muscles, like a fisherman fighting to reel in a catch of the day. Her strong legs absorbed the blow and they landed running.

At the next, Danny saw Rhys call a taxi with his free hand, like a rodeo rider, desperately trying to counter his shifting weight. It was a momentum-busting mistake from his better-fancied stablemate. Now just a few lengths ahead, Rhys began working vigorously, sitting lower in the saddle, in a vain attempt to make up for ground lost. Meanwhile, Danny was now niggling Silver Belle, encouraging her to keep in touch and maintain her interest in the pursuit, though he knew a mere shake of the reins wouldn't be enough to make her mind up. Without a whip, he knew there was no chance she'd catch the leading pack.

'Come on girl,' he growled, strong arms rowing with increasing urgency, bordering desperation. She met the next fence on a good stride, pinging it. It afforded them both a moment's breathing space as she'd made a few places, overtaking some stragglers on the retreat. Yet still they had seven rivals to pass, many leading fancies for the race and, from his years as a form expert, Danny knew those wouldn't come back to him. He had to get after them, still twelve lengths off the pace-setter with half a circuit to go.

And then disaster, as the mare was forced to tighten up as a tiring rival meandered into her path and as a result, she met the fifth from home all wrong. She breasted the fence, parting the birch and sending plumes of dead leaves in the air.

Some jockeys would've given her a severe telling off by asking her for maximum effort. But Danny knew that would only serve to upset her rhythm so soon after the error and, in any case, it was too early to set sail for home. Instead, he ran a calming hand down her plaited mane. Once she appeared to regain her composure, he began pushing her forward as the field progressed downhill towards the end of the back straight. Rhys was now within spitting distance and fading tamely, clearly given up the ghost after a series of serious blunders from the now-weary second favourite Lost Arctic.

Danny felt like easing off too. After all, without a whip, there was no way Silver Belle could trouble the leading protagonists from where she was currently sat in seventh. And then, something suddenly occurred to him. Clinging to a renewed glimmer of hope, he began to push with added vigour. Passing Rhys, he slapped his pal on his back protector and motioned for his whip.

Rhys' scowl vanished as he saw who it was and he wasted no time threading the whip through to Danny's outstretched whip hand. He hastily gave the mare a couple of sharp reminders to keep her focused. The response was instant, finding untapped reserves, she carved through the field, overtaking rivals on either side.

'Go Jacko!' came from behind.

Supporters began to voice their approval from the stands as Jackdaw struck the front. Danny, buoyed by the spurt of energy, kept up momentum on the lightly-weighted fourth favourite as the field crested the rise at the farthest point on the track. He gave her another crack on her powerful, yet compact behind, just to ensure the message got home. She sustained the Arazi-like forward move, sixth, fifth, fourth. But at what price?

Danny knew few horses could quicken more than once in a race and perhaps this was Silver Belle's one and only burst. They'd yet to embark on the lung-burning climb served up by the home run. From past visits, he also knew danger lurked round every corner at Cheltenham – a true test of jumping – and while they could enjoy a moment's freewheeling on this downhill stretch, they were fast approaching the notorious third-last obstacle where runners would hurtle into it in a bid to build momentum before they embarked on the climb to the line. Many came a cropper here and Danny wasn't prepared to take any undue risks. He went in short and popped it neatly and safely, unlike two of his rivals ahead, one unseating, the other's jockey let out a terror-fuelled shriek, struggling to keep his mount from kissing the sodden turf.

'Don't you fucking dare give up on me,' he gasped, as he felt the tiny mare begin to down tools. It was all about impetus on the stiff climb for home and he threw everything forward. He growled into her ears as they took third. She handled heavily and he had to keep correcting her to keep straight, like driving on a flat tyre.

He slapped her sharply on her flank. Fearing her tank had run dry, he had it in his mind to opt for safety by getting in tight and popping the final fence. Three. . .two . . . But Silver Belle had other ideas. Lit up by the firm slap, she left the ground a stride early, standing off the fence what felt like a mile out. A split second was all that was needed for Danny to adapt to the sudden change in plan, fearing they wouldn't make the other side together. But her compact hind legs coiled like a spring, sent the pair soaring and she cleared the fence with daylight to spare, inspiring Danny to dig deeper himself to match her Herculean effort. They now held a chance, albeit slim.

He afforded the briefest of glances over to the far rail where clear leader Jackdaw had drifted. Despite being less than fluent at the final fence, Jackdaw held a couple of lengths advantage on the run for home. He never doubted the mare beneath him was tough as teak and she found more from somewhere.

Danny pictured Sara's ashen face watching from a hospital bed. He couldn't let her down, not again. He summoned energy and strength from reserves he didn't know he had but this was a two-way effort. *Don't give up on me girl!*

He glanced over again and could see Jackdaw's stride shorten, petrol gauge teetering on empty. He also caught a red flash of the lollipop stick marking the finish line up ahead. 'Come on,' he growled, though it was drowned out by the thousands roaring on the favourite ahead. He heard little, though, now barely conscious. His thoughts increasingly fragmented as he pushed himself on, mind starved of oxygen, instinct now the driving force.

Silver Belle began to drift off a true course, veering towards the centre of the track, as she gave everything in pursuit. A couple of slaps on her quarters straightened her up again and she had closed to within a length of her target. The former second had tired off the scene. It was now a two-horse race.

The racecourse speakers bellowed out the closing stages. 'Hotpot Jackdaw far side, the gutsy mare Silver Belle nearside and closing. The favourite's all out and looking for the finish line as Silver Belle keeps coming, the grey just won't go away. A hundred yards to go and Jackdaw is clinging on by a half-length, Silver Belle, with Danny Rawlings in an all-out drive, getting to the leader, memories of Dessie's '89 fightback. Nothing in it close home.'

Danny pushed her neck forward, mindful of the head-bobbing finish.

'Oh that's tight,' came the commentator, 'a barnstorming duel fitting to kick off the Cheltenham Festival. Jackdaw and Silver Belle pass the post as one. Staying on for third is Thrifty Merchant.'

'Photograph. . . . photograph,' came the stewards, above the yells of delight and applause of the appreciative onlookers. Danny collapsed forward and loosely hugged the sweated neck of his charge.

'Well done,' escaped his lips between rapid breaths. 'Well done.'

But she was breathing even harder than he was and her movements were heavy, like a punch-drunk boxer, forelegs trembling slightly.

With his last ounce of energy, he quickly dismounted, easing the load on her back. He checked her over, like a concerned parent. In his eyes, Silver Belle was the bravest horse he'd ever sat on, she just took a bit of understanding from the saddle that's all.

Kelly had run up the woodchip path in front of the stands to meet the pair. She threw a rug over the mare, whose grey coat would lose body heat after such an ordeal, like a marathon runner wrapped in foil after the line. The mare's breathing had steadied and found a rhythm, much to his relief.

The roar of the crowd was replaced by a murmur of palpable anticipation as the judge in the stewards' room pored over the photo image of the two rivals a course-width apart. Danny knew it was all done by computer now and a mere pixel between them on the monitor would be enough to separate the two. Dead-heats were rare these days.

'And here is the result of the photograph.' The crowd fell eerily quiet. 'First, number twelve, Silver Belle.' Danny's gloved fist punched the air. 'Second, number three, Jackdaw, third was number eight, Thrifty Merchant.'

Danny longed for Sara to lead them in but knowing she was recovering in hospital was enough for him. But the six-figure purse attached to first prize would mean nothing if the child she was carrying hadn't survived the terrible ordeal. And, although all around him cheered and congratulated him on this greatest success of his racing life, his mind was strangely elsewhere.

He smiled and touched the peak of his cap in acknowledge-ment of the clapping public lining the chute. Danny held one rein, Kelly the other. They led the little heroine into the enclo-sure marked 1st and graciously accepted the cheers.

'Make sure you weigh in after all that,' Kelly said, spotting the TV crew lurking to grab an interview with the winning jockey. 'Have you got a phone?' Danny asked.

Kelly handed over her mobile and Danny punched in the number for the ward nurse at Salisbury General. He stuck up five fingers to the approaching interviewer, Jimmy Bowers, a rubber faced wag who generously held back for Danny to make the call.

'Nurse Rogers,' a female voice said.

'I'm ringing to ask about Sara Rawlings, she was taken in this morning, I'm her husband.' The nerves had returned.

'She's fine, tests have come back clear.'

'And the baby?' Danny said, mouth arid.

'We've carried out a scan,' she said, 'and all is well. Her blood count is A1 too.'

'Thank God for that,' Danny sighed. 'Tell her I love her.'

'I will. Oh, and congratulations.'

'What for?'

'We're all glued to the telly in the ward, you're on it right now,' Rogers said. 'You'll be our first celebrity visitor.'

'Cheers, anyway, send my love to Sara, better weigh in.'

As Danny flicked the mobile shut, Bowers thrust a mike in

his face. 'What a cracking finish Daniel, it must be a dream come true for you.'

Danny looked down the lens of the camera and said, 'Sure is.'

He carried the saddle and tack into the glass-fronted weighing room before hurriedly changing into jeans and plain black shirt.

CHAPTER 28

Danny wasted no time stuffing his kitbag and forcing the zipper. He swiftly left the scene of victory and joined Kelly, who'd finished hosing Silver Belle down, in the horsebox. He made a detour to Salisbury General and, leaving Kelly to tend for the needs of the mare in the short-stay car-park, he hurriedly followed signs to ward 2B. He poked his head around the door. Sara was dozing with the muted telly showing them lining up for the Champion Hurdle.

Sara's eyes opened and she managed a smile as Danny approached the bed. A drip was attached to her arm and some colour had returned to her cheeks.

He leant forward and kissed her on the lips. 'Got here as soon as I could.'

'Did they tell you, the scans are fine.'

'Yeah,' Danny said, emptying his lungs. 'Been worried sick. Puts it all into perspective.'

Sara's smile returned, as if relieved by Danny's reaction.

'We'll get on to finding a potential yard to put a deposit on, once the prize-money clears. In no rush, though,' he said. 'Joint decisions all the way from now on.'

'I'll have a good look on the internet when I get home,' she said. 'Something to keep me busy while I fully recover. Got to find a place with room for friends to stay, because we'll be out of town, views over the valleys would be nice,' she said, staring off into the distance as if recollecting a dream. 'As well as some lovely Persian rugs and a fireplace, a proper one with oak surround. I spotted lovely drape curtains–' She stopped and shifted to face Danny. 'Are you still listening, Danny?'

His eyes were fixed on the portable TV attached to a bracket on the wall. 'Sorry love, they're just jumping the last in the big one, can I?' Danny asked, finger hovering above the mute button.

'Go on.' Sara sighed and shut her eyes, saying, 'We'll need two tellies as well.'